W9-ATM-871

"Would not a broken mainmast put our departure for Europe off even further?"

Rose asked astutely.

"Oh, what is another day or two when you are making such a hit in London?" Bennet replied.

"A hit? I am no such thing. I am probably the most talked-about woman in town."

"Yes, that is what I meant," Bennet said, staring into her eyes. They reminded him of the sea.

"Do be serious, Mr. Varner," she said sternly. "You cannot want to be in the company of an infamous woman."

"My friends call me Bennet." He rested his elbow on the table and his chin on his hand to study her better.

"What do your enemies call you?"

"I see to it that I have no enemies," he said with that determined smile of his, and Rose wondered if he did not make them or if he simply eliminated them.

Dear Reader,

It's June, so start thinking about your summer reading! Whether you're going to the beach or simply going to relax on the porch, don't forget to bring along a Harlequin Historical® novel. Since publishing her very first book with us in 1993, Laurel Ames has gone on to write eight books, which critics have described as "hauntingly good," "cutting edge" and "endearing." Her latest, *Infamous,* is a delightful Regency about a dashing nobleman and spy whose silly and snobbish mother and sister do their best to foil a romance between him and the one woman he feels is worth pursuing—a beautiful and *smart* country heiress who's hiding secrets of her own.

Tori Phillips returns this month with *Midsummer's Knight,* the sequel to *Silent Knight.* Here, a confirmed bachelor and a wary widow betrothed against their will switch identities with their friends to spy on the other, and fall in love in the process. In *Runaway* by Carolyn Davidson, a young woman who becomes a fugitive after an act of self-defense is discovered by a kind cowboy, who takes her back to his parents' Missouri home as his "wife."

And don't miss *Widow Woman,* the first historical title by long-time Silhouette Special Edition® author Patricia McLinn, about a feisty female rancher who must win back the heart of her ex-foreman, the man she once refused to marry and the unknowing father of her child.

Whatever your tastes in reading, you'll be sure to find a romantic journey back to the past between the covers of a Harlequin Historical® novel.

Sincerely,

Tracy Farrell
Senior Editor

Please address questions and book requests to:
Silhouette Reader Service
U.S.: 3010 Walden Ave., P.O. Box 1325, Buffalo, NY 14269
Canadian: P.O. Box 609, Fort Erie, Ont. L2A 5X3

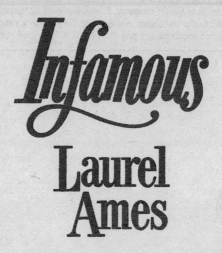

Infamous

Laurel Ames

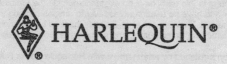

HARLEQUIN®

TORONTO • NEW YORK • LONDON
AMSTERDAM • PARIS • SYDNEY • HAMBURG
STOCKHOLM • ATHENS • TOKYO • MILAN • MADRID
PRAGUE • WARSAW • BUDAPEST • AUCKLAND

If you purchased this book without a cover you should be aware
that this book is stolen property. It was reported as "unsold and
destroyed" to the publisher, and neither the author nor the
publisher has received any payment for this "stripped book."

ISBN 0-373-29018-7

INFAMOUS

Copyright © 1998 by Barbara J. Miller

All rights reserved. Except for use in any review, the reproduction or
utilization of this work in whole or in part in any form by any electronic,
mechanical or other means, now known or hereafter invented, including
xerography, photocopying and recording, or in any information storage
or retrieval system, is forbidden without the written permission of the
publisher, Harlequin Enterprises Limited, 225 Duncan Mill Road,
Don Mills, Ontario, Canada M3B 3K9.

All characters in this book have no existence outside the imagination of
the author and have no relation whatsoever to anyone bearing the same
name or names. They are not even distantly inspired by any individual
known or unknown to the author, and all incidents are pure invention.

This edition published by arrangement with Harlequin Books S.A.

® and TM are trademarks of the publisher. Trademarks indicated with
® are registered in the United States Patent and Trademark Office, the
Canadian Trade Marks Office and in other countries.

Printed in U.S.A.

LAUREL AMES

Although Laurel Ames likes to write stories set in the early nineteenth century, she writes from personal experience. She and her husband live on a farm, complete with five horses, a log spring house, carriage house and a smokehouse made of bricks kilned on the farm. Of her characters, Laurel says, "With the exception of the horses, my characters, both male and female, good and evil, all are me and no one else."

For Ma and Dad, whose unfailing support
and enthusiasm have encouraged me
to write far more than I ever thought possible.

Chapter One

London, February 1815

"Men are the most arrogant, helpless and stupid creatures on the earth," Miss Gwen Rose Wall said out loud as she strode along South Audley Street into a brisk head wind, strangling her reticule with both hands. "Especially my brother, Stanley." Her almost military gait caused her brown wool pelisse to flap open, cooling her heated anger to a becoming flush by the time she found the house number she was seeking on one of the corners. Its generous size, the tripartite Venetian windows and long side portico distinguished Varner House from the other residences on the street. However, it was not this grandeur that daunted Rose from entering, but a series of shouted expostulations in a high-pitched female voice. Though the content of the expletives was shrouded by the stout brick walls of the house, it was clear the woman was neither being attacked nor in pain, but was extremely angry. When the screeches momentarily ceased, Rose shrugged and began to ascend the steps under the portico, thinking that once she paid this duty visit her time in London would be her own, no matter what Stanley said.

A youngish man dashed out, putting on his hat and skipping down the steps so rapidly he collided with Rose. He would have overbalanced her backward had he not caught her in his arms. He stared at her with such a look of surprise and friendliness that Rose stared back, wondering if he recognized her. But his boyish face, creased with laugh lines and alight with a pair of merry blue eyes, was unknown to her. She found herself to be holding his hat, which she must have caught as it tumbled from his head. His long black hair was hanging over his brow now in tempting disarray and she had the most maddening urge to run her hands through it to stroke it back in place.

"Bennet!" shrieked the voice from the open doorway. "You come back in here this instant and explain.... What do you mean by kissing female persons on the front steps?"

A small hatchet-faced woman appeared with her fists clutching a silk shawl closed. Her perfectly black hair seemed unnatural planted on top of a face so seamed with age and frustration.

"I wasn't kissing her, Mother." He finally released Rose. "I was running her down in my haste. So sorry, miss—uh miss—?"

Rose cleared her throat and handed him his hat. "Miss Gwen Rose Wall."

"I am Bennet Varner, and this is my mother, Edith."

"I know. I mean, I was coming to pay a call on my godmother, Edith Varner."

"Wall? Wall? I swear I must be godmother to half of England. Who is your mother?"

"Mrs. Eldridge Wall." When this failed to elicit a spark of recognition, Rose added, "Who was formerly Miss Maryanne Varner, a rather distant cousin of yours, I believe. But I see I have caught you at a bad time. Perhaps another day would do better. I'll leave my card with you.'' Rose flicked this out of her reticule and handed it to Bennet, who accepted it eagerly.

"Nonsense," Bennet said. "You must come inside. Too cold a day to be standing about on the steps." He took her arm and pulled her up the remaining steps and through the door past his mother, who was staring at him as though he had taken leave of his senses. "And I've given you a fright," he added.

"But you were going out, and in some haste, as I recall," Rose protested as she surrendered her pelisse to the butler and tried not to gape at the grand staircase leading to the next floor, which must contain a ballroom, she surmised, to do justice to so much carved and polished oak.

"Oh, I wasn't going anywhere important."

"You said you had an appointment," his mother accused as she followed them into a cheerful morning room where a fire blazed on the hearth and a modish young woman sat petulantly at an escritoire.

"My sister, Harriet Varner. This is Miss Gwen Rose Wall from…"

"Wall," Rose supplied. "It is near Bristol." Rose seated herself on the sofa Bennet indicated. He claimed the seat beside her, totally ignoring his mother, who had planted herself on a nearby chair.

Harriet stared at Rose appraisingly and Rose felt the girl to be adding up the cost of her blue wool walking dress and weighing it against her own filmy muslin gown and pearls. Harriet's was a ridiculous costume for February, even the last day of February, Rose decided. Harriet was pretty enough, her sharp features still softened by the bloom of youth, but she had been ill-advised to crop her hair so short. That sort of wavy, flaxen hair was much better left long rather than attempting to tame the remaining short locks with a curling iron.

"I said, are you making a long stay in London, Miss Wall?"

Rose jumped at the imperious question from Mrs. Varner.

"Only a week or so, until we have arranged passage. I am accompanying my brother and his wife on a...a sort of grand tour." Rose could not admit to playing nursemaid to a young bride. She was not yet twenty-three herself and only her mother could think such an arrangement suitable.

Bennet jumped up and tugged at the bellpull. The butler burst into the room as though he had been standing with his hand on the doorknob. "Tea, Hardy, and some cakes. Perhaps a suitable wine," Bennet said, rubbing his hands together. "Oh, I expect you know what we need."

Rose smiled at Bennet's clumsy orders and she thought that Hardy was tempted to do so as well. She had already put Mrs. Varner down as a shrew and she suspected Harriet also gave her brother a hard time. Why else would he have been escaping the house so hastily? He did not strut or put on airs like her brother, but moved quickly and naturally. And he was strong, she thought, the memory of those arms holding her so safely causing her to stare at him raptly. She forced her attention away from him. No matter how much she thought she could like him, she must not, she reminded herself.

"I expect you know the roads are a bit torn up still," Bennet offered.

"Where?" Rose asked, remembering their recent drive from Bristol.

"Europe."

"Where in Europe?" she asked, thinking his comment unnecessarily vague. "France?"

"Pretty much all of it. Perhaps I should explain I am

in the shipping business, so I have occasion to get news—"

"Not *in* business," corrected Harriet. "Bennet has interests, as we all do. He is not directly involved in business."

"Oh, I see," Rose said as she watched Bennet roll his eyes heavenward. Rose smiled, for it did not matter to her that Bennet was in trade. Nor did it matter to him, but it obviously caused Harriet some pain and made his mother wring her hands nervously.

The tea tray was brought in and Edith Varner began to serve. "And how is your mother, Miss Wall? She is still…alive, I assume."

"Yes, of course," Rose said as Bennet cringed. "She is arranging to move into our house in Bristol, thinking that Stanley and Alice will like to have Wall House to themselves. She wrote to you that the three of us would be stopping in town. But perhaps her letter was misdirected."

Edith looked guiltily toward the stuffed escritoire, and Rose schooled herself not to glance in that direction.

"It is too bad you are not making a longer stay," Mrs. Varner said. "Or we might be able to arrange some entertainment for you. As it is…"

"A ball!" Bennet decided.

"A what?" Harriet demanded. "But you just said—"

"How long could it possibly take to arrange? A day or two, no more. I can have my secretary help you. Besides, your birthday is coming up on March third, Harriet. We must celebrate that."

Bennet ignored his gaping sister and mother to pace about the room and throw out suggestions as to whom to invite, what musicians to engage, as though someone should be taking notes. Rose was glad it was not her responsibility. She liked Bennet quite well as a man, but as a brother or son she thought he might leave much to be desired.

"I shall arrange everything," Bennet decided, seating himself and taking up his teacup, then turning abruptly to Rose. "Are you sure I did not hurt you when I ran into you?"

"Of course not. I am used to pushing about thousand-pound horses. I do not hurt easily."

"Ah, you ride. We will go tomorrow. I have a stable full of hacks champing at the bit for exercise."

"I could not impose in such a way."

"You would be doing me a favor. What is your hotel? I shall call for you at ten."

"Greeves Hotel, but I..."

"That is no more than a mile from here. What a happy coincidence."

"But I do not know what Stanley, my brother, may have planned."

"I shall bring horses anyway. At least you and I may ride."

"Bennet," his mother admonished. "With no chaperon?"

"With a groom, of course," Bennet added.

"I should be delighted to ride," Rose said for no other reason than to see Edith Varner's expression turn sour again.

Bennet looked thoughtful for a moment. "You know the season is just starting, Miss Wall. I would encourage your party to spend a month with us at least to get a proper taste of London before venturing off to foreign parts. Why, you can stay at Varner House."

This offer brought such sharp gasps from Edith and Harriet that Rose hastened to say, "We simply cannot impose in such a way. It will not be worth the bother of removing from our hotel to here, for I am quite sure Stanley has secured passage for us by now.''

''Oh, I shall speak to him. He should leave that up to me. If you want decent accommodations I will get you staterooms on one of my ships.''

And so it went until the prescribed half hour was up. Then Rose asked if the butler could call a hack for her. Bennet immediately sent round for the carriage and insisted on delivering her to Greeves Hotel himself, giving her a running account about all the buildings they passed as they made their way down Oxford Street.

Rose was careful not to mention a liking for bonbons or diamonds, for she feared Bennet would simply stop the carriage to hop out and purchase some. He was a strange man, not at all what one would expect of a London smart. Rose decided he was some sort of cit, with a family aspiring to society. She could almost feel sorry for Edith and Harriet. Almost, but not quite, for she had no doubt that if Bennet had not dragged her into the house, both mother and daughter would have refused to acknowledge her. What of that? She had been snubbed before and was quite used to it. She rather thought she had grown a thick enough skin to carry her through any situation.

Rose had thought Greeves Hotel a rather grand structure with all its rows of windows and wrought-iron railings, until she had seen Varner House. But Bennet had given specific directions to his coachman, so Greeves could not be too pedestrian. Though why she would care what Bennet Varner thought was beyond her.

''At ten tomorrow,'' he said, kissing her gloved hand as he helped her down from the open carriage. ''I shall hope to meet your brother and his wife.'' He was gone then in a flurry of orders to his driver and a spin of carriage wheels. Rose stared after him as she walked up the steps and through the double doors into the lobby. They were on the third floor and the long climb gave Rose time to consider just what Bennet Varner's game was. Could he be smitten with her? She knew she was pretty, but she did not think about it much since she knew she would never marry. Bennet might be boyish, amusing and sweet in the middle of a crisp February afternoon, but what was he like when drunk? That was what mattered. She shrugged off such thoughts and went to unpack her riding habit and shake out the wrinkles from the dark green velvet. At least she could look forward to a ride the next day.

"Sir, just three more," the spectacled young man said as he deftly slid documents under the poised pen of Bennet Varner. Any possible boyishness was wiped from Varner's face as he perused the papers with a knit brow. He focused his gaze on the contracts and tried to put out of his mind the surprised green eyes of Miss Gwen Rose Wall as he had held her on the steps of his house. Her eyes were more of a blue-green, he decided, picturing them in his mind and causing his secretary to clear his throat to get his attention. Bennet signed a document without reading it at all. That look she had, like a startled doe, her russet hair brushing her shoulders, her pert nose, those eyebrows drawn in concern and those luscious lips…

"Sir? Sir? Are you unwell?"

"Fine, Walters, I'm fine." Bennet cleared his throat. "Is the *Celestine* still in port?"

"Yes, due to sail tomorrow."

"Her departure will be delayed," Bennet said absently.

"Some special cargo you have engaged?"

"No. She needs her…her mainmast replaced."

"Her mainmast? It's the first I have heard of it. I would have thought Captain Cooley—"

"He doesn't know it yet," Bennet said firmly.

"But, sir."

"I feel quite strongly that the mainmast is about to go and I want it replaced. I'm sure you can handle all the necessary arrangements." The piercing look Bennet shot at Walters sent him scurrying from the room, leaving Bennet to get back to a contemplation of Rose. He must stop her from taking ship for Europe by whatever means he could.

Through the half-open door he watched Walters dispatch a messenger to inform Captain Cooley of his fate, then draft an order for the new mast. Probably they could find one in London, but Bennet would stubbornly insist on his course of action even if Walters had to send to the Highlands for a tree. He meant to delay the *Celestine,* and with good reason.

Bennet pushed aside the dull paperwork on his desk and thought once again of those blue-green eyes and that burnished hair like fine silk. Resignedly he put on his hat and greatcoat and walked through his secretary's office without a word, leaving Walters to rehearse in his own mind the Banbury story he would feed to Captain Cooley when the man came storming up from the docks.

"I don't care if we are distantly related," Stanley said as his long strides carried him down the hotel stairs the next morning. "You cannot just go off riding alone with a perfect stranger."

Rose looked up to her brother, a serious young man with brown hair and sincere blue eyes. "I am not going alone. My groom is coming," she said, glancing at the slight youth who followed silently in their wake.

"Martin is just a boy. What sort of protection would he be?"

"All the protection I need. He is..." Rose's protest trailed off at a warning look from Martin's sharp brown eyes.

The boy moved around the brother and sister, holding the door open. The street in front of Greeves Hotel seemed to be full of riding horses. Bennet dismounted from a fidgeting black brute and tossed his reins carelessly to his groom, an older man who already seemed to have his hands full.

"I brought enough hacks so we could all ride, or you can have your pick of horses."

Rose introduced the two men, embarrassed by her brother's stuffiness. Bennet seemed not to notice he was being sized up by Stanley, and pointed out the most dangerous-looking of his beasts as a little fresh if Wall had a notion for a brisk gallop. Rose did not choose the dainty mare that would have been a good mount for Alice, had she the slightest interest in riding, but the strong-boned gelding with the white blaze, who met her gaze with interest. Martin replaced Bennet's groom as escort and poor Stilton had to lead the mare back to Varner House.

Conversation was brief and confined solely to the points of the horses as they made their way through the noisy streets to Hyde Park. When they reached this landmark Rose knew she must be smiling foolishly as the full expanse of the park broke upon her gaze. "I had not thought there could be so much grass in all of London," she said to Bennet with delight.

"Oh, the city isn't all cobbles and paving stones."

Bennet let Rose set the pace and try out Gallant's long strides. Rose smiled at Stanley, who cantered at her side on Victor, and he grinned back. The only time they were in perfect accord was when they were on horseback, for they did both love to ride.

Rose glanced back at Bennet and Martin who seemed to have fallen into conversation. Why this should worry her was beyond her. Martin had far more discretion than she. But there was something so disarming about Bennet

Varner. His friendliness, she supposed. She would have to be careful.

As Stanley urged Victor into a gallop, Rose fell back slightly, sacrificing a faster run to talk to Bennet. "You keep a fine stable, sir."

"Call me Bennet. I know it's unfashionable, but everyone does."

"Who usually exercises your horses?" Rose asked, matching Gallant's steady trot to the black's capricious jogging and head tossing as best she could.

"I do, or the grooms. A bit of town training is good for the young ones. Settle down, Chaos," Bennet said firmly and the black rolled a wary eye at him.

"You train your own horses, then?"

"As much as I can manage. Business keeps me in town a good deal, so I bring my young favorites with me. Your brother is a bruising rider."

"It is the one thing he does really well. I shall have no fear in placing the breeding stock at Wall into his hands."

"I take it that task fell to you before?"

"Before he came of age Stanley was at school the better part of the time. Now…"

"Are you meaning to move to your house in Bristol with your mother?"

"I had hoped to stay at Wall and help him, but he does not want my help. And I am certainly no comfort to Alice. I suppose it will have to be Bristol after all."

"That will be a pure waste of your talents."

She looked inquiringly at him.

"I mean, unless you marry yourself," he hastened to add.

"That will not happen," Rose said, still sorting out what talents he was talking about.

"London is full of men who will fall in love with such a face as yours, even if you have no fortune."

"As it happens I have just as large a portion as Stanley, from my mother. And therein lies the problem."

"Problem?" Bennet gave her a blank look. "Beauty and fortune, not to mention a good seat and excellent conversation."

Rose did not blush at his mention of her seat and cast him a speculative look. "How would I ever know if a man wanted me for my conversation or my face, or even my seat, so long as the money is in the way? No, I will not marry. I feel I can go on quite well myself. And if Bristol is too dull, in a few years I shall be old enough to set up a horse farm for myself."

"You will never be old enough to do that. And you can be sure of your man if he has an equal or better fortune," Bennet replied with a satisfied smile.

"Perhaps I prefer to maintain my independence." Rose eased Gallant into a canter, thinking to interrupt the conversation.

"Perhaps he would let you," Bennet said, matching Chaos's stride to Gallant's and riding dangerously close to her side so as not to have to shout. "Not every man insists on taking control of his wife's money."

"It is not a worry I will have. I will not marry and that is that," Rose said, shaking her head. She brought the animal back to a more sedate trot with no more than a small tug on the reins.

"After I have removed every impediment?" Bennet asked with a grin.

"Not every one. I do not like men," she said, slowing Gallant to a walk.

"All men?" he asked in surprise as he trotted past her.

"All the ones I have had occasion to meet."

"And how many is that?" Bennet teased, pulling up his horse to try to intercept the gaze Rose resolutely directed straight ahead.

"Too many."

"I see. What a fortunate circumstance, then," he said as Rose rode past him.

His pause caused her to look around at him. "What is?"

His blue eyes glittered with mischief. "Why, I too have been pursued by fortune hunters until I confess I am quite marriage-shy myself. I too have decided never to marry."

"That seems an odd coincidence." Rose pursed her lips.

"Yes, it does to me as well, but there you have it. Since we are both confirmed bachelors, there is no impediment to our friendship."

"Friendship? I can think of one."

"Look, your brother is stealing a march on us. Race you to the edge of the park."

Rose spurred her horse to try to overtake Bennet before he came up with Stanley. In at least one feature the two men were alike. They knew when to run away from an argument they were destined to lose.

"I have not had such a ride since hunting season," Stanley said, patting Victor's steaming neck and letting the horse cavort playfully, before bringing it down to a walk beside Bennet and Rose.

"You must make yourself free of my stables whenever you have time to ride. You can see they need the exercise." Addressing Stanley, he added, "I have also put your name down as my guest at White's and Boudle's, so feel free to drop in there when in need of some solitude, or some companionship."

"That is most kind of you," Stanley said sincerely. "I fear we shall not be in town long enough to take advantage of so much hospitality."

"You must at least stay for my sister's coming-of-age party. She and Mother would be pleased to have family there. Oh, and I had meant to tell you, my ship *Celestine* is in port and the cabins are not booked. I beg you to make use of them if France or Italy is your destination. Otherwise they would travel empty."

"Varner, I am overwhelmed. I will pay for passage, of course."

"I had offered rooms at Varner house but Rose would not hear of it. We get so little company."

"But you have done so much," Stanley said. "You must come visit us at Wall when we return. We shall be back in time for hunting season."

"I should be delighted." Bennet smiled at Rose in that self-satisfied way that said he had charmed her brother completely.

By the time they returned to the hotel Bennet's groom was back to take charge of the horses, leaving Bennet free to dine with Stanley at White's, and, Rose presumed, introduce him to his cronies. She went upstairs, shaking her head and plotting how to get the better of Bennet Varner. He was a provoking rogue. She supposed she should have expected some sophistication from a London male, but intelligence had been a surprise, though he masked it well enough. She had never known a man like him, and found to her surprise that she was looking forward to a third meeting just to match wits with him again.

"Where is Stanley?" Alice asked from the settee as Rose whisked into the parlor that was common to their two suites.

"Gone off with Bennet Varner to his club. Do you feel well enough to shop? We are invited to a ball at Varner House, and I have my doubts that I own anything elegant enough to do the occasion justice."

"Stanley was going to take me shopping."

"But if he goes with you it will take forever," Rose

said, unbuttoning the frogs of her jacket. "You know he cannot make up his mind about such things. Then he gives those heavy sighs when he is tired of waiting for you."

Alice frowned in thought. "I suppose we could make a start. I shall need some new gowns."

"Also we may be here some few days until the *Celestine* is ready to sail." Rose opened the door into her bedroom and her maid, Cynthie, took her coat.

"Then we are going?" Alice asked with a pout.

"Of course," Rose said. "What made you think we were not?"

"Stanley." Alice followed Rose into her bedroom. "He said if I was meaning to be sick for days on end I might as well do it at home."

Since Rose had had some such thoughts herself, she felt a little guilty at Alice's tearful reply. "Don't worry. I will bring Stanley up to scratch." Rose selected a buff walking dress, and stepped out of her riding skirt. "I have been promised Europe and I mean to see it. I have no intention of wasting the whole season here in London."

"But I never had a London season. Neither did you, if it comes to that. Would it be so awful to stay just a few weeks?"

"If we do not embark for France within a fortnight I shall return to Wall or Bristol," Rose vowed, emerging from the top of the dress.

"But why are you so dead set against London?"

"Because I might meet...any number of fribbles and fops. You know I have no patience with such men." Rose adjusted her hair in the mirror and glanced at Alice to see if she believed her.

Alice shrugged and went for her reticule and pelisse while Rose sent Cynthie to tell Martin to find them a hack. Stanley had caviled at paying passage for four servants— his valet, two maids and a groom—especially when there would be no horses involved. But Rose had held out for Martin's quick usefulness as a footman and general dogs-body and finally prevailed when Alice begged them to stop arguing over so trivial a matter.

The young women spent a successful afternoon at the modiste and mantua makers' shops. Rose found two evening gowns that needed no alterations, but Alice chose to have hers made from scratch and risked not having any for Harriet Varner's birthday ball. When the carriage returned them to the hotel, Alice grabbed one small parcel of ribbons and left Martin and Rose to transport the large stack of bandboxes to the third-floor suite.

"What do you think of Bennet Varner?" Rose asked her groom as they trudged up the stairs.

Martin darted her an uncertain glance. "He's a quick'un, miss."

"Yes, I thought so myself. Though he acts the part of a jovial carefree fellow, I find myself expecting some hidden agenda."

"But what could it be, miss? No one in London knows—"

"No one we know in London knows anything about what happened at Wall five years ago, but many people go to London."

"Are you thinking of Lord Foy?"

"The war was over last year. I cannot imagine where else Axelrod Barton, Lord Foy, would be except London. Surely not at that Yorkshire estate that he described as moldering into the rock from which it was built."

"But what are the chances of meeting him? It's such a very big city, miss."

"I am sure you are right, Martin, and I have nothing to fear. Ten to one Axel is still tripping about Vienna or haunting the gaming hells of Paris."

"Besides, even if you were to encounter him, he knows nothing."

"He remembers nothing. There is a difference and I should not wish to jog his memory."

"I shall keep an eye out for him, miss, and warn you if he's about."

"Martin, don't say anything to your sister, Cynthie. No need to alarm her unnecessarily."

"Yes, miss," Martin agreed as he deposited the boxes in the common sitting room for Alice and Rose to sort out.

Susan and Cynthie, the two maids, unpacked the treasures and the women spent a profitable hour planning several toilettes. Rose and Alice got on better when they spoke of trivialities. Rose truly had no intention of marrying, but she saw no point in being a dowd either. She had money and meant to enjoy it. She also knew that the best way to put forward their tour was to get Alice tricked out as soon as possible and in good twig for the crossing.

The chance that they could actually be traveling to where she might meet Lord Foy did not disturb her so much as encountering him in England. He was not likely to be touring museums or ruins. So long as they avoided British society abroad she would be safe. Therefore, the sooner they left England the better.

Bennet Varner sighed and paced from door to window for the twentieth time, looking out on the dismal courtyard below Viscount Leighton's small room in the group of apartments known as the Foreign Office. Leighton growled and cast his pen aside, running his hand through his fair hair in exasperation. It suddenly occurred to Bennet he was annoying his best friend.

"You always get like this where there's a woman involved," Leighton complained. "Will this be another of those uncomfortable seasons when I am forever worrying about Foy blowing your head off?''

''That's only happened once, and if you recall he merely wounded me,'' Bennet said, throwing himself into one of the wing chairs pulled close to the small grate.

''Only because he knew you would not have him arrested for that. If he could have killed you with impunity he would have done so. And that was over your sister. Every time you make up to a woman, Foy seems to appear to take her away from you. When will you two stop this stupid competition? It started at school years ago, and you have never grown out of it, either of you.''

''I don't know what you mean. Besides, my first meeting with Lord Foy was when I saved your skin on the playing field. Are you forgetting that?''

''I would like to. So what is this new inamorata like?''

''I don't know what makes you think—''

''Heavy sighs from a man normally tied to his desk when he is not crawling about one of his ships.'' Leighton pushed his papers aside and rose from his desk.

''She's my mother's goddaughter, just arrived from the country.''

''An innocent?'' Leighton rifled through his desk drawers.

''Yes, in many ways, but not stupid. She is already suspicious of me.''

''Suspicious of you, a man without the sense to know when his intended has taken another man as her lover.'' The slight man extended his search to the corner cupboard.

Bennet hopped up to pace again.

''Sit down. I'm sorry I said anything. Aha.'' Leighton held up the brandy decanter triumphantly, sloshed some of the liquid into two glasses and handed one to Bennet as his friend paced past him. "What are you doing that she is suspicious of?"

"I'm trying to keep her in London and having a damned hard time of it."

Leighton seated himself by the fireplace and jabbed at the small blaze with the poker. "Why keep her here, where Foy may get at her? You can follow her wherever she goes. A few weeks of dalliance in the country might be just the thing to ease your nerves."

"To Paris?"

"Oh, that's another matter, but the rumors may be completely false. When you think about it, does it not seem entirely fantastic that Napoleon could have any thought to leave Elba? France is facing economic ruin, the peace negotiations are nearly completed. Probably it is all a hum."

Bennet threw himself into the other chair again. "Perhaps if I warn her of our suspicions she can delay her brother's departure—"

"No, that you must not do, for we do not know what sort of economic panic such news would cause if it were to get about. You know what fools we aristocrats can be."

"If I cannot tell her I will simply have to deceive Rose."

"Rose, a country rose?" Leighton mused. "When may I meet this latest paragon of yours?"

"Harriet's coming-of-age party tomorrow night. I don't suppose you are in the market for a wealthy wife?"

Leighton looked sharply at him. "Not a chance, Bennet. Remember, I know Harriet. Besides, she always said she was going to marry Foy when she was old enough."

"Yes, I suppose there's no stopping that now. Will you come anyway?"

"Yes, so long as there is no pressing business here, I will attend. I must meet the woman who has thrown you into such a fuddle."

Chapter Two

Rose breakfasted in bed, a luxury she now allowed herself since Alice was not an early riser, and, judging from the hour at which Stanley had stumbled in, she rather thought he would be abed till noon. Of course, at Wall, she would have been up and riding two hours ago, but she was on holiday and should try to enjoy herself. She could enjoy herself now that Varner had expanded her horizons. Rose decided she could like London quite well now that she knew there was such a delightful place to ride.

Cynthie helped her into her green riding habit again, and Rose promised herself that she would buy another if Bennet appeared today. He had said they would ride every day, but it would be just like such a careless fellow to forget and leave her standing in the lobby of Greeves Hotel with Martin on watch in the street.

She spent the remaining hour before ten o'clock writing a long letter to her mother in the comparative privacy of the lounge off the lobby. Rose had just handed this over to be mailed when she saw the horses from the window and looped up the tail of her habit to go down the steps. Bennet leaped to her elbow and helped her to mount Gallant so solicitously she decided she would rumble his lay today. She would, at least, take up yesterday's argument where he had interrupted it.

They had brought Victor for Martin to ride, and the two grooms kept a respectful distance back from Bennet and Rose.

"No horses for Stanley and Alice?" Rose asked, looking innocently around from her perch atop Gallant.

"Your brother told me Alice does not ride." Bennet flicked an imaginary speck of dust from his plum-colored coat.

Rose wondered if he had deviated from his usual black riding jacket for her benefit. "Did he also tell you he planned to have such a bad head from staying out late drinking that he would not be able to sit a horse today?"

"No, I surmised that myself," Bennet said proudly.

"You were with him, then?" Rose asked as she steered her horse through traffic.

"Yes, for part of the evening. I left him around midnight."

"I cannot say that I like Stanley taking up gambling and drinking. I know all men do it, but that does not make it a safe pastime."

"If you are worried that he will get into fast company, I assure you my friends would never fleece a guest of mine." Chaos gave a little jump at a bright red curricle, but Bennet's grip turned to iron and brought the animal under control. The man's leg muscles bulged tautly under his buff riding breeches.

"You have a high opinion of your friends, sir. I shall reserve mine until I meet them."

"Hah, I see. A recommendation from me is worthless, as you have decided to mistrust me."

Rose stared at him to have her mind read so accurately,

then turned her attention back to the last thoroughfare to separate them from their destination.

"I have surprised you, haven't I?" Bennet prodded as they approached Hyde Park.

"Yes. As I was about to say yesterday when you galloped away to avoid the remark, you are not at all trustworthy."

"Yes, when you said you could think of one reason we could not be friends. I saw the barb coming so thought I would avoid it until I could think of a rejoinder."

Rose laughed. "You are a jump ahead of me today, and yes, you did surprise me. It will not happen again," she assured him as she urged Gallant into a trot.

"That I can believe. Why do you not trust me? And do not waste time dissembling."

Rose looked at Bennet thoughtfully. He was riding carelessly with both reins gathered in one hand and not paying any obvious attention to his horse, yet the beast was minding his subtle leg signals much better than yesterday. It struck her that Bennet rode as naturally as a soldier, and her experience of soldiers should make her dislike him. But she could not think of a clear reason to do so. She urged Gallant into a canter, using Bennet's own trick against him. The horses would be used to having a brisk canter as soon as they got to the park, would expect it if they rode here again, she thought. Why did she not trust Bennet Varner? At the end of fifteen minutes and on the other side of the vast park she was ready to bring her mount down to a walk again and answer him, even if it meant never riding here with him again.

"All of this, the horses, your kindness to Stanley, the offer of your ship, why?"

"I did not think courtesy required a reason," Bennet replied, his dark eyebrows arched in surprise over those innocent blue eyes of his.

"You have been more than courteous, you have been kind in the extreme, and charming enough to allay the suspicions of a brother, who though dense around women, can generally take the measure of a man."

"Hah. Is that a compliment or an accusation?"

"You decide. It is your motivation that is suspect."

"I'll take it as a compliment. My motivation is quite simple. I am, in the general way, bored silly by society and the women thrown at my head by a well-meaning mother and sister who think it is high time I married. To encounter a woman who is no danger to me is refreshing in the extreme. That is why I thought we could be friends, because I am no danger to you, either."

Rose stared at him and felt herself smiling at those laughing eyes. If he was not telling the truth, his performance at least deserved the compliment of her pretense of belief.

"And something else," he added.

"What?" she asked, wishing she could really have such a friendship.

"I enjoy jousting with you. Do you know how rare it is to find someone able to hold her own in an argument?"

"Unfortunately, yes."

"So there you have it. I am in some need of companionship of the abrasive kind, someone who does not agree with me at every turn just because I am as rich as Croesus."

"You are not."

"Not what?"

"As rich as Croesus."

"How would you know?"

"If you were you would hire a man of business and not be at all involved in trade." Rose lifted her chin as though his vocation mattered to her.

"It is precisely because I am involved in trade that I am so rich."

"No matter how much your sister would like it to be otherwise?" she chided.

"Rose, don't tell me you won't countenance an acquaintance with a cit. I had not thought you so stuffy."

"On the contrary," Rose said, deciding to change her tack, "I regard your involvement in trade to be the most stable thing about you. It is your avocation I disapprove of."

"Gambling? I assure you I—"

"No! Gammoning people into thinking you a charming, empty-headed fellow when in truth…"

"In truth, what?" he prompted with a grin.

"I haven't figured that out precisely, but I will."

"I shall anticipate the moment. Bring sweet Alice to tea this afternoon if you wish to extend your study of my character. Bring Wall, too, if you can manage it. Mother wants to meet him, even though he is safely married."

"Is she looking for a husband for Harriet?"

"Always. I scared off one suitor by challenging him to a duel. The offers since then have not been as forthcoming."

"I should think not, if they are in danger of being shot."

"Actually, I was the one who was punctured. It was a pure waste of my claret. I should have let him carry Harriet off to Yorkshire."

"That is a very hard thing to say of your own sister. How old was she?"

"Seventeen."

"Not old enough to know her own mind."

"Old enough to know better than to get involved with a man like Foy."

Rose halted her mount and pretended to be checking

the tightness of the girth. Bennet looked back in some concern, dismounted and went to help her down. "What is it?"

"Nothing. Martin, check the cinch," she called. "I shall walk a little way."

"I've said something to disturb you. Do you find it unnatural that I do not love my sister?"

Chaos followed behind Bennet like a large dog.

"No, of course not. It is I rather who have spoken out of turn. To condemn you for something I know nothing of is ill-done of me."

"Well, I was going to mention that, but as you have admitted your fault I am left with no barbs to fire."

Rose managed a brief smile, and she almost told him she knew Foy. But no, he would find out soon enough. Why ruin this day, when Axel was likely to ruin the next?

"Tell me what is wrong," Bennet begged, looping the reins over his arm and taking her hand between his two.

"The engagement and duel, this all happened years ago." Rose said, shaking the mental image of Axel's piercing brown eyes from her mind. "Surely it is past history. Perhaps Foy did not even survive the war," she said hopefully.

"No such luck. He was wounded several times and kept turning up like a bad penny to cut up our peace. This time when he begs for Harriet's hand I shall agree."

Rose became conscious of her surroundings and began walking again, forcing Bennet to surrender her hand. "That might make Harriet like you better, but if you did not think him worthy of her then…"

"It is not that Axel has become more acceptable, but that Harriet has managed to descend to his level. I must get her married off before she causes a scandal that I cannot squelch."

Rose's glance flew to his face.

"No, do not ask me what all she has been up to. By emulating her intimate acquaintances she has become very jaded. She may merely be trying to get revenge on me for being in control."

"Perhaps, if you talked things through with her, there might be a reconciliation."

"Harriet forgive me? Not a chance. Not with Mother on her side, and Harriet is like Mother in that respect. The catalog of my wrongs never has anything erased from it, but grows with time like the national debt. I doubt I could ever be forgiven for all my offenses."

"You are joking."

"Except that this birthday ball may wipe out a few. You should have your invitation by now. You are coming, of course."

"You make it difficult to say no. But then we must be off to Paris." She watched the smile fade from his face as he halted again.

"Do not go," he begged.

"But I must. I must go whenever Stanley and Alice are ready to leave." She signaled to Martin to bring Gallant, and Bennet helped her to mount.

"Help me convince Stanley to spend the season in London. You can stay in Varner House. Mother and Harriet would love to have you."

"Now that is an untruth," she said with her usual pert smile as she watched him swing up onto Chaos.

"Then stay to keep me from boredom."

"To argue with you? I think you will find that grows stale after a bit."

"Bantering with you? Never."

The look in Bennet's eyes could not be misread. He was not joking this time or making game of her. She smiled sadly and shook her head. One mention of her to Axel and he would revise his opinion about that. She urged Gallant into another canter, and the horse responded willingly to have two such treats in one day. What a strange man Varner was, to trust her with confidences about his family that if repeated would do them a great deal of discredit. She would not repeat them, of course. Rose never gossiped and took pains to say the best of people. She was well aware what careless chatter could do to a woman's character, how it could mar her very life. Was Bennet Varner naive or merely the first frank man she had ever met? She would have liked to further her acquaintance with him just to puzzle that out.

Bennet left Rose reluctantly at the hotel and wondered if he should risk delaying the ball just to buy a few more days. No, a celebration at Varner House would be no particular lure to the Walls, at least not to Rose. They would simply shrug and board the next packet. Just as the promise of a fine ship might not hold them. There was the possibility of making London so interesting for young Wall that he did not mind dallying in town, but Bennet caviled at introducing Stanley to any new vices just to serve his own ends.

He returned to South Audley Street, as he did frequently, to a house in pandemonium. Bennet heard his head groom sigh heavily as Bennet surrendered the reins to him and mounted the steps, prepared to untangle whatever setback was making his mother shriek in that disconcerting way. Had she only known, she could have gotten better work from the servants if she maintained her dignity rather than screaming at them like an angry fishwife.

For all her pretensions to society, Bennet felt his mother's plebeian tantrums more of an impediment to the family's acceptance than his involvement in trade. After quieting the seamstress and bribing her to finish Harriet's gown by the following day, after soothing the ruffled feathers of Mrs. Marshall, the housekeeper, and convincing Armand, the chef, not to pack up and leave, he cornered his mother and sister in the morning room.

Harriet was sprawled on the sofa, crying over the dress, which she pronounced ugly beyond words. Her tears would have been more convincing if she had not been wearing an expensive new blue walking outfit.

"Then wear one of your other dresses."

"I have worn them all. The only thing that will make the new dress acceptable is a proper necklace of diamonds."

"And I suppose you know just the ones to set it off. Very well, write down who has them and his direction and I will have Walters pick them up tomorrow. They will be your birthday present. By the way, you have sent an invitation round to the Walls, haven't you?"

"Well, I have invited them, though I do not see the need." Edith spoke now, two spots of color still remaining in her sallow cheeks from her recent tantrum. "They are, after all, just country cousins. What if they embarrass us with their dress or speech?"

"They won't, Mother," Bennet assured her absently as he picked up the *Times*. Just to discomfit her he glanced critically at her black bombazine. It was an affectation, this wearing of black three years after his father's death, when she would have looked better in some other color. But like the dyeing of her hair, Bennet put it down to bad advice from someone.

"I'm inviting Axel, then," Harriet said in the subdued silence that followed.

Bennet raised an eyebrow, and was about to say "why not?" but decided too prompt an acceptance of her suitor might make Harriet suspicious. "If you must." He sat and tried to focus on the financial news.

"If you get to invite the wallflower and company, I should be able to ask my friends. After all, it is my party." Harriet seated herself at the messy escritoire and pulled a list toward her.

"What did you call her?"

"A wallflower. Those dowdy clothes. And can you imagine her playing nursemaid to a young bride? She must be odd indeed."

"If I hear that title fastened on Miss Wall I will know where it came from, and I won't forget your maliciousness."

"In another day you will not have any say in what I do. I shall be in possession of my own fortune and I may marry Axel if I wish."

"Yes, I suppose you may, but do you not think you ought to shop around a bit first? Tomorrow you become one of the most marriageable young ladies in London, and I should think you could do a great deal better than Foy. Don't you think so, Mother?"

"Harriet is in love with Axel. Aren't you, Harriet? Why else would she have run off with him?"

"It has been four years," Bennet said, trying to bury himself in the paper. "May I point out Axel has made up to several other women since then, every time he lands back in London, in fact."

Harriet's blue eyes were ablaze with anger. "It does not seem like four years. It was my coming-out season and I remember every moment of it."

"I too recall the entire season with nauseating clarity, especially that bullet I took for you."

"That was your fault, Bennet," his mother informed him.

"Don't tell me you favored that havey-cavey elopement."

"It was better than having you break Harriet's heart by not letting her marry Axel."

"Well, I will no longer be the impediment."

"What if he does not ask me, Mother?" Harriet rose, clenching her hands together dramatically. "What if Axel's feelings have changed, or he has been too put off by Bennet?"

"Oh, he'll ask you all right," Bennet interrupted. "He needs your fortune more now than ever. Oh, by the way, I have made an appointment for both of us to see Barchester tomorrow morning. The reins of your future will then be put in your hands, Harriet. Have you engaged a man of business?"

"Not...not yet."

"Do you wish Barchester to recommend someone?"

"Certainly not. Is it necessary to have such a person with me tomorrow?"

"Not really, unless you mean to change banks immediately."

"I haven't decided yet."

"Let Barchester know when you do and where you want your monies deposited. He can arrange everything."

"I don't want him to do anything. He always treats me like a child."

"He means no harm by acting fatherly. Most women of independent means do not care to handle their own affairs."

"Most women do not have such an unreasonable guardian. I suppose you will charge me rent now to stay here?"

"Do not be absurd. You are still my sister, but I've no doubt you will be married within the month and off my hands for good."

"Must you both bicker like this?" their mother demanded. "You give me a splitting headache."

"I have tried bickering alone and it just doesn't work,"

Bennet quipped, sending his mother charging from the room, grumbling to herself.

Harriet waited until their mother was gone before she giggled. "Why do you bait her, Bennet? She cannot defend herself."

"And I cannot help myself. If only she realized how much we enjoy arguing. Seriously, Harriet, I will be placing a great deal of wealth at your disposal tomorrow. I hope you have considered that it might be wiser to keep control of it yourself than turn it over to a husband—any husband, including Axel."

"I know what I am about. I am not the green girl I was at seventeen."

"No, I realize that. There will also be investments to discuss. You will have to decide how you want to manage those."

Harriet walked dreamily to the window and stared out at the redbrick residences across the way. "I think once I am married I will set up a proper town house. I consider it highly unfair Papa left you both Chesney and Varner House."

"Hasn't Axel some residence other than his lodgings and that estate in Yorkshire?"

"He has a house near Epsom, but I require one in London."

"I am looking for a house for the Walls to rent. I can have Walters make inquiries for you...if you wish to make use of his services."

"Why are the Walls looking for a house?"

"To rent merely. They cannot stay in that hotel forever, and Mother has made it abundantly clear she does not want them here."

"But I thought they were on the point of embarking for Europe, at least before you introduced them to the social whirl of London."

"One invitation can hardly constitute a social whirl—oh. I forgot to tell Mother I asked them to tea today to make her acquaintance before your birthday ball."

"She won't like that."

"Yes, I know, but perhaps you can tell her for me. A diamond necklace should be worth one favor."

"Very well, I will tell her," said Harriet, walking in a businesslike way toward the door. "Just make sure my diamonds and my dress are ready by tomorrow afternoon."

"I have nothing else to concern me at all."

"Nothing but that nasty shipping business."

"That nasty shipping business keeps you both in fine gig."

"But must you flaunt it?" she asked with her hand on the doorknob.

"The world is changing, Harriet. I and other men like me helped win this last war. Don't ask me to be embarrassed about that. Didn't Wellington himself come to dine?"

"One evening."

"Well, he did have a war to fight. Now go and tell Mother the Walls are coming and I expect you both to be polite to them."

"If we must. But they are such encroaching mushrooms."

"You have not even met Stanley and Alice yet."

"Are we expected to entertain every country dowd we are remotely connected with?"

"Why not?"

"Why not? I have better things to do with my time."

"Just tell Mother."

Harriet ducked out of the room. Sometimes, just for a moment, Bennet thought he had got through to her and made some impression. There was sense in her some-

where, but then she would quote their mother or one of
her fashionable friends and turn his stomach. No, he did
not love his sister anymore. She had changed into some
creature he disliked exceedingly.

When the Walls were shown into the elegant gold salon
there were already two guests present, enjoying their tea,
Lady Catherine Gravely, and her daughter, Cassandra. After the coldly polite introductions it became clear to Rose
that the other two women were intimates of Harriet's and
had been invited to amuse her, since conversation with
the Walls was not expected to. It was also clear who had
tempted Harriet to savage her hair so badly, for both
women sported a head of tight curls.

Every time Bennet introduced a topic Rose or Stanley
might care to discuss, Harriet changed the subject to some
personage they did not know, thus shutting them out of
the conversation. Poor Alice took everything in with such
wide eyes, Rose knew they would put her down as a simpleton. Lady Catherine and Mrs. Varner were no help. The
former stared speculatively at Rose any time she opened
her mouth and the latter seemed interested only in her
daughter's gossip. If Edith remembered Rose's mother at
all she never made reference to her.

Rose was annoyed and in the mood to show it, but she
liked Bennet Varner and did want him for a friend. She
admired the way he had charmed her brother and sister-
in-law, no matter how much she suspected his motives.
And here he was, sending her embarrassed grimaces because his sister and mother were snubbing them. She
could at least enjoy that repartee with him. She gazed
about the lovely ground floor salon that was used only for
tea. She could imagine the elegance of the rooms that
must lie above. And yet she felt sorry for Bennet Varner,
always having to apologize for his mother and sister.

When Stanley cleared his throat meaningfully, Rose gulped her tea and was about to make some excuse to get them away early. Suddenly Harriet did mention a name they all knew.

"Lord Foy?" Alice piped up. "Wasn't that the man you were engaged to, Rose?"

Stanley choked on a gulp of tea and Rose paused with her cup halfway to her mouth. Bennet looked at her in inquiry.

"Foy...Foy..." Rose pretended to muse. "Is his name Axelrod Barton?"

"Yes," confirmed Cassie, her red lips parted in surprise, the bodice of her white muslin gown straining as she turned her plump form the better to stare at Rose. Rose was surprised to discover the look of utter disgust Lady Catherine bestowed on her own child. She knew there were women who hated their children, but she had never actually seen it before.

"Yes, it must be the same man," Rose confirmed. "He was a subaltern whom Father brought home one winter. I believe he was recovering from a leg wound."

"Shoulder," corrected Stanley, nervously clearing his throat.

Rose shrugged and silently thanked her brother for his attempt to draw talk away from the engagement.

"By engagement," Cassie asked playfully, "you don't actually mean...?"

Rose stared at her as though she had not comprehended. The figured muslin Cassie wore was meant for a younger girl, or perhaps a slighter girl, and did not become her.

"I fear it was just a schoolgirl passion," Rose said lightly. "You must know how entrancing those red uniforms can be. Was I sixteen or seventeen? I cannot recall, but when I considered seriously marrying a soldier, I thought of all the worry Mother had gone through and I backed out of the engagement. Foy understood.''

This speech damped the interest of the others but failed to appease Harriet, who was staring at Rose as though she wished her to disappear from the face of the earth. Bennet's gaze was not one of condemnation as Rose expected, but one of sympathy and understanding.

''Then there was that dreadful incident,'' Alice said, taking a provoking bite of cake so that everyone had to hang on her words until she had swallowed. Stanley gave one of his impatient sighs.

''What incident?'' Lady Catherine finally demanded sharply with more than casual interest.

''Colonel Wall's untimely death,'' Alice replied knowingly.

''Yes,'' agreed Rose. ''The marriage would have had to be put off for a year anyway, so we mutually agreed to part.''

''How did Colonel Wall die?'' Harriet asked, her intense gaze darting between Rose and Alice, ''if I'm not being too personal?''

''He was trampled by a horse,'' Stanley said without elaborating.

''That is why I never ride,'' Alice added. ''Nasty, dangerous beasts. I wonder you did not shoot the stallion, Stanley.''

''Perhaps I would have, if I had been there, but Rose was right. It was not Redditch's fault that Father and Foy decided to ride him when they were in their cups. He's a little wild around men he doesn't know, anyway. I assure you he behaves perfectly for me.''

Rose wondered if part of Stanley's tolerance derived from thinking he had tamed a beast his father could not handle.

''Still, to keep a killer horse...'' Cassie shook her head

in condemnation as though she knew something about horses, when Rose was quite sure from Cassie's stout figure that she did not even ride.

"But it was an accident," Bennet said. "I would never get rid of one of my beasts if it accidently threw Harriet and broke her neck."

"Bennet!" Harriet cried, incensed. "That is the most unfeeling remark you have ever made."

"No, I don't think you can be right there. It comes nowhere near the time I compared you to the opera dancer. Then there was the incident at the East India Docks…"

"If you tell anyone about that I shall—"

"Stop it, Bennet," his mother commanded. "To upset your sister in this way is very ill-mannered."

"So sorry, Mother. Sometimes I forget everything you taught me about manners."

Mrs. Varner had the conscience to look abashed at this. "You must excuse my son," she said finally to the Walls. "Sometimes his rather misplaced wit takes him beyond the bounds of what is pleasing."

"Humor is always pleasing," Rose said, giving Bennet a grateful smile for drawing fire upon himself. "And anyone should be able to take a joke so long as it is made in good fun. And as much enjoyment as we are deriving from the tea, I fear we must be going soon. Alice's dress is nowhere near completion and I am sure you must have a thousand things to see to before tomorrow night."

They did not linger over their departure. Bennet would have sent them home in his carriage, but Stanley said they would find a hack.

"What an old tartar the mother is," he said to Rose in the carriage. "I suppose we must go to this thing, seeing as Bennet has been so obliging."

Alice stared at her husband, her limpid blue eyes out-raged. "Surely you do not mean you would rather not?"

"Not if we are to be subjected to so much frostiness from Mrs. Varner and that other old dragon! Those two chits were not much better. I think they might have spoken to you, Alice, just for the sake of politeness."

Rose sighed. If Stanley noticed being cold-shouldered, then it was blatant indeed. "Perhaps they will when they know her better. Ten to one she will be so busy dancing tomorrow night she will not even have time to converse with them, but there is no real need for me to go."

"No, I think you must, Rose. After all, she is your godmother," Stanley said firmly.

Meaning, Rose took it, that if she cried off, he would as well. That would leave Alice in floods of tears and with her to blame.

"Yes, I suppose I must. After all, an evening can last only so long. Then we will finalize our arrangements for Europe."

"Mmm," Stanley replied.

Chapter Three

The next day, in spite of Rose's sporting a new pearl-gray riding habit with a modish top hat, Bennet did not come to ride. He did, however, send Stilton with two mounts. Martin conferred with the older groom, making arrangements for returning the horses, Rose supposed.

They sprang Victor and Gallant as soon as they reached Hyde Park, and the carefree ride reminded Rose of their rides together at home. Her feelings for Martin, when she bothered to analyze them, were those of an older sister. She had wrested him and his sister, Cynthie, from a workhouse when their parents had been carried off by influenza. Having made herself responsible for them, she felt closer to them in many ways than to her own brother and mother. At least they had no secrets from each other, which was not the case with her own family.

Martin drew rein first to walk Victor near one of the ponds and let him get a short drink. Rose let Gallant lower his mouth to the water also, but the large gelding only played in it, flapping his lips at the icy ripples. She missed the provoking conversation of Bennet, but was unwilling to say so.

"I imagine Mr. Varner is busy today," Martin suggested.

"Yes, I am sure that he is always busy, today especially."

"I made some inquiries about Foy yesterday. He did survive the war."

"I know. His name came up at tea yesterday. But Stanley and I were so engrossed in distancing ourselves from him, we never got to hear what they were saying about him."

"He's on the hunt for a wife, done up, by what I could make out."

"That's not much of a change from five years ago."

"They say he will make a match with Varner's sister if Varner will give his consent."

"He will give it." Rose scratched her mount's withers then turned to Martin. "I keep feeling I should warn Harriet about Axel."

"How can you do that without giving yourself away?"

"I do not know. Yet I must do something. Perhaps I should tell Bennet."

"You can't do that either."

"I think I can trust him far enough to tell him how rotten Axel is without going into specifics."

"I wish we were well out of this town. Now that we know Foy is here, France is looking better and better to me, even if I don't know the lingo."

"To me as well. Perhaps we should hope for a disastrous evening. That might convince Stanley that London is not as much fun as he thinks."

"That depends on how disastrous. If Foy is pursuing the Varner chit he is like to show up at this ball."

"I am well aware of that possibility, but I will be on the lookout for him. To be sure there will be a hundred

people there. I should be able to avoid one man. If all
else fails I will hide until it is time to leave.''

Martin nodded and suggested they ride on toward
Green Park now that the horses were rested.

"Walters!" Bennet shouted as he came into the office,
tossing a paper at his secretary and casting his hat aside.
"Trace this shipment back to its source. I want to know
who sent it, who paid for it and who delivered it to the
dock.''

"Now?'' Walters asked as Bennet went into his inner
office and attacked his desk, a drawer at a time, making
a mangle of the papers inside and finally knocking onto
the floor the stack of documents that had been carefully
arranged on the blotter.

"It's only a matter of national security. Yes, of course,
now.''

"A trunk full of books?'' asked Walters, peering at the
bill of lading as he gathered up the contracts.

"With a heavy bottom. There was enough gold under
those French plays and poems to finance a small army, or
a large army for a few days.''

"Where was it going?''

"Elba.''

"Good Lord!'' Walters said, his arms full of documents
as he stared myopically at the shipping order. "And on
the *Celestine*.''

"The matter is now in the hands of the Foreign Office.
Get cracking, Walters. We need that information.''

"Right away, sir, but you will be terribly late if you
wait for this.''

"Late for what?''

"Your sister's ball, of course.''

"Oh, my God. I had completely forgotten. I'll rush
'round there and fly up the back stairs to change. You

know Leighton at the Foreign Office. Seek him out and give him the information, then come to the house. Oh, did you…?''

''I picked up the necklace and earrings and delivered them to Varner House.''

''Excellent! They had them in good time?''

''Carried them 'round myself before noon.''

''You are a paragon. Give yourself a raise. I must go. Have a footman interrupt me tonight, whatever you learn. I must know.''

Gwen Rose sat observing the dancing couples in utter and unremitting boredom. She looked down again at her ivory silk gown with the scallops of seed pearls. She was impeccably dressed and had her hair gathered up in a Medusan knot of curls, restrained by a silver riband, yet no one had asked her to dance all evening. Nor was any gentleman likely to without an introduction. Several men had cast curious glances in her direction as she sat alone almost within the embrace of a large parlor palm she had struck up a friendship with. She was grateful for its company and it did seem more likely to converse with her than the dozen dowagers who were similarly ensconced in the corners of the Varner ballroom. At least its conversation, if it had any, would have been neither silly nor malicious.

She did not know how it was that she always imagined people to be talking about her. Perhaps because they so often were discussing her at the assemblies around Bristol. Typically it would be the duty of the hostess or even the hostess's daughter to introduce newcomers about until they had struck up a conversation that seemed promising. Neither Mrs. Varner nor Harriet had made the slightest effort to ease the Walls into society.

Fortunately Stanley had become acquainted with half a

dozen men from the clubs and could make Alice known
to their wives, one of whom was not much older than
Alice and took her under her wing. Rose supposed she
could have trailed after them, but since Alice never
thought to include her it would have taken some effort to
attach herself to them. And she frankly found the palm
better company.

The Varner ballroom, which extended out over the
ground floor portico, looked much as she had suspected
it would, glittering gold in the light of hundreds of candles
and richly alive with music. She could see through the far
doorway into the refreshment salon, which had red wallpaper. She would dearly have loved to go there to get
something cool to drink and to look at the paintings on
the wall. But women looked so singular when they moved
about a room this size alone. The worst part would be
when they had to go in to supper. She would wait until
near the end so she would not be so conspicuous for not
having a partner, but then it would be hard to find a place
to sit. Perhaps Stanley would think to save her a seat, if
he remembered to leave the card room at all. Trapped
again, she thought as she sighed heavily.

She had hoped Bennet would put in an appearance, not
that he would have time to joust with her. Probably his
tardiness was what had the Varner women so disturbed as
they whispered between themselves, casting occasional
dark looks at Rose. Edith looked like a black crow in her
silk, and Harriet's dress was far too old even for a woman
celebrating her twenty-first birthday, the bosom revealing
the spareness of her breasts. Rose mentally took herself
to task for being critical. It did not matter that she did not
say these things out loud. She should not even be thinking
them.

When the Gravelys arrived Lady Catherine was impeccably dressed in lavender silk and traded insincere kisses

with both Varner women. Cassie was wearing a white gown trimmed with scarlet scallops and large red silk flowers to set off, Rose supposed, the exquisite necklace of rubies at her throat. They were jewels more appropriate to an older woman, but would have looked misplaced against Lady Catherine's stark-white skin. Whatever else one said of Cassie she did have the most creamy skin. On second glance the rubies shone like drops of blood around her neck, and with the cropped hair, the specter of the guillotine loomed in Rose's mind. Rose wondered if the association was particular to her or an intentional ploy of Cassie's for attention. A sharp look from this miss warned Rose that she had been staring too long at her, but so had others, so Rose did not take herself to task again. If they were going to bore her, what did they expect?

She was attempting to ignore them by mentally coppicing the hedgerows around Wall, since she was quite sure the hired men were not doing so in her absence. She had rounded the horse pasture, had gotten past the stream and nearly to the stone fence when someone entered the room who caused every head to turn.

She hoped desperately that it was Bennet and she could at least exchange a bored smile with him. But the man wore a scarlet coat, and for a moment Rose's eyes blurred with shock. It was Axelrod Barton.

Rose tried to shrink even farther into the plant's embrace. She would wait for Foy's attention to be diverted and slip toward the refreshment salon. Surely it had a door into the hall and she would be able to make her escape. But Axel surveyed the room like a hunter picking out his prey, his fair head thrown up arrogantly, his brown eyes slicing through the crowd, his tanned hand gripping the hilt of his dress saber. Rose felt his speculative gaze come to rest upon her. Perhaps he would not recognize her after five years. She had changed much more than he. She tried to avert her eyes, but it was as though he compelled her to look at him. When she did meet his gaze he nodded and ran the back of his hand along the faint scar on his jaw.

Rose covered her hand. The ring that had made that scar was no longer there, but it felt as though it was. She had thrown that mark of his possession back in his face. She reminded herself that she was free of Axel, that he could do nothing to hurt her, but she knew that was not true.

She sent him in return a cold, challenging look and he came to her with his wicked lip-curling smile. It was the nicest thing about him.

"You remember me," he said, taking her hand and kissing it possessively.

"I could scarcely forget you."

"You nearly did for me. You and that ring and that stallion of yours. I tell you, Rosie, never in all my years in the Peninsula have I seen the like of your efficiency at mayhem."

"Must you go on about it?" Rose asked, looking distractedly at the attention they were drawing.

"What? Have I offended your maidenly sensibilities?"

"At one time or another you have offended all my sensibilities."

"Dance with me. I think it would be so much more amusing to argue with you while you are concentrating on your steps."

"I am not dancing," she said firmly, daring him to dislodge her from the palm tree.

"Never say you don't remember how, for I recall quite distinctly the dancing at our engagement party."

"Of course I remember how. I simply am not dancing tonight."

"Why not tonight?" he demanded, compelling her to

rise to her feet so as not to have a tug-of-war with him over her hand.

"Don't be so stupid, Axel. If I dance now they will think I have been wanting to dance all evening."

"And haven't you?" he asked with a laugh.

"Yes, of course, but I don't want to let them know that," Rose said, nodding toward the Varner women.

"But—no! This is all too complex for me. You will dance," he said, placing an arm forcibly about her waist when the players obligingly struck up a waltz. "You owe me that much."

As Axel whirled her down the floor Rose caught a glimpse of Harriet's flushed and angry face, and an almost jealous look from Cassie. Certainly Mrs. Varner knew the man who was pursuing her daughter was waltzing passionately with his former fiancée. She whispered something to Lady Catherine just as they danced past. Lady Catherine's face looked as though it had been cut in stone, for all the expression it bore.

"You have grown even more lovely with the years," Axel said in his caressing way.

"Fustian."

"A lady would return the compliment. Do you not still find me handsome?"

Rose glanced up at him and had to admit that she did not. "I find you dissipated."

"Then I have achieved my aim."

"If looking dissolute were a worthwhile object." Rose turned her face away, desperately searching for Stanley, or Alice's petal-pink gown.

"But women love it." He bent to whisper in her ear. "The more scarred and disheveled I am, the more I have to fend them off." His sun-bleached blond hair fell mockingly over his brow from its central part.

"Not all women," Rose corrected, trying to push herself back from his embrace without tripping. "At least one woman sees you for what you are."

"And what is that?"

"A spoiled, selfish blackguard—"

"Yes, of course."

"You're impossible," she whispered viciously.

"I give you impossible. What else?"

"And dangerous."

He gripped her even tighter. "Most certainly. I commend you on your excellent reading of my character. Though I think you should have mentioned what a fine dancer I am."

"I had no intention of complimenting you, sir. I think very ill of you. And do not smolder, Axel. It makes you look childish."

This last remark seemed to shake his poise. "I am a dangerous man," he warned.

"I know that," Rose said, fixing him with her angry green eyes.

"Then why do you not act like other women?"

"Seek you out, you mean? Common sense. A coiled snake has a certain fall-from-grace fascination about it," she said with disgust. "That does not mean I would stretch out my hand to pet it."

"You are piercing my hand with your nails," Axel complained.

"I will draw blood in a moment if you do not put some space between us."

"Any other woman in the room would be enjoying herself. They are all watching you."

"I am well aware of that. I detest being the object of so much scrutiny."

"I can take care of that." Axel spun her into the hallway and dragged her toward the only closed door. It turned out to be the library.

"This is the outside of enough," Rose complained as Axel kicked the door shut and turned her wrist around behind her back to hold her close to him. "Release me or you will regret it."

"I don't think so," Axel said as he captured her mouth in a hungry kiss.

But Rose had one arm free and that was enough. She drew back and punched him in the throat as hard as she could manage. Axel went to his knees, gasping for air.

The door opened and Bennet appeared, seeming startled to see a guest of his in difficulty. "Are you—Axel, what happened?"

"He cannot talk now. He is choking," Rose informed Bennet, as though it were an everyday event.

"I can see that. Perhaps we should get him some water," Bennet said, searching the glasses and decanters on the side table.

"Oh no, let's not. I mean, it's only Axel. He'll be fine."

"Brandy!" Axel gasped, staggering to his feet and supporting himself with a hand on the edge of the desk.

"See," Rose replied.

"Still," Bennet said, repressing a chuckle, "I think I should do something. Can't have him expiring in the library."

"Oh, very well," Rose agreed. "I will get some." She exited in no particular hurry.

Axel gulped from the glass Bennet put in his hands and had a renewed fit of coughing that lasted several minutes.

"Well, perhaps brandy wasn't the best choice," Bennet decided. "What happened?"

"She punched me in the throat," Axel complained hoarsely.

"No! Really?" Bennet bit his lips to keep from laughing outright.

"Yes, ow!" Axel was still feeling the injured area.

"Dangerous woman," Bennet observed sympathetically. "Shall I call my carriage to take you home?"

"Devil take you, Varner!"

"He probably will, and you as well," Bennet said, refilling Axel's glass and pouring some wine for himself.

"See that this doesn't get about."

"Would a host gossip about his guests? Besides, I do not even know the lady."

"Just see to it. And I want a word with you later," Axel said menacingly as he left the room.

"As soon as you feel up to it." Bennet sat down at his desk and laughed at the thought of Rose fending off Axel so efficiently. But then, she knew Foy. He had to keep reminding himself of that. The two of them probably knew each other better than he knew either one of them, and that was a sobering thought.

Where the hell was Walters? He wanted to know what was going on. He went to the small side door and unlocked it. Opening it, he stared down the dark back stair that came out in the stable block, but there was no unusual activity so he closed it.

Music flowed into the room as the hall door opened and Rose spun in. "I could not find any water. Will champagne do? Oh, he is gone."

"You do not seem much bereft."

"I am not, actually. Had he still been here I might have felt compelled to apologize." Rose fingered her injured arm.

"To Foy? No, my dear. I feel sure he had it coming. Did he bruise your wrist?" Bennet came to take the glass from her and put it on the desk.

"Probably, but I wear gloves most everywhere."

"I am sorry, Rose," he said, keeping hold of her hand. "If only I had not been detained."

"Oh, do not regard it. Axel and I always clash. I only hope I have not distressed Harriet."

"How could that be so?"

"She saw Axel dancing with me."

"She will get over it."

Rose sighed. "What...what did he say about me?"

"That you are a dangerous woman. But I had already surmised that."

"My antagonism toward Axel is of long standing, but I do not know why he thought he could get away with dragging me in here."

The smile suddenly left Bennet's face. "Did anyone see you leave the room with him?"

"Bennet, everyone saw."

"Then you must go back in on my arm."

"I do not care so much for myself," she said, letting him take her arm, "but if there is talk, Stanley will never forgive me."

"Do not worry. We shall put a stop to it."

As they entered the ballroom during an interval between two dances, the buzz of talk and the subsequent lull that followed them through the room convinced Rose she had been the subject of conversation. She scanned the crowd for some friendly face, or at least a familiar one. There was only Alice standing near Cassie, and Axel talking earnestly to a stone-faced Harriet. Fortunately Stanley was nowhere in sight—probably still in the card room.

Bennet ignored them all. He spoke to the musicians and had them strike up a waltz. Rose admired the masterful way he got just what he wanted. Other couples joined them on the floor after frantically checking dance cards and discovering that this waltz was nowhere on the program. Rose wondered how much of the gossip was about her hasty exit with Axel and how much sprang from what he might have said about her. It hardly mattered. She could not show her face again in London. But the Walls were poised to launch themselves toward Europe. They should be able to stay ahead of even Axel's agile tongue. And in four or five months she would go to live at her mother's house in Bristol, a city that had run its length gossiping about her.

It was worth facing them all down to stand up just once with Bennet Varner, the only man she had ever met who was worth talking to. She forgot about the rest of them and focused her attention only on him and the music. These few minutes made up for the whole interminable evening. He smiled at her and she sailed around and around almost as though they were one being. Only his stopping signaled her that the music had ceased as well.

''Come, I shall lead you in to supper.''

''Surely there are many with precedence over me.''

''None, in my estimation. At any rate I have no idea who they would be.''

Rose let Bennet escort her into the formal blue and white room, fill her plate with all manner of delicacies and supply her with a glass of iced punch. The table seemed to go on for miles and no one sat close enough to disturb them. Except for an occasional glare from Harriet or Mrs. Varner, Rose could have imagined she was some quite ordinary girl enjoying a first flirtation with an extraordinary man. He rattled on about the *Celestine,* his ship, and how much fun she would have in Italy, just as soon as the mainmast was replaced.

''The mainmast?'' she asked, swallowing a bite of lobster cake the wrong way. ''But that sounds rather serious.''

''The work of a day or two—no more.''

''You make everything sound so easy, when actually I am quite sure it is an enormous undertaking, to change a mast and get it fastened to the ship.''

"No, were you thinking that the deck held it up?" he asked, standing a candle in an aspic jelly and watching it fall over.

"Yes, well, I have never thought much about it. I have stayed in Bristol, of course, and watched the ships but I have never been on one."

"What holds the masts up is all of the rigging. It is most important that for every line pulling forward there is one pulling backward with an equal amount of tension. The same thing left to right."

"It all makes such perfect sense when you explain it, but does not that put our departure off even farther?" she asked astutely.

"What do you mean?"

"All that rigging will have to be taken down, then put back up again."

"Oh what is another day or two when you are making such a hit in London?"

"A hit? I am no such thing. I am probably the most talked-about woman in town this night."

"Yes, that is what I meant," Bennet said, staring into her eyes.

"Do be serious, Mr. Varner," she said sternly. "You cannot want to be in the company of an infamous woman."

"My friends call me Bennet." He rested his elbow on the table and his chin on his hand to study her better.

"What do your enemies call you?"

"I see to it that I have no enemies," he said with that determined smile of his, and Rose wondered if he did not make them or if he simply eliminated them.

"You have one—Axelrod Barton, Lord Foy. He is looking daggers at you this very moment."

"Like yours, my antagonism with Axel goes back so

far he is like a bunion. It feels odd when he is not rubbing at me.''

Rose laughed and then sobered herself. ''Unfortunately Axel is more dangerous than a bunion. He is at home here and I am the outsider. Whatever he says will be believed.''

Bennet forcibly drew his gaze away from the slender mounds of her bosom and got lost in Rose's eyes again. ''Oh, I think if you are accepted by my family your character will bear scrutiny.''

''If my acceptance hinges on your family's approval, then it is fortunate that it does not matter to me what people think.''

''I can take care of Mother and Harriet. But if you do not care what people think, then why did you come back into the library when another woman would have run off and had the vapors.''

''Because I do care what you think of me…friend.''

''And I care—what is it?'' Bennet said impatiently to the footman whispering in his ear. ''I must leave you for a few minutes, Rose. Forgive me.''

The glow of Bennet's safe aura lasted only a moment after he followed the footman out. Rose now found herself to be the object of scrutiny from so many pairs of eyes she felt she had to do something. She brushed at an imaginary stain on her gown, then got up in mock frustration and went upstairs to find one of the chambers prepared for the ladies to withdraw into to relieve themselves or repair torn hems. She was not lucky enough to find an empty one so she did not stay to listen to the idle chatter. The talk seemed rather forced after her entrance.

She crept back down one flight and stole into the unoccupied library. Such a delightful room, a fire burning in the grate and her pick of books. She chose a volume of Diderot's encyclopedia and seated herself in the high-backed armchair turned toward the fire. She curled her legs up in the chair, thinking that the cozy leather must have embraced Bennet often. The dark paneled room said Bennet to her, from the highly polished furniture to the shelves and shelves of well-used books. No matter how much she tried to apply herself to the text her mind kept wandering to her friend and that provoking smile of his.

She thought she must have dozed, for a sudden draft awakened her and subsequent covert sounds of liquid being poured indicated that whoever had come through that oddly placed side door was no burglar but was quite at home. The hall door opened and she heard confident steps.

"Gaspard, what news?" Bennet demanded in perfect French.

Rose gaped in the privacy of her chair as Gaspard revealed plans to free Napoleon from his island prison. He mentioned half a dozen ships, *L'Inconstant* by name, and a thousand men.

"They managed to evade the British cruisers then," Bennet said. "Amazing." Bennet's contributions to the conversation, though in fluent French, were noncommittal. None of the news, though he demanded details, seemed to be much of a surprise to him. Rose listened to his inflection to see if she could tell if he were a part of this heinous plot, but she could not.

The door was flung open again and Rose thought the room was getting a trifle crowded. Her danger of being discovered was great, even if she made no sound.

"Leighton, come in," Bennet said. "You are very late."

"I just got Walters's message," the new voice said excitedly. "I had to dispatch a flurry of reports just in case."

"Gaspard seems to have little doubt his news from the fishermen on Elba is true."

The door to the library thumped open again and Rose moaned inwardly, drawing tighter into the cover of the wing chair.

"Bennet, I want to speak to you now," Axel demanded drunkenly.

"Not now, Foy, can you not see I am engaged?"

"This cannot wait."

"Oh, very well. Leighton, take Gaspard, go to your office and await me there."

This last was spoken in English, Rose supposed, for Axel's benefit. To her relief at least two of the men left by the exterior door.

"I am not asking permission this time. I am telling you. I mean to have Harriet."

"Yes, of course," Bennet replied. "Brandy?"

"What do you mean? She told you?"

Rose heard glasses being filled and wondered what Bennet was playing at.

"We discussed all this when I turned her inheritance over to her," Bennet said calmly. "She is responsible for her own fortune now. It was nice of you to come to ask formally for her hand, but there was really no need."

"But I didn't," Axel replied.

"But surely you intend to," Bennet countered.

"You cannot stop me."

"I do not mean to. I only stood in your way four years ago because of her young age. Since her attention has remained fastened on you all these years, I see now that I was wrong."

"You admit you were wrong?" Axel asked incredulously.

"Yes, her love for you, compared to the length of most affairs in London, amounts to a grand passion. Without a doubt, you and Harriet belong together."

Rose heard their glasses click together, but she did not imagine Axel was participating in the toast.

"We do? Yes, of course we do. So there are no settlements to work out?"

"Not between the two of us. You have only to deal with Harriet. Do you plan a large wedding?"

"I—we haven't decided yet."

"Allow me to put one of my traveling carriages at your disposal for your honeymoon. Also Harriet has taken a notion to have a London house. I can be no end of help to you there."

"I prefer to make my own arrangements, if you don't mind."

"Not at all. Just let me know if I can be of service."

"I—I will."

The door opened and closed with less assurance this time and Rose breathed a sigh of relief. If only Bennet would leave now. She heard him chuckling to himself. So, he was not really foisting his sister on such a villain as Foy, but was making a May game of the man. She heard footsteps coming toward the fireplace and closed her eyes as if in sleep. She detected a slight gasp when Bennet discovered her, but maintained her pose. He said nothing, but she could feel his weight on the arms of the chair, his breath on her forehead, then his lips on hers. Her eyes flew open.

"Wh-what are you doing?" she stammered as she shrank into the chair.

"Waking a very appealing sleeping beauty."

"I do not think you really believed me to be asleep."

"Of course, you were asleep. Otherwise I might suspect you of eavesdropping."

"No one could have slept though Axel's incoherent ranting."

"Aha, that should have been my line, not yours."

"Very well, I was pretending to be asleep to avoid embarrassment." She stood and closed the volume.

"For you or me?"

"For both of us. And as long as I have been accused of *spying*—" she laid an accusing emphasis on the word but Bennet only grinned at her "—what do you mean by handing your sister over to such a rake?"

"But if I make it easy for him, he may decide he does not want her. Believe me, I know Axel."

"I know him too."

"I have been trying to forget that," Bennet said with the first edge to his voice that she had ever heard. He put down his glass and deliberately kissed her. And she let him, only coming to her senses when she realized this was just the sort of thing she would have killed Axel for. But Bennet was nothing like Axel. Still, this was not a kiss of friendship, and she had to put him in his place.

When he finally released her she sniffed and said, "In your own way you are just as ruthless and manipulative as Axel."

"Something tells me I should take offense at that," he replied, trying to get close to her lips again and finding a volume of Diderot thrust in his face instead.

"Something tells me you won't. I must go and find Stanley and Alice. It is time we were taking our leave."

He did not try to detain her but chuckled again as he replaced the volume on the shelf. It was in French and if he knew anything about Miss Gwen Rose Wall, he could make a guess that she was not just looking at the pictures. He went over his conversation with Gaspard in his mind. Even if she spoke of it, and he did not think she would, she was scarcely likely to spook their quarry, not before the trap had been sprung. He really must remember never to underestimate her again.

Chapter Four

The next day Rose and Martin had ridden alone again and Rose decided to go with Martin to return the horses to Varner House. They rode around the corner past that larger side portico to the stable block off the alley. Rose was not surprised at the opulence of this part of the house. She was just complimenting Stilton on the facilities when Bennet drove in with a high-stepping team that required all the efforts of his tiger to subdue while Bennet jumped down in order to be the one who lifted Rose from the saddle and set her gently down on the paved brick courtyard. "I'm sorry I missed our ride today. Surely you were not going to walk back to the hotel."

"I had some thought of getting a hack and going shopping down Oxford Street on the way back," she replied, stepping out of his embrace.

"Did you enjoy your ride?"

"Immensely, since I did not have to fend off either Axel or you."

"I must apologize for my behavior last night. I was…drunk."

"I know when a man is drunk and you were no such thing."

Bennet, looking boyish in his somber attire, blinked at being contradicted. "Excited then. I lost my head."

"That's not much of an excuse for your behavior in the library last night," Rose said, turning her back.

"Stealing a kiss?" Bennet walked around in front of her, blocking her retreat from the stable block. "Is it my fault you are utterly irresistible...friend?"

Rose noticed that both grooms and the tiger were pointedly ignoring them, meaning they could hear every word. "That was not a kiss of friendship," she whispered urgently. "Martin," she called. "Please go find us a hack."

"Don't bother, Martin," Bennet countered. "I will take you back to your hotel or shopping if that's what you wish." Saying that he lifted Rose into the curricle, which seesawed slightly behind the agitated team. He had swung her about so effortlessly it almost made her giddy. She should resent that, but somehow she found that she liked to be a bit dizzy when in Bennet's company. It let her say things she would never think to say to another man.

Bennet hopped in, grabbed the reins and spared no more than a backward glance to make sure Martin and the tiger had swung up behind. "Now where were we?" he asked Rose as he feathered the turn into the street.

"In too public a place to discuss anything private," Rose reminded him.

"I'm sure I can rely on the discretion of my tiger just as you trust Martin."

Rose stared at him, wondering how much of her connection with Martin he divined. "It was not your loss of control that worried me the most."

"What then?" Bennet glanced at her in such apparent innocent good humor she felt unable to upbraid him about the presence of the Frenchman in his library. If he were guilty of clandestine activity against the government would he be likely to have the effrontery to invite her condemnation? The answer was yes. From her brief experience of Bennet Varner, there was little he would not dare and nothing he could not carry off. She must not let herself be as swayed by his charm as everyone else was. Beginning to feel her long silence had grown awkward, Rose scrambled in her mind to find some other flaw with which to upbraid him, but she could not.

Bennet grinned at her speechlessness. "Do you go to the party at Lady Catherine's house tonight?" he asked absently.

"No, why should they invite us?"

"Because it would be the gracious thing to do for the relatives of a close friend, which is precisely why they have not."

"You sound as though you resent them as much as..."

"As much as I dislike my own mother and sister? That was what you were about to say, wasn't it?"

"Yes, but then I remembered my manners."

"You won't have much use for them in London," Bennet said, passing a string of carts and running the danger of locking wheels with a mail coach before he nipped back to his side of the street. "You will meet a great many people here who will be gracious to your face, but who will talk about you unmercifully behind your back."

"And how are they different from people anywhere else?" she asked, clutching the side of the curricle as he feathered another corner. It suddenly occurred to her that they were not going to Greeves Hotel, that they were not, in fact, even going in the right direction.

She was about to point this out to Bennet when he turned a look of genuine surprise upon her. "You have been the subject of gossip before?"

"Yes," she said guardedly. "The breaking of an engagement, even when done by mutual agreement, is bound to be a cause for gossip."

"Was that the only reason for the gossip?" He asked it casually, as though it were a matter of little interest to him. But Rose read it as an invitation to confide in him. Had there not been the tiger pointedly ignoring them, she might have been tempted, but there were Martin's feelings to consider as well.

"You know what Axel is. I offended his pride by crying off. Even though he took the ring back with relief, he gave it about that he was the one who jilted me and hinted at some dark reason for his decision."

"Yes, putting all the blame on you without saying anything actionable."

"As though I would take him to court when all I wanted to do was forget…" Rose ran out of breath, and Bennet looked at her with concern.

"Forget Axel? Impossible. He is like a boil on one's neck. It is impossible to forget him even when he is a thousand miles away."

Rose laughed nervously. "Does Lady Catherine entertain often?"

"Nearly every week. She needs material and that is the easiest way to get it."

"Material? Whatever do you mean?" Rose stared about at the shops they were now passing, mapmakers, chandlers and an excise office.

"For her rumor mill. When I said Harriet had fallen under some bad influence it was the Gravelys I was referring to. They have taught her to be spiteful with a smile, playing people against each other for amusement—the sort of social torture I would like to warn you of."

"In order to be hurt by them I should have to care what they thought, what anyone thought of me, and I do not."

"Does Alice?" Bennet asked, drawing a conscience-stricken look from Rose.

"Yes, but she is an innocent. What has she to worry about?"

"Last season they took Miss Robin Coates on as their protégée, led her into excesses that became too dangerous. Now they have dropped her. She will never receive another invitation from either family, and no word of explanation."

"But what has that to do with—"

"Ah, here we are," Bennet said with satisfaction, and he pulled the team to a halt on the dock.

"But where are we?" Rose demanded, letting him swing her down from the curricle all the same.

"The *Celestine*. I was sure you would want to inspect her."

"And if I feel that the staterooms are too small?" Rose looked critically at the three-masted schooner with its green and gilt trim.

"Why, we can have them enlarged. Of course, we shall have to throw part of the cargo overboard, but it's only money. Actually I knew they were to remove the old mast today, so I thought you might like to watch." Bennet looked up at the intricate block and tackle arrangements and nodded.

"You are impossible!" Rose said as she let him take her arm to help her along the crowded quay.

"Just when I was congratulating myself on how agreeable I was being."

"You know what I mean."

"Shall I carry you? I would not want you to trip on your riding habit and fall into the Thames."

"I can manage," Rose said as she threw the tail of her long skirt over one wrist and skipped up the planked gangway.

"This is Captain Cooley," Bennet said. "Miss Gwen Rose Wall will be sailing with you to Europe."

"Aye, if we ever get out of port. It's yer own ship and all, but to be replacin' a perfectly fine mainmast..." Cooley shook his head grimly as the chocks squeaked and the men heaved. The mast was belayed with stout ropes until the pulleys could be repositioned, run out and fastened to the mast again as the huge billet of wood swayed ponderously over the deck. A man in a carpenter's apron was excitedly crawling about underneath the many tons of wood, making Rose's flesh creep. Cooley went over at the seaman's excited exclamation and lay down on the deck himself to examine the butt of the mast. He rose again and waved his hand, shouting some order that started the pulleys to squeaking again.

"Well, I'll be blasted! Beggin' yer pardon, miss. It beats me how you knew that mast was cracked afore I did, Mr. Varner. You can see the interior crack from the base. It would probably have riven into splinters in the next storm. You are a wonder, sir. Yer father would've been proud of ye."

Rose thought she had caught a look of surprise flit across Bennet's face before his usual aspect of cheerful confidence reasserted itself. If Bennet had known the mast was cracked then this had not been a deliberate ruse to keep her in London a few more days. But if, as she surmised, it had been a lucky guess, it meant Bennet was still suspect. What could he hope to accomplish in a few days or a week—the liberation of Napoleon? The realization hit her in a warm rush. If Bennet were trying to contrive that, then he must know Europe would soon be a very dangerous place for the English, or was it just that he could not afford to let her and her knowledge loose on the Continent?

Absurd! She was much more of a danger to Bennet here in London than in Paris. She could and probably should march right into the Foreign Office and tell them what she had overheard. She went over in her mind how she would tell it, how she would probably be unsuccessful in gaining an audience with anyone of importance, how they would disbelieve her even if she got someone's ear. She would appear a fool, but what did that matter where the safety of the country was at stake? She considered for no more than a moment confiding in Stanley. He was so unused to trusting her judgment in any matter of importance that she knew he would only say she must have misheard and dismiss her concern.

"Seen enough?" Bennet's abrupt question caused Rose to jump.

She cleared her throat. "We have not seen the cabins yet."

"I think you will be quite pleased on that account. Let me go down the companionway first so that I may assist you."

"I do not need any help," Rose insisted. But the effort of bunching up her riding skirt and trying to keep it tucked about her so as not to expose her ankles left her with only one hand to hang on to the ladder. She could not see her feet, and one misstep caught her off balance. She let go of her skirts but too late to avoid a tumble backward into Bennet Varner's arms. After her initial gasp she clutched him around the neck and looked accusingly into his eyes. "Knowing you as I do I might almost think that was no accident."

"Of course not. I bring all my *chères amies* here, hoping they will fall down that ladder into my arms."

"You can put me down now."

"What?"

"Miss, are you all right?" Captain Cooley called from the deck.

"We're fine," Bennet shouted back.

"Harrumph. I was askin' Miss Wall."

"I'm all right, Captain Cooley. Thank you," Rose called. "He seems to have your measure," she said quietly to Bennet.

"He's like a father to me."

"Exactly."

When Bennet finally did set her on her feet again, it was some minutes before the warmth of his touch could be driven from her mind. He hefted her as though she weighed nothing. Bennet Varner was neither an office recluse nor a society lapdog, but a man capable of physical prowess, and Rose did not believe he had got that way just training horses.

"Do the cabins meet with your approval?" he asked after she had meticulously looked through all of them. They did have small windows but she was agreeably surprised by their scrubbed and polished look.

"They are much more spacious than I ever dreamed. Shall I have our trunks sent down?"

"Not quite yet. They would only be in the way for the moment," Bennet said as he conducted her to the ladder. Rose made him go first for she was quite sure ascending was much easier than going down, especially if there was no one staring up your dress. And she must get the hang of it, for Bennet would not always be there to catch her.

Rose turned her face into the breeze and inhaled deeply. She could imagine clinging to the rail as the ship plunged between waves like a frisky horse, tossing its head and glorying in what it did best. Bennet came to stand behind her. She could almost feel the heat of his body vibrating through the slight space of air that must remain between them.

"Do you not fear seasickness?" he asked, quite out of tune with her romantic thoughts.

"Not in the least," she said with a smile.

"I did not mean you, of course, but your sister-in-law seems of a delicate constitution."

"Oh, I am sure Alice will be sick, but it will not be as bad as being shut up in a carriage with her the whole way from Wall. On the ship she can have her maid to mop her brow with lavender water."

Captain Cooley strolled over to see them off the ship. "Seasickness? Not unless it be a rough crossing. If you are used to a horse galloping under you, the *Celestine* will seem like a cradle."

Rose almost laughed out loud at the look of woe this caused on Bennet's face. "But I suppose we will be delayed weeks over this mast, sir," Rose said ingenuously.

"Weeks? Bless you, miss. No. This is but a trifle. We could sail day after tomorrow if we was not waitin' fer a cargo." As this last was said with a somewhat accusing glance toward Bennet, Rose surmised that the delay was deliberate.

"Thank you, Captain Cooley, for letting me see the *Celestine*. I can look forward to the voyage with a quiet mind now."

Cooley clicked his heels together, bowed and kissed her hand for good measure.

"What a gentlemen," Rose said as she negotiated the narrow gangway. She did not refuse the hand Bennet stretched to her as she made her way down the ramp to the quay nor the strong arms that lifted her into the carriage.

"I suppose you think it rather archaic for a bride to need the comfort of a sister along on her wedding trip, and not even her own sister at that."

"It's as good a way to escape home as any," Bennet replied, getting in beside her and taking the reins from his tiger.

"Disabuse yourself of the notion I came willingly. My mother insisted upon it."

"Your mother?" Bennet queried as he skillfully turned the curricle in the tight area of the wharf and set off.

"Yes, I think she wanted to dislodge me from Wall, make me give up the management of it. Perhaps she and Stanley even conspired to rip me from my moorings in this fashion."

"Then you do not really want to go to Europe?" Bennet asked hopefully.

"Oh, for lack of anything better to do, but no, it was not my idea."

Rose glanced at Bennet's profile, watching the wheels grind behind his so innocuous eyes. She wondered if he would now try to give Stanley and Alice a disgust of the voyage, or failing that, the Continent itself.

"I was thinking," Bennet said, "since you have no engagement for tonight you might like to use my box at the theater. It's a new play and I think you might like it. You can at least be sure your pleasure will not be interrupted by the appearance of Mother and Harriet, since they will be at Lady Catherine's rout."

"Will you not be using your box?"

"No, I must attend the blasted party, as well. The Gravelys and Varners have been running tame in each other's houses for years. It would be remarked on if I were not there."

"Perhaps I shall take advantage of your generosity. My enjoyment will be especially enhanced by the thought of you trapped by Lady Catherine and Cassie."

"I nearly was, you know."

"What do you mean?"

"Trapped into marriage. Cassie was one of those maidens who was being thrown at my head."

Rose snorted a surprised laugh, as they tooled through the business district.

"I know. It would take much to lift her, let alone throw her, but she was not always so undesirable. Seven or eight years ago she was much sought after."

"But not by you?"

"Never in earnest. Ah, here we are."

Rose turned to look in surprise not at the facade of the hotel but at a modest sign reading Varner & Son, Shipping Agents on a stately four-story brick building.

"Sentimental or optimistic?"

"What, oh, the sign. I really could not bear to change it. I shall be a moment only."

"May I come in with you?"

"Of course, if you have an urge to visit a shipping business."

Bennet helped her down, and after showing her upstairs to his spacious office, requested his harried secretary to produce some tea. The man gaped for a moment before he snapped out "Yes, sir" and ran off.

As Bennet sat at his desk and began signing documents and laying others aside, apparently oblivious to Rose, she wandered about the room examining the port maps, tide charts and shipping schedules on the wall. There was a tide chart for every major port and a large folio of maps of harbors. After glancing through this Rose realized that Bennet Varner, if he wished to do so, was in a position to make England very vulnerable. He could land a French fleet in any harbor he chose. When the tea came she sat in one of the chairs by the fireplace and idly reached into a large trunk for a book. She came up with a volume of French poetry.

After reading a few verses, she searched through the jumble of volumes, wondering why they had been tossed into the trunk so carelessly. They were all in French.

Jammed into one corner of the buckram-lined trunk was something shiny.

The clerk came to confer with Bennet about a visitor and Bennet chose to receive him in the outer office.

Left alone Rose removed all the books. It was just as she had suspected. The trunk had a false bottom and she was quite sure it had once contained several hundred pounds of gold beneath these books, for she extracted a gold sovereign from the crack. She replaced the bottom and tossed the books back in as carelessly as they had been before. Then she chose a play by Moliere and pretended to be deeply engrossed when Bennet returned.

"You may take that with you if you like."

"It was not all I thought it would be," she said, laying the book aside. It might have to be a trip to the Foreign Office after all, she decided. Talk was one thing, but this was actual physical evidence.

When Bennet returned Rose and Martin to the hotel, her brother was coming out with Alice by the arm. Bennet helped Rose down without the customary hesitation of his hands on her waist.

"Rose, you will never guess. We have been invited to Lady Catherine Gravely's," Alice said excitedly. "At least Stanley and I have. I suppose she forgot about you."

"Lucky Rose," said Stanley.

"I have been invited to make use of Bennet's theater box and I think I will."

"Alone?" Stanley and Alice asked in unison.

"Of course not. I shall take Martin and Cynthie with me. They can sit in the back of the box and be tolerably amused."

"Oh, well, that's all right then," Stanley said. "Have you dined yet, Varner?"

"I was just thinking about a late lunch at the club,"

Bennet replied. In a moment Stanley had replaced Rose in the curricle, and when Rose saw Bennet pass the reins to her brother she knew lunch would be postponed until Stanley had tested the paces of the team.

"I can't think it's the thing for you to be taking your servants to the theater," Alice said with a pout, following Rose in the door.

"They have names, Alice, and feelings," Rose said, nodding toward Martin, whose impassive face displayed not the slightest discomfiture at being talked about as though he were deaf.

"To be sure they will not even understand the play," Alice insisted as they walked up the stairs.

Rose flushed at this direct insult. "I expect they will understand it a great deal better than…" Rose saw Martin purse his lips and shake his head behind Alice's back. "Than many who profess to be better educated," Rose said, provoking a slight grin from Martin and a puzzled frown from Alice.

"I suppose if you must have chaperonage they are better than nothing."

"Very much better than many an escort I could name."

The first act had been hysterically funny and Rose's enjoyment had been unmitigated by any care except the constant scrutiny of many of the gentlemen in the pit and all of those in the boxes. After examining her gray silk evening gown to make sure nothing was amiss, she had insisted on Martin and Cynthie drawing their chairs far enough forward to warn any intruder that she was not alone. By candlelight Martin would pass for a man, and Rose had no doubt of his courage and willingness to defend her in the face of a much greater threat than the ogling of a bunch of quizzes. She dressed Cynthie well enough that only her shy demeanor marked her as a lady's maid rather than a lady.

During the first interval Martin obtained ices for them, and Rose felt like a child at a fair as she, Martin and Cynthie discussed the intricacies of the plot.

During the second interval Axel appeared, thrusting his way through the curtain at the back of the box and sliding into a seat beside Rose as smooth as a snake, twisting his scabbard out of the way with a flourish.

"Axel! What on earth are you doing here? How did you even know—"

"I saw you from the pit."

"Just so we both know where we stand, I have a knife in my stocking and I know how to use it."

"Whew! You don't give a fellow much of a chance to be sociable."

"We both know we are beyond that," Rose said with dignity.

"That's no reason to threaten me."

"I'm surprised you were not invited to Lady Catherine's," Rose said tensely, eyeing Cynthie, who had shrunk into the corner and stopped breathing. Martin put his arm about his sister protectively and tried to shield her from Axel's regard.

"I was. I'm surprised you were not. Are you not offended?" Axel swiveled his head to glance at the maid, who gasped and whimpered.

"Why should I be, for I am much more amused here."

"Can you not get rid of those two, or at least keep that girl from sniveling?"

"I had much rather you went back to Lady Catherine's party."

"A lot of dull talk. We had better entertainment in Spain."

"Wars are not meant to be entertaining."

"I promise you I can be far more amusing than Bennet Varner. I saw you in his curricle today. What is the attraction?"

"This theater box, for one thing, and I was enjoying it tolerably well until you came to sit on my pleasure."

"I had no idea your favors could be bought so cheaply." Axel grasped her gloved hand and kissed it. She did not return his fervent pressure.

"He also has the most magnificent horses in London."

"Horses, always your weakness. Now I see. I was afraid you were actually attracted to him."

"I have no intention of ever marrying anyone. I told him that. He is merely being kind to his mother's godchild."

"You? I did not know there was a connection. Did he tell you I almost killed him in a duel once?"

"He may have mentioned something of the kind."

"Mentioned it in passing, did he? The little gutless...I'll wager Varner has never killed as many men as I have."

Rose regarded him with impatience. "I'm quite sure he has not killed any."

"Unless he did it on the exchange. What a damned dull dog. Why do you frown at me?"

"Other than you talking over the lines of the players, I was just thinking what an odd society where a rake and a killer, such as yourself, has the entrée and an innocent man is held up to ridicule."

"Innocent? That's a laugh. Varner's involved in some damned deep doings, I'll tell you that right now. You had best distance yourself from him in case he is arrested."

"I don't know what you mean."

"Frenchmen visiting the house and his office in the middle of the night. I mean to find out exactly what is going on."

"The war is over. There could be a hundred explanations for a man involved in trade to have dealings with the French."

"I can think of one that is not very appetizing." He finally dropped her unresponsive hand and took up her fan. "Do you want me to tell you what that is?"

"I feel sure you are going to whether I wish it or not," she whispered.

"There are a few Englishmen who did not let the inconvenience of a war interfere with their business. They profited, in fact, profited from the buying and selling of information. While we were sweating our guts out in Spain, Bennet was living in luxury—"

"You have absolutely no proof for such an accusation," Rose said with more heat than conviction.

"Not yet, at any rate. But by morning Mr. Bennet Varner may find himself in irons."

"It strikes me that would be a stupid thing for you to do if you finally mean to marry his sister," Rose countered.

"If you knew Harriet better you would realize that nothing would please her more."

"But the scandal..."

"Then she would have to marry me and stop all this simpering and demurring—"

"Axel, you sound almost as though—she turned you down!"

"Will you hush? She says she is having second thoughts. She's making all sorts of silly demands—control of her finances. Have you ever heard the like?"

"Yes, from myself several years ago. I had not thought she had so much sense."

"It's that brother of hers. He can't legally control her anymore, but he's playing games with her mind." Axel clenched his hand and broke two ribs of Rose's fan.

"I still think attempting to discredit Varner will put the death knell to your chances with his sister. She may not care about him but she does have some regard for an unblemished name."

"Don't we all?" Axel cast the fan aside.

Rose stared at him, trying to decide if the cut was deliberate or merely careless. "No, I don't anymore. What you did to me was despicable."

"I was angry." His eyes smoldered and seemed to be boring through her. "Perhaps it is you who have been planting ideas in Harriet's head."

"I have scarcely spoken to her, and she loathes me. Even you should be perceptive enough to realize that. If you want the truth of it, that ill-fated waltz you stole from me is at the root of the problem."

Axel stretched his arm along the back of her chair. "You may be right," he said slowly.

"Then why did you do it?"

"I could not help myself. I never could keep control where you were concerned." One creak of his chair and a sudden movement toward Rose brought Axel face-to-face with Martin's small but lethal-looking pistol barrel.

"For God's sake! You let that child have a gun?"

"Not only that, but I taught him to shoot," Rose said.

Axel stared at Martin as though trying to conjure up some memory. "You were there," he said slowly. "You were there in the stable that night."

"Unfortunately, sir, I did not have a gun then," Martin said in a clear voice.

Suddenly Axel's gaze shifted to the quietly weeping maid and recognition lit his eyes, like a fox surprised in a hen yard with blood on his whiskers.

Rose looked piercingly into his face and enjoyed watching the sweat glisten on his brow. "I imagine you are by now feeling a bit de trop, Axel."

"He wouldn't dare fire," Axel said, licking his dry lips.

"Accidents do happen," Martin stated.

"Another time, then." Axel rose slowly, presented his back to Martin and walked out of the box.

Three sighs of relief followed his departure. "Good work, Martin."

"I'm sorry, miss. It was a reaction. Now he remembers Cynthie."

"At least he knows we mean business."

The curtains to the box were pushed open again and Martin swung the pistol toward the surprised face of Bennet Varner, who immediately put up his hands. "And here I was thinking you needed a better escort."

"Sorry, sir," Martin said as he thrust the pistol back into the waistband of his livery.

"Best make sure you haven't left the hammer on cock," Bennet warned as he seated himself beside Rose. "We would not want any accidents."

Rose valiantly contained the giggle that sprang to her lips every time she thought of Bennet's expression. "So, how was the party?"

"Dull, compared to your company. Does your servant often threaten gentlemen in theater boxes?" Bennet asked, glancing over his shoulder at the apologetic Martin.

"We are all a bit on edge," she confided. "We just had a visit from Axel."

"I saw him leaving Lady Catherine's and detached myself as quickly as I could."

"He made it sound as though he came here by accident."

"He had a charming chat with dear Alice. I surmised that she revealed your location. What are his designs?"

"I'm not sure even Axel knows. He seems bent on marrying Harriet, so annoying me is just a pastime."

"I don't like it. Where Axel is involved women seem to get...hurt."

"What women?" Rose asked distractedly, wondering if she should warn Bennet about Axel's suspicions. But just because Axel was a villain did not mean he was stupid. What if he were right about Bennet Varner?

"There was Trudy Wilcox, the banker's daughter. I was twenty and still listening to Mother at that point. I can see why Axel wanted her, heiress to a fortune. She finally married a lawyer."

"And was delivered of a seven months' child?" Rose guessed.

"How did you...?"

"I know Axel. How many were there?"

"Three. Lady April Dell was reported to have died of a fever. I expect I'll never know what really happened. And now Robin Coates is an outcast."

"These were all women in whom you had shown some interest?"

"Not a serious interest. Remember, I'm a confirmed bachelor."

"Small wonder, with Axel taking every woman you show the slightest liking for."

"But what would be his motive? In the case of April and Robin there was no fortune to speak of."

Rose stared at him, but the question was genuine. He really had no idea what was going on with Axel. Raised in a household full of women, with no brothers, perhaps such competition was foreign to him. "Always you look for motives where there are none."

"What do you mean?" he whispered, totally unconscious of how sensual his voice was when she could feel his breath on her ear.

"A motive is a thing a thinking man or woman has.

Don't make the mistake of classifying Axel as a thinking being.''

''He's intelligent—malicious but intelligent. Even drunk, if he ever is really drunk, you can see him calculating.''

''Calculating to be sure, but not like a man. He has the low cunning of an animal, operating on instinct, not motivation.''

''But if he was taking them away from me, then I am a danger to you.'' Bennet moved backward as though his very touch could harm her.

Rose regretted saying anything, for she did not want to lose this closeness, this friendship that already surpassed any she had ever known. ''No, I have been able to allay his suspicions. He thinks I am interested only in your horses, your ships and your theater boxes.''

''And are you?''

She hesitated a moment before answering, ''Yes, of course.'' Then she reveled in that look of shock that preceded his easy grin. ''Perhaps I failed to mention your witty conversation.''

''Perhaps you shouldn't. I have not been very witty tonight,'' Bennet whispered as he moved closer again. ''No wonder Axel feels he has to wrest Harriet away from me if that is the game he has been playing.''

''And you did not even realize it,'' Rose drawled, fascinated by Bennet's so sensual lips as they moved closer.

''No,'' he said. ''I thought it was all some fanciful notion of Leighton's.''

Rose hesitated at the name of the other man who had been in the library that night. Perhaps she could investigate him and not have to accuse Bennet.

Sudden applause made Bennet jerk back again and look around, as though he was surprised to find himself in a theater. ''It's over.''

"And I have missed most of the act thanks to Axel," Rose moaned.

"And me."

"In your case the interruption was more amusing than the play."

"In any case I had better take you home before I start operating on instinct."

As they exited the box into the hallway, a dandy came yawning out of the neighboring box, and Rose had some misgivings about his having been close enough to hear Axel's conversation, if nothing else. Was he yawning to prove he had not?

"Boring play, Varner," the slight, balding man said. "I swear I slept through the half of it." The man patted his thinning brown curls back into place.

"I wouldn't know, Dowd. I missed most of it myself." After an uncomfortable pause when the dandy seemed disinclined to move, Bennet was forced to say, "Let me present Miss Gwen Rose Wall. This is Magnus Dowd, a…a business associate of mine."

"Charmed," Dowd said, taking her hand and kissing it in a fishlike manner, making Rose eternally thankful for gloves.

"How can you say it was dull?" Rose asked. "I laughed the entire way through the first act."

"It had no substance."

"One looks for humor in a comedy, not meat."

"It presented too light a fare for me, and so I shall tell anyone."

"Good night, Dowd," Bennet said, dragging Rose away.

"What an odd little man."

"So much for that play," Bennet said as he conducted her through the crowd. "Dowd will kill its chances over luncheon tomorrow. By the evening the theater will be half-empty.''

''How can one man have such influence?''

''His comments are barbed with ridicule. Because they are witty, people assume they are true.'' Somehow Bennet's carriage managed to be one of those first in line outside the theater.

''So the playwright, the actors, the theater will all suffer because he has decided not to like the play,'' Rose said as he helped her in. ''That is absurd.''

Bennet waited for Martin to help Cynthie onto the opposite seat. ''True, but the play is by an unknown. Dowd has nothing to gain by being fair. If it were someone who was generally accepted he would take the safe path and give it a nod of approval, perhaps even effusive praise.''

''Even if it were no good?''

''Yes. Think of it as a model of our society.''

''I find it more like animal behavior. Where is the virtue of attacking someone for no reason? He would be better employed defending an unpopular theory.''

''He is not employed. That is the problem. He has money but no vocation. He is not creative himself. The only way he can draw attention is by tearing something down.''

Rose was thoughtful for the rest of the ride home, wondering if Dowd would find employment tearing down her character. But there was very little Dowd could do that Axel could not, so the scandal she had put to rest in Bristol was bound to surface again in London. It was only a matter of time.

Chapter Five

Rose had let Cynthie sleep on a daybed in her room and was kept up many hours listening to the girl's sobs. The child was as shaken as though the attack had happened yesterday, not five years before.

After a late breakfast Rose issued forth to church with Cynthie and Martin for escort. She was not a devout person, but she felt that one of them ought to go, to pray for fair winds or something, perhaps a putrid throat for Axel, which might turn into a fatal inflammation of the lungs. If ever there was man who deserved a slow, horrible death it was Axel Barton.

They walked there in spite of the cold and afterward she took Cynthie and Martin to a tea shop for lunch. They had such good times, just the three of them, with no posing or pretending. They would come with her to Bristol when she went to live with her mother. The horses would be a problem. There was no stable convenient to the house in Bristol and the thought of her beautiful horses, so used to the lush pastures at Wall, stuffed into a stall day and night had about decided Rose to leave them in her brother's care. "What will you need Martin for, then?" Stanley had asked. Cynthie and Martin separated? Or

Martin and Rose taken from their horses. The only alternative was to set up for herself and keep both of them
with her, but then her mother would be alone.

When they returned to the hotel Rose was informed by
Alice that the Varners would dine with them in their suite
that night. Something to look forward to, she thought, as
she undid her bonnet and seated herself at the small escritoire in her room. So long as Bennet would be present
Rose did not care how many reluctant relatives he dragged
along. She began to wonder where this fascination with
Bennet Varner would lead. He was a puzzle to her. Once
she divined why he was trying to delay their departure,
especially if it was a nefarious motive, would she lose
interest in him? But she rather thought the mystery was
the least part of his charm.

In the broad light of day it seemed fantastic to her that
she could even suspect Bennet Varner, and her arguments
against Axel the previous night had in part convinced her
that she was being overly suspicious. Perhaps Bennet was
just what he professed to be, a bored merchant who enjoyed dalliance but nothing so serious as marriage. He was
the perfect medicine for her melancholy. She could say
anything to him, for when she left London she would
probably never see him again. She pushed the thought
aside to focus on the fantasy of a long ocean voyage with
him standing behind her, with his arms around her.

After forcibly evicting this picture from her mind, she
took up again her mother's letter informing her of the
progress she had made in removing to Bristol, and ex-
pressing her surprise at the length of time the party had
lingered in London. Rose penned a reply that they had
been so warmly received by the Varners that it would be
ungracious to rush off after having just become acquainted, but that they still meant to sail for Italy and
France. That was only two-thirds of a lie, for they had

been warmly received by Bennet. Axel's presence in town she failed to mention. Stanley, if he thought to write at all, would probably skirt the subject, and Alice corresponded only with her parents.

When the table in the sitting room had been laid and the hour for dinner finally arrived, Bennet came alone. His face looked serious for once but he smiled at sight of Rose. Now that was a smile to give a maidenly heart an extra leap or two.

"Did you miss riding today?" he asked as he sat beside her, watching the waiters bring in several laden trays.

"We must rest a day. It's only fair that the horses do as well."

"Until you came to town mine rested two days out of the three. They look forward to you riding them now."

"They cannot know me yet," Rose said, blushing at the compliment.

"It's really too bad you are not staying the whole season. The pair of you would have my beasts whipped into shape in another month or two. Also there are plays you will miss, assemblies, balls. I could probably get you an invitation to anything you would care to attend."

"You've been far too kind, already," Stanley said. "Try this lamb. It is nearly as good as what we have at Wall."

"It's a treat for me—us to have company," Bennet said.

Stanley did not notice the slip and began to talk of his plans for Wall. Bennet decried Stanley's having to wait a year to put forward some of his schemes for the improvement of his stables, flocks and herds, and went so far as to offer to trade breeding stock. Stanley began to look thoughtful.

So that was it, Rose thought. Bennet would make Stanley want to stay in England, if not London. "Have you ever been to Paris?'' Rose asked to distract Bennet. He might succeed in throwing a rub in the way of their tour, but she would not let it be easy for him.

''Why, no, never,'' Bennet replied, and something about the answer made her suspicious.

''Venice?''

Bennet shook his head no.

''Is that not rather odd for a merchant?''

''Too busy.''

The more Stanley and Bennet spoke of Wall or Chesney, the more Rose threw in remarks about Europe, though she had frequently to overextend credulity in connecting her interjections to their conversation. Stanley ignored her, but Bennet had often, she thought, to bite his lip to keep from laughing. When Bennet left it did not seem to Rose as though four hours had passed.

Stanley looked sagely at Rose and said, ''I think the fellow is interested in you, Rose. I think you might try to be a bit more engaging. Speak of horses or hunting rather than Paris or Venice.''

''For the moment I don't think there is anything I could do that would discourage Bennet Varner,'' Rose said with a laugh.

''So there, he is interested. Nice catch for you, though one wonders why such an affable fellow isn't leg-shackled already.''

''Leg-shackled?'' Alice queried.

''Just an expression,'' Stanley replied. ''You already like his horses, Rose.''

''Believe me, I can see the advantages of such a match, particularly because of his horses,'' Rose said with a grin, ''but I do not think his affections can be permanently engaged.''

''You may just be wrong about him, Rose. You can't judge all men by—well, you know what I mean.''

"By what?" Alice demanded. "I hate it when you two have private conversations about things I don't know."

Rose considered for a moment how much she could divulge to Alice. "When I broke my engagement with Axel, he was not at all a gentleman about it. He said some very unkind things, and he did not just say them to me. He repeated them to others."

"I simply meant that Rose need not think all men cannot be trusted," Stanley replied to the pouting Alice.

"But I have talked to Lord Foy, and I do not see how you could have been so cruel as to throw him over, Rose."

"Alice, Foy had not a feather to fly with even in those days," Stanley replied knowingly. "Father never should have suggested the match."

"But to be cast aside because he was poor... I find you very mercenary, both of you."

"If you knew the negotiations your father engaged in over your hand, you would not be calling us mercenary," Stanley quipped impatiently.

"Well, if that is what you think, you can just go to Paris alone, Stanley Wall." Alice plunged into the larger bedchamber and firmly slammed and locked the door.

"Oh, Lord," Stanley said. "What made her take such a maggot in her head? You know, being married isn't all it is cracked up to be. Perhaps you should not dangle after Bennet Varner."

"Do you want me to see if I can reason with her?" Rose asked.

"Believe me, Rose, there is no point in even trying until those floods of tears are at an end. I think I shall look in at some of the clubs."

"On Sunday?"

"That is the charm of London," Stanley said, searching

out his hat and gloves. "There is something to do any day of the week."

"Stanley, you do still mean to go to Europe, don't you?"

"Would you rather not?" he asked hopefully with his hand on the doorknob.

"I...I think it would be wise to go. It is a chance we may not get again. In a year or two you and Alice will have a child and not want either to drag it along or leave it behind."

"Not at this rate, we won't," he said as he left without answering her question.

Cassie regarded her reflection in the mirror of the chamber put aside by the Moltons for the ladies to rest, repair torn flounces and refresh themselves. If she held her head up just so, without turning it from side to side, there was only a creamy expanse of neck and no sign of a second chin. The black ruffles on her white gown were daring, but were the perfect foil for her rich skin. Her rubies were the pièce de résistance, resting warmly around her milky throat. But the white rosebuds in her hair were beginning to wilt from the excessive heat of the apartments.

The door opened and she saw Harriet, via the mirror, lift one dainty foot from under her dress of gold satin to kick the door shut behind her.

"What is the matter now?" Cassie asked, adding another touch of scent to her elbows.

"Axel! He's flirting with Robin Coates."

"What can you expect? You did turn him down. Come to think of it, why did you refuse his proposal? You have been yearning to marry Axel Barton ever since he shot Bennet over you."

"Bennet says I can have my pick of men now."

"You could have had your pick before, except for

Axel. Now that he is served up to you on a platter, you don't want him.''

"He was also making after that Wall woman at my birthday party. Perhaps Bennet was right about Axel being unreliable.''

"Listen to yourself. Taking advice from the brother who 'destroyed your happiness forever.'" Cassie clutched her hands to her ample bosom in a schoolgirl imitation of her friend.

"Bennet is different now,'' Harriet said, tramping about the room and kicking a footstool out of her way.

"What do you mean? Has he perhaps finally decided to settle down himself?''

"I suppose that might be it. He has certainly lost all interest in my affairs.''

"If you accept Axel and Bennet were to propose to me we could make it a double wedding.'' Cassie turned in her chair to see what effect this suggestion might have on her friend.

Harriet laughed. "Not likely. They cannot come within ten paces of each other without showing their teeth.'' She spun around to ease the creases in her gown and examined the rows of gold trim along the bottom for loose threads.

"Mama says Axel is only making over Rose Wall to take her away from Bennet, just as he took Robin Coates. If we could get rid of the Walls, both Axel and Bennet might settle down to marriage.''

"Bennet dined with them tonight at their hotel.'' Harriet gave her neckline a tug and pushed her breasts up to see if she could get any mounds to show. "Can you believe he actually expected Mama and me to go with him? Fortunately we had this invitation to fall back on. It's frightfully dull here, but at least we don't have to listen to Rose and Bennet chatter and laugh.''

"It's hot, as well, and I have drunk too much already.

My feet are swelling." Cassie thrust her feet in their tight slippers out in front of her.

"I do wish the Walls would be gone to France. Mama warned Bennet not to encourage them. All it took was a single invitation and it looks like they may be fixed here for the season."

"Surely not. I do not understand what Bennet sees in that rail of a person. A good wind would blow her away."

"She's horse-mad like him." Harriet looked at her face in the mirror over Cassie's shoulder, and pinched some color into her cheeks. She glanced at Cassie's rosebud complexion.

"Do you think if I learned to ride Bennet would take more of an interest in me?" Cassie asked, trying to pull in her stomach.

"Oh, I don't know," Harriet said as she plopped down on the bed. "There must be something we can do to dislodge these upstarts."

"That should be no great trick for Mama." Cassie pulled the most wilted of the rosebuds from her headpiece. "She can get rid of most anybody. The trouble is we don't know them well enough to know what skeletons may hang in their closet."

"But if there are none we could perhaps always create one?" Harriet asked, a predatory gleam in her eyes.

"Harriet, there are always skeletons. At least that is what Mama says."

"Alice Wall is simple enough to be flattered into divulging any confidence. We will make up to her. I suspect there is more to that broken engagement than Rose Wall let on."

"And her brother was covering up for her. But Alice would have been too young to have heard any of that."

"It is surprising what children hear and are willing to

repeat. We will take her shopping with us. That should do the trick.''

"That will get the Walls out of the way, but it does not solve your problem.''

Harriet sighed heavily. ''Cassie, do you think I should marry Axel?''

''I...I think perhaps not.''

''Why not? Axel is still the most interesting man in town.''

''At least not until Bennet has offered for me.''

''Why should I wait for you to snare Bennet? You have been at it this age.''

''When Bennet Varner marries, Axel will not be forever competing with him for women.''

''You mean he may settle down?'' Harriet asked.

''Not necessarily. But I think he would restrict his activities to casual affairs.''

''He will not have any more casual affairs if I have anything to say in the matter, and if I marry him, I intend to be the one in control.'' Harriet rose and checked the mirror one last time.

''Would you expect him to be absolutely faithful to you?'' Cassie asked, toying with her reticule.

''Oh, I don't know. Part of his charm is his experience.'' Harriet licked her pink lips. ''When I think of all those women! You know he told me he made love only to virgins when he was in the Peninsula.''

Cassie stared at her on hearing this bit of news. ''One would not have thought there would have been enough for him.''

''And they were not all willing.'' Harriet bit her full bottom lip and let it slide through her teeth as Cassie cast a worried look in her direction.

''He tells you about the women he's made love to?''

''Only by number,'' Harriet said, tweaking a curl into

place. "Apparently there were so many he cannot recount their names."

Cassie gnawed one fingertip. "We should go back down."

"If we must," Harriet said as she opened the door, "but if there is no one to talk to, let us get your mother to take us home."

Bennet arrived at Greeves Hotel on Monday with his groom and horses only for Rose and Martin. Rose wondered how he knew her brother had not meant to ride. Perhaps they had discussed it the night before. Perhaps Stanley had bowed out to give Rose more opportunity to entrap Bennet Varner. Rose smiled at the thought, for she had no such notion. On one of the first really warm days of March she could think only of spring and flowers. Even international intrigues seemed to slip from importance.

As they rode through the streets to the park Rose thought Bennet seemed preoccupied, certainly not his usual jovial self. By this time he would normally have started to work his wiles upon her, leading her along with some bit of nonsense that distracted her from the horses and their usual canter. But today she took control and let Gallant break into a ground-covering gallop that startled some early risers. A few guardsmen looked as though they thought it was a runaway, and meant to pursue her, but when Rose heard hoofbeats it was Bennet who brought his horse up alongside her. She tugged tentatively and Gallant gave her control, coming smoothly down into his trot, but giving a prance to show that he could have gone on forever. Chaos whinnied and shook his great black head in challenge, but Bennet curbed the urge to race with no more than a firm tug.

Bennet's expression was unreadable. Perhaps he was disturbed because he had not been able to dragoon his mama and sister into eating dinner with them the previous evening. He might even now be attempting to frame an apology. No, that could not be it, for he had left them in high good humor the night before.

Perhaps Napoleon's escape, or the invasion of England, or whatever Bennet was plotting was not going well. She thought over what Axel had said about Bennet Varner, but Axel was wrong about so many things she had trouble crediting him with any clarity of thought. She disliked that she still found him charming, since she knew the worst of him.

"Dowd's letter appeared in the *Chronicle* today," Bennet finally said.

"Dowd?" Rose asked vacantly.

"That popinjay we met at the theater the other night."

"Oh, I think if he did not care for the production he might have kept it to himself rather than spoil everyone else's enjoyment of it."

"He thanked the entire production staff for putting him to sleep. He has not rested so well in weeks."

"The little worm. If he missed part of the play it was not from sleeping. I suspect he was eavesdropping on Axel's visit to our box."

"Did you cover any dangerous ground in your conversation with Foy?"

"I have been trying to recall," Rose said as she slowed Gallant to a walk. "Nothing was said that would reflect on me, and there was dead silence after Martin pulled the gun out."

Bennet smirked. "A creeping sort of creature is Magnus Dowd. He will flatter you to your face and tell tales on you when your back is turned."

"Is that to be a warning to me of what to prevent or what to expect? For it does not sound as though one could stop such gossip."

"No, one cannot do more than try to be aware of it."

"Axel did say something about you." Rose guided her horse along a row of plane trees and watched Bennet closely as the sun threw bars of gold and shadow through the bare limbs across the track in front of them.

"About me stopping Harriet from marrying him?"

"He touched on that and seemed to think the solution to getting her out of your influence was to have you arrested as a spy."

"A what?" Bennet jerked so abruptly that Chaos fought him for the bit.

Bennet's surprise was genuine and the peal of laughter that followed would have convinced anyone else of his innocence. The horse shook his head at these doings.

"He seems to think you have unsavory French connections," Rose added.

"Foy is a fool to think that all Frenchmen are imperialists. They do not all worship Napoleon."

No denial that he knew Frenchmen. That was wise. "So if he went with such a tale to the Foreign Office you would be able to protect yourself from arrest?"

Bennet grinned at her. "Most certainly, though I cannot be so sure of keeping Axel out of Bedlam where they would be sure to want to restrain him."

"That might not be such a bad place for him. Could you manage it?" Rose asked with a straight face.

"Are you serious?" Bennet asked in boyish delight.

"No, but I wanted to assess how powerful you are."

He smiled sadly. "Not all powerful men abuse their power."

"How refreshing to hear that."

There was silence for a time while Bennet seemed to be engaged in some sort of internal struggle. "I wanted to mention to you that you will not be returning to Greeves Hotel."

Rose looked at him inquiringly.

"Your brother and I have found better accommodations for you."

"What on earth do you mean?" she asked, staring at Bennet's profile. "Surely the *Celestine* embarks within the week."

"She is waiting for a cargo. In the meantime my secretary has found a house you may have on short lease in South Audley Street. It will be so much more convenient...for the horses."

Rose had opened her mouth to blast him, but since he was clearly expecting her to be angry, and no doubt had rehearsed an abundance of arguments to persuade her of the advantages of the house, she merely said coldly, "How very considerate of you."

The look of surprise and relief this bland pronouncement wrought satisfied her that her brother had connived to get her out of the way so that the removal could be made without her opposition. She would handle Bennet the same way she was learning to handle Stanley, by pretending the entire affair was a matter of indifference to her.

"By the time we return your trunks will be installed," Bennet continued uneasily. "The house is fully staffed and you will not have to lift a finger."

"How delightful." Her voice tinkled in the cold air like breaking glass. "I can hardly wait to see the place."

"You're angry, I surmise," he said.

"Whatever makes you say that, Bennet? Don't most women like to have things managed for them, taken out of their control and be handed about like a china doll who cannot move her own legs?" Rose asked, a flush of anger rising to her face in spite of her viselike control on her temper. She unclenched her hands to keep Gallant from jabbing his mouth on such a tight rein.

"Yes, but not you. I told your brother it was not the best way to handle the situation, but he insisted."

"Why, then he shall have all the credit and not you."

"Credit or blame? I don't like the way you are taking this, like the calm before the storm. I have the feeling you are going to murder someone."

Bennet's supposed fear of her was a compliment of sorts. That, along with his knowing her well enough to know she would be offended, began to tickle her sense of the ridiculous. "I have the feeling I am going to murder someone, too, but I haven't yet decided whom. Most of the blame does fall on you, of course, your unnatural kindness in the midst of an unkind city, your repeated attempts to keep us here. A more suspicious woman might believe you had designs on her fortune or her brother's." Rose glanced at him sharply.

Bennet gaped, then grinned. "I would be hard put to find a more suspicious woman than you, but I assure you I have no such motives."

"What then?" She stopped her horse. "Let us be frank for once, perhaps for the first time in our brief and amusing relationship. Why do you want to keep us here?"

Bennet halted Chaos and turned to face her. "I have a good reason—more than one in fact."

"Oh, more than one! That makes it all right, I suppose. Of course, you are not at liberty to say what those are."

"How did you guess?" He smiled charmingly, making Rose even angrier.

"Because it goes along with all the rest. When can you tell me?"

"I can make all known to you in a week, no more."

"The truth now would be better received than more lies later." She spurred the horse forward, less angry at Bennet than at herself for letting her temper show, but she liked Bennet and she would rather not see him again than feel that she could not trust him. Axel had been every bit as charming and he could not be trusted out of her sight. Her own father had played her mother false for years. Why should Bennet be any different?

She hesitated at the edge of the park, for she had no idea where to go from here. She had half a notion to ride back to the hotel, but she would only make a fool of herself if she did. So she waited and Bennet rode up and said, "This way."

The house was half the size of Varner House and, like most of the other town houses in London, scarcely more than a generous room wide. But the salons and bedrooms were no less elegant than those of Varner House. Rose's praise of the house was so effusive that neither Stanley nor Alice guessed how hurt she was by being tricked into the move. Stanley pointed out that it had no stable, but that scarcely mattered since Bennet's house was nearly across the way. Alice emphasized the size of the three salons on the first floor, which Rose took to mean she had some aspirations of entertaining. For the first time Rose began to see the advantages of being a mere sister-in-law. Not being the mistress of the house, she could enjoy such entertainments without worrying about them or taking any of the blame if they were disasters.

The gentlemen went off to lunch at one of their clubs, leaving Alice to mollify Rose, as Stanley had evidently mollified Alice by renting the house. As Cynthie hung up Rose's gray riding habit and exclaimed over the elegance of her new bedroom, done up with an ivory wallpaper covered with rosebuds, Rose quizzed Alice on how they had managed to keep such a delightful surprise secret from her.

"Well, you see, Stanley thought you might not quite

like it, since it seems to throw a rub in the way of our expedition to Europe.''

''Merely a delay, Alice, not a rub,'' Rose said, pulling a blue wool dress over her head. ''You are not disappointed, Alice?''

''No, it was my idea. That is, when Varner offered the house so obligingly, and at a more modest fee than we are paying at the hotel, it seemed perfect. Plus we shall be able to entertain here.'' Alice went to the window to glance up the street toward Varner House.

''But whom will you invite? We scarcely know anyone in London.''

''The Varners, the Gravelys and all their particular friends.''

''What about…Robin Coates?'' Rose said, deliberately choosing a name she knew was ineligible.

''Oh, no, she is not at all the thing. The Varners no longer receive her, since she is considered fast.''

''How confusing,'' Rose said, sitting down to brush the tangles out of her hair while Cynthie buttoned her. ''Just last year she was a bosom friend to Harriet and Cassie. One can only think their affections are easily engaged and disengaged.''

''What are you saying?'' Alice turned to stare at her in the mirror.

''That however delightful these people are as company or acquaintances we cannot expect them to be lifelong friends. London is not a place that fosters lasting friendships.''

''You are so gloomy, Rose. If you have had a lonely life at Wall, I promise you, I do not mean to follow in your footsteps. I mean to make as many friends as possible and invite them all to stay with us. And we shall visit them in their country places.''

''But what about Axel? Will you invite him?''

Cynthie dropped Rose's riding boots noisily.

"Since he is very nearly engaged to Harriet I see no reason we should not invite him as well," Alice said, her small chin thrust out.

"But she turned down his proposal."

"She is merely being coy. I had a long cose with Axel at Lady Catherine's party and I find him to be a much wronged gentleman. In fact, I think I shall speak to Harriet on his behalf."

Rose stared at her in so much surprise, Alice continued. "Perhaps you could put in a good word for him."

Knowing it was pointless to argue with Alice, Rose said, "I will think about it."

As they descended the stairs she thought about what she should have said, that even if Harriet were her worst enemy there was no word of encouragement she would give her in marrying Axel Barton.

They had barely settled themselves in the bright morning room facing the street when Axel called, as though he knew he was being spoken of. In the dim light of the hall he looked handsome still, a man just losing his edge, a soldier teetering on the brink of his prime with only one way to go. "And how has Rose taken to her surprise?" he teased, strolling into the room and letting the sunlight play off his hair.

"You cannot imagine how delighted I was," she lied as she motioned him to the sofa. "To not even be bothered with the packing was a treat. Have you seen the house before? It is lovely."

"I am...familiar with it," Axel said, swinging his saber out of the way with a flourish as he sat down and crossed his legs. "I came to take you delightful ladies for a drive."

Rose raised an eyebrow at him. "I fear we are too

interested in exploring our new domain to even consider it."

"I should adore to go for a drive," Alice countered, jumping up from her chair. "You may stay home if you wish, Rose. For though it would not be proper for you to drive with Axel alone, it is perfectly acceptable for a married lady to do so."

Axel smirked at Rose as Alice flounced upstairs to get her reticule and pelisse.

"I do not know what kind of game you are playing with Alice but be forewarned that Stanley is an excellent shot."

"You always did cast me in the worst possible light."

"My judgment was always vindicated by your performance. Surprise me and act like a gentleman or I promise you that you will regret it."

"Threatening me again? 'Tis a good thing I'm a soldier or you might set me all atremble. Besides, what possible designs could I have on sweet Alice?"

"One hates to think," Rose said, wondering if this sudden interest in Alice was a ruse to get close to her or if Axel really did mean mischief. "Perhaps I shall go with you after all." She could see by the smile that split across his face that this had been his plan all along, but she went upstairs for her pelisse and hat anyway.

Alice tripped down the stairs and took Axel's arm, then pouted when she realized Rose meant to accompany them. Rose observed the curricle and team standing at the curb. They were not inferior beasts by any means, but would have been no match for Bennet's bays. The groom who held their heads wore black livery with scarlet facings.

Axel drove them through the parks with which Rose was now familiar, but these were all new to Alice, so she frequently exclaimed in delight at even these bleak winter prospects. The roadways and walks were more crowded

with carriages and riders at this hour of the day, so Axel
had to halt the team frequently in traffic even if there was
no one he or Alice wished to chat with.

"Alice," Rose complained. "These horses will get sick
if we keep them standing like this in a cold wind. We
must get them back into the streets."

"Always with you it is the horses first," Alice complained. "You care a great deal more for them, even
strange horses, than you do for me."

"That's not true. But you might have some consideration for Axel, who has to hold such a restive pair."

"Oh, I am sorry. Let us drive on then. What else is
there to see?"

"I thought you might like to visit some of the shops,"
Axel suggested.

"See, Rose, Axel doesn't care about the horses," Alice
said, thinking she had complimented her host. "For they
will be standing an hour if we stop to purchase anything."

Rose saw Axel open his mouth, then close it, and
chuckled to herself. Perhaps Alice would have been safe
from him after all. Once her sister-in-law became entranced with a hat in a Bond Street shop Axel helped her
down, and, not giving Rose a chance to alight, said, "We
shall drive around the block and pick you up here, Alice."

Axel signaled the groom to wait on the sidewalk with
no more than a motion of his arm.

"So, you have bought this conversation at great pains,"
Rose commented. "What is it you wished to discuss?"

"Merely wanted to know how you are enjoying your
stay."

"Very much until you appeared." She studied the fa-
cades of the buildings just to annoy him. "So if you go
about London telling everyone I am fast, as you did in
Bristol, it will be sure to cast a pall over the visit."

"Would that bother you? I thought you said you did not care."

"Not for myself, but it would be upsetting for Alice. However, it would merely put forward our departure. You don't mean to dog our steps to Italy or France, do you?"

"If I never see those countries again, it will be too soon."

"Owe money there as well, do you?" Rose gibed.

"If I did not need both hands to drive..." he said through gritted teeth.

"What would you do? Hit me? You're not above it in private, but I think even you would stick at such abuse in a public street."

"There is no other woman on earth who can provoke me to it."

"If you recall, you do not require any provocation but what comes from a bottle."

"I'm a better man than your father ever was."

Rose looked straight ahead and sniffed back the threatening tear. "Yes," she said, "unfortunately, you are."

"I did not mean to argue with you," he said, casting a worried glance at her profile.

"What did you mean by all this? You haven't much time. We are very nearly to the shop again."

"I'd be surprised if such a silly widgeon as Alice could make up her mind in that length of time. See, she is still inside. I just hope the curricle will hold all the boxes."

"So, you have no designs of Alice. Why bother with us at all? We can only call back unpleasant memories for each other."

"I...I mean to settle down and marry. At least I did until you filled Harriet's head with tales about me."

"What?" Rose stared at him. "Have I this right? You are accusing me of gossiping about you?"

"Why else would she refuse me? She was hot enough to marry me four years ago."

Rose looked closely at the still attractive but rather battle-worn face and almost slipped into a feeling of compassion. She could have told him that he was not so dashing as he used to be, but he would not have believed her anyway.

"Is she in love with you?" Rose asked, curious to know how Harriet felt about Axel.

"Love? What does our class know of love? It's always the money we have to secure, and unless I miss my guess she has a great deal more than you."

"Axel, your reputation for debts, gaming and...other pursuits must be common knowledge in London. If Harriet is reticent it has nothing to do with me."

"So, you have said nothing to her?"

"Axel, she looks down her nose at me. We cannot have traded more than a dozen sentences the whole time I have been here."

"I suppose what's more to the point, will you promise not to say anything in future about...about what happened at Wall?"

"You were eager enough to talk about me if you recall."

"But you never said anything in your defense." A puzzled frown marred his face. "You never made any accusations."

"I remember it very well."

"Why did you keep quiet?"

"I had nothing to gain by trying to destroy you. Of course, that did not stop you."

"I swear I will not utter another word about you, if you promise not to warn Harriet off me."

"I said nothing then. Why should I now?"

"Revenge." The word curled off Axel's tongue like an old friend.

"That would not change the past. Is that why you brought me out here, to make a deal?"

He glanced at her, that wicked smile looking sheepish on his lined face. He still had it, that roguish appeal. Rose found herself hoping he did settle down before he lost it, for that was all he had going for him.

"Now that I think on it, you can say nothing against me, without risking what I will say about you. We are both in check."

"If that is the way you prefer to think of it. There's Alice."

"No matter. We have an understanding. I don't suppose you could put in a good word for me?"

"In good conscience I'm afraid not, but Alice has some such notion."

"What?" Axel gaped and nearly forgot to halt the team.

Alice came to be helped in while a shop assistant stuffed bandboxes about their feet and handed Rose one to hold on her lap. She rather thought Axel would not be tempted to drive with her sister-in-law again.

When they returned Alice went to lie down for a nap and Rose asked for tea to be brought to the book room, a windowless but cozy retreat tucked between the back of the stairs and the diningroom. She had been rather surprised that Axel was as much afraid of her as she was of him. She was offended, too, that he thought she would stoop to his tactics. But she did venture to feel a bit more optimistic about their stay if Axel really meant to reform, or even pretend to reform.

Rose wandered from room to room, examining each suspiciously. After the book room was a sumptuous dining room, then the breakfast parlor on the end, which would be warm from being over the basement kitchen. The next floor up consisted of three beautiful salons and the one above that of no less than six bedrooms and two dressing rooms. The servants' quarters must lie above that. The house was not, she thought, as she came back to the ground floor, your typical hired lodging. The quality of the furniture and fittings was expensive and not a jumble of castoffs. The place had been decorated with some care, albeit in a rather masculine style. Moreover, it had a familiar air about it, as though she had been there before or had visited it in a dream.

The feeling was strongest in the small book room. Some arrangement of the inkwell and blotter said "Bennet" to her. She examined the volumes on the shelves. More than half were in French or some other language than English. Bennet had used this room. She was sure of it without having to ask. She sat in the single wing chair in front of the grate and had her tea, wondering how she'd had the misfortune to fall in love with a man who might be a spy at the worst, and at the least was just a flirt, a pleasant fellow with not a serious intention to his name.

The chair embraced her as naturally as he had, as though she belonged in its arms. She really did fall asleep this time and spent her exhausting dream trying to escape Bennet Varner, but he always had the fastest horse. Like everything else, he had seen to that.

"Rose, wake up. We were looking all over for you," Stanley said with his hand on her shoulder.

"Oh, I must have fallen asleep." Rose glanced at the hearth but the fire had gone out.

"You've less that half an hour to dress for dinner. We are invited to Varner House."

"This is very sudden," Rose said as she got up and walked out into the hallway.

"Sudden? No," Stanley said as he ran through the morning room and started up the stairs. "We were invited last night. Didn't Alice tell you?"

"She must have forgotten to mention it." Rose tramped up the steps, thinking it would be a treat to see Bennet again. Some surprises were pleasant.

She put on her new dress, the peach one with the ivory ribbons. She had been saving it, but she needed cheering up. She walked on one side of Stanley as he led Alice up the street toward Varner House. He was telling her about a race meeting he'd been invited to, and Alice's only concern seemed to be how much of a damper this would throw on her social life. Once she ascertained that she could hold dinners without him or accept invitations with Rose as escort she quickly lost interest in the expedition.

They were received a bit icily by Edith Varner, and Harriet seemed petulant as they gathered in the gold salon. As soon as Bennet arrived, of course, the room overflowed with goodwill.

"How are you enjoying the house?" he asked cautiously as he greeted Rose.

"Very much, especially your little book room," Rose replied, staring up at him. At his surprised look, she continued. "It is your house, isn't it?"

"Why, yes. I had it furnished for when we have guests. Varner House just isn't big enough." Bennet threw up his arms in mock despair, though Rose guessed the Varners very seldom had overnight guests.

"His business acquaintances use it," Harriet explained.

"Foreign business acquaintances?" Rose asked.

Bennet looked peeved and Rose was satisfied that she had both surprised him and annoyed him. "The French ambassador stayed there once," he replied, as though that should impress her.

"Oh, well, that explains it then," Rose said. She

thought Bennet was about to drag her aside and demand exactly what that explained, when Lady Catherine and Cassie arrived with Axel. Rose had the feeling they were all intimates. The smile Lady Catherine bestowed on Axel held what was for her an uncharacteristic warmth. Lady Catherine was once again tastefully dressed in mauve but Cassie was trying out the affectation of a red gown trimmed in gold. She looked like nothing so much as a stout general.

A man called Leighton was the last to arrive, and Bennet disappeared for a few moments after introducing him. Rose studied Leighton's fair, innocent face, not quite willing to believe that such wholesomeness could disguise treachery. Then she glanced at Axel. At least Foy looked like what he was, a dissolute soldier. His appearance was the only honest thing about him.

Bennet returned, and, at the prompting of his mother, escorted Lady Catherine to the green dining room. Axel immediately took Edith Varner's arm. Rose hated protocol, for they were not even numbers and she would have to go in alone. To her surprise Leighton offered her his arm. Perhaps he perceived her as the next eldest. She smiled graciously anyway and forgot about what the others were doing. She could see by the peevish surprise on Edith's pinched face that Bennet had rearranged the name cards. Rose and Leighton were on Bennet's right hand with Stanley and Alice on his left. The enemy, as Rose regarded the rest of the party, was at the other end of the table. The green dining room on the ground floor was small by Varner standards, seating no more than a dozen comfortably.

"Varner!" Edith said a bit too loudly. "I thought I told you to invite that nice Mr. Dowd, the one with the theater box next to ours. He knows all about plays and will be able to instruct Alice on what she should see."

"Leighton is the only real drama critic I know," Bennet replied as he served himself from the platter of cutlets being held for his inspection. "Dowd is an amateur meddler. He has done more to set back the development of drama in London than any other single individual."

"That is rather harsh," Harriet replied. "And you are always condemning us for gossiping."

"That's not gossip. It's a fact, and I have told him so to his face."

Cassie cast a speculative look at Leighton, curled her lip in scorn, then turned her attention back to Axel, who was on her right. Harriet's petulance seemed to increase with each of Cassie's titters. Well, what did she expect, Rose thought, if Harriet had indeed turned Axel down? She should be wise enough to realize Axel was only flirting with Cassie to try to make Harriet jealous. Rose received a portion of capon from the placid Hardy and wondered how the man retained his composure.

Lady Catherine cast her obelisk gaze about the table, examining each of the guests in turn. Rose watched her inscrutable masklike face as she dismissed the Walls and Leighton as uninteresting and even Edith Varner as dull. It was a pretty mask Lady Catherine wore, but a mask all the same. Rose was trying to guess her age. At least forty-five with a grown daughter like Cassie. The woman held her head up to prevent any sagging of jowls from giving her away. Perhaps even fifty. The dainty way she picked at her greens and turbot, only pretending to eat, explained her spare, fragile-looking figure. One would never have guessed she was any relation to the buxom Cassie, whose portions nearly overflowed her plate. Lady Catherine smiled at Axel's antics, curled her lip at Cassie's inept attempt at dalliance, passed over Rose as though she were of no consequence—to Rose's relief—and settled finally on a study of Bennet.

By the end of the second course the now furious Harriet was making up to Stanley, who was beginning to sweat inside his collar. Whereas Rose was enjoying herself immensely. Little brother might find London not so much to his liking after another week of these stupid games. Rose had initiated a fervent discussion with Leighton, who recited for her a brief history of drama and criticism and gave her the opportunity to completely ignore Bennet, leaving him with no one to talk to but Alice. Her revenge was complete.

Leighton invited Rose to the theater the next evening but was rudely interrupted by Alice, who said it would not be proper for Rose to attend alone.

Rose almost choked on her cream tart at the thought of Alice setting herself up as a duenna.

"It was on my lips to invite you as well, and your charming husband," Leighton said. "Varner will not come, of course, or if he does he will be late, or leave early. I do not think he has ever seen a play in its entirety."

"We cannot all be men of leisure," Bennet countered.

"Don't let him fool you, Miss Wall. I have a very important position at the Foreign Office. Bennet may work all day long, but I frequently work the night through as well."

Rose was brought back to earth by this reminder. What better time to test Bennet's veracity? She turned to him for almost the first time that evening. "So that's why you pooh-poohed Axel's accusation," Rose whispered.

Leighton looked an inquiry at Bennet.

"Lord Foy seems to have taken it into his head," Bennet said, "and I do not know where he got the idea, for it is the most nonsensical—"

"Cut line, Varner," Leighton demanded.

"Axel thinks," Bennet whispered, leaning across the corner of the table, "that I am some sort of spy."

Leighton happened to be taking an incautious sip of wine, which choked him as it tried to pass a laugh in his throat. It was some moments before he could recover himself enough to speak. "That's a good one, Varner. Wait until I tell everyone."

Both Lady Catherine and Edith Varner were looking suspiciously toward their end of the table, so Rose sobered herself and tried to look bored. She did not want to cause any resentment at the good time she was having. She stared pointedly at the hunting prints and still-life paintings on the walls. But she had learned nothing, except that Leighton might be as good at dissembling as Bennet.

The party moved back into the gold salon across the hall and Lady Catherine immediately ordered Cassie to the pianoforte. The large girl pouted for a moment, eliciting the remark from her mother than it was ungracious to make people beg to hear her play. The performance began with a great deal of mechanical dexterity, but little inspiration, Rose thought. But Rose did not play herself, so she had no right to judge. A servant, under the guise of refreshing the brandy decanter, whispered something to Bennet, who nudged Leighton, and they both left the room.

Rose listened until the end of the piece and escaped into the hallway before Cassie began her encore. On the pretext of finding a bedchamber she tiptoed up the stairs to the first floor and heard voices coming from the library door. Some of the language she was hearing was distinctly French. "He has most definitely landed at Cannes and is making his way north."

"That is incredible!" Leighton said.

"It is just as I expected," Bennet replied.

"Is our source reliable?" Leighton asked.

The Frenchman replied that the news came with a shipment of brandy.

A door opened somewhere and Rose scurried back
downstairs. She had been feeling so relieved just an hour
ago. What if Leighton were in this thing with Bennet, this
plot to return Napoleon to the throne? It was fantastic to
suspect him, as well, for Rose did not even know Leighton. That was the point: she did not really know Bennet
Varner either, except that he had far more subtlety than
any man she had ever known.

She returned to the salon with an unquiet mind to find
Alice at the pianoforte and Stanley turning the pages for
her. At least those two had patched things up. But if Stanley was willing to make peace by giving in to anything
Alice wanted, then Bennet could manipulate Stanley and
Rose through the gullible Alice. Rose shook her head.
Why would he bother? Unless he did have a genuine concern about the three of them being caught in a war of his
making. And if Leighton worked at the Foreign Office,
there really was no point in going there. She listened distractedly through the rest of the performance, declined to
play herself and thus put a mercifully quick end to the
evening, for with Bennet gone, there was no one to encourage them to stay longer.

Chapter Six

Rose and Martin presented themselves at the stable behind Varner House at five minutes before ten o'clock. She could see at least one advantage to their new location. They could call for the horses rather than sit waiting in the lobby of the hotel. She was being given a tour of the row of stalls by Stilton, who named each of his dozen charges and gave Rose their history. She was interested to find a descendant of Wall's old stud, Valor, and was surprised that Bennet had not mentioned it.

"I just had him brought up from the country a day ago," Bennet said from behind them. "He should be rested enough for a ride if you've a mind to try him. Ordinarily I would say he was a man's ride, but I feel sure you can handle him, Miss Wall."

"I never boast of prowess on horses," Rose replied, watching the young chestnut being saddled by a stable lad. "There is no surer way to invite a spill. Perhaps you would be interested in developing a breeding program with the Wall line?"

"Most definitely," Bennet said, a wicked grin spreading across his face. Stilton turned abruptly to polish one of the brass catches on a stall door, biting back a grin, Rose was sure.

"I had meant with the horses," she said severely.

"So had I," Bennet returned with a look of such mystification a stranger might had concluded him innocent of innuendo.

"I begin to wonder if you mean anything you say, sir," Rose replied, conceding the point to Bennet.

As soon as the colt was saddled Bennet lifted Rose onto Bright Valor's back as effortlessly as though he were placing a child there. The colt danced a little, trying to balance Rose's slight weight, prompting her to conclude that he was unused to a sidesaddle. Perhaps Bennet meant to have his revenge for the previous night by getting Rose unseated in Hyde Park. That would do her no credit. She patted the horse's withers reassuringly and addressed him in a comforting undertone as Bennet and Martin mounted.

Once they had left the streets behind and gained the green expanse of the park, Rose relaxed her grip on the reins and let the colt stretch his legs as far as a canter only. For the next twenty minutes she thought of little except the horse and making sure he had a successful first ride with a lady. He tended to prance rather than spook at brightly painted carriages, and whinnied to unfamiliar horses, asking, she supposed, if they would like to go for a romp. He was no coward, but a playful, sportive creature, and Rose knew she must be wearing a silly grin at his antics. It was her experience that most falls were as much the rider's fault as the horse's, and she wanted this particular horse to do well. When she convinced Bright Valor she really did want to walk and had leisure to glance at Bennet, he was grinning as well. So he had meant for the horse to please her, or was Bright Valor one more string tying her to London?

When they finally dismounted on a long avenue of trees

to walk their mounts, she gave a sigh of relief and laughed at Chaos, who followed Bennet like a great black dog. The image was very much a metaphor for Bennet's dealings with the world. He mastered chaos and made it look easy. At times like this she had trouble casting him in the role of a villain. Still, there was the Frenchman and that incriminating trunk. Yet Bennet had made no excuses about Gaspard and had left the trunk sitting openly in his office for her to discover. Did he think her too stupid to be suspicious, or was he baiting her? But to what purpose?

She became conscious of him clearing his throat.

"I asked am I forgiven?"

"For what?" she replied blankly.

"For tricking you into moving to Change House."

"Is that what you call it?" she asked, playing for time. She was not sure she did forgive him.

"Father bought it with money he earned on the Exchange."

"Yes, and invited his business acquaintances there, so they would not be insulted by your mother and sister." Rose paused to look at a bed of bulbs, just pushing their way through the ground.

"You're very astute. Mother still pretends he merely did not want her bothered with entertaining dull company."

"Just as she pretends he moved there in order to take a mistress."

"She never told you that." Bennet sent Rose a suspicious look.

"No, Cassie mumbled it to Axel last night." Rose proceeded along the path. "She does not guard her tongue at all."

"Actually my father did tread the straight and narrow, though I would not have blamed him much for seeking more tender companionship than Mother's. Once Lady

Cat set Mother's foot on the bottom rung of the social ladder, Mother thought of nothing else but advancement in that quarter."

"Lady Catherine, you mean? She must be powerful indeed."

"She is much more adept at gossip than Cassie ever will be. Lady Cat, as she is called at the gentlemen's clubs, has been mentoring Harriet in that skill."

"Have you no influence over your sister?" Rose asked sympathetically, all the time wondering if a spy would trust her with such confidences.

"Not even when I had control of her fortune. Now it is hers to bestow as she will. I wash my hands of her."

"I do not always get on well with Stanley but I know that in a pinch I could count on him no matter what I had done."

"You deserve loyalty, Harriet does not. And you never answered my question."

"What question was that?"

"Am I forgiven?"

"My dear sir, one can be punished and still never be forgiven."

"Are we still talking about me?" he asked gently.

She stared at him for she had been thinking of herself. "And even if one is forgiven, the incident is never really forgotten," Rose continued.

"I told them you would not like to be surprised." Bennet kicked a stone from the bridle path.

"Deceived, you mean. And yet you conspired with them against me. I tell you it made me feel very…alone. As though someone for whom I had a great regard had been gossiping about me behind my back. It did not destroy my liking for you, friend, but it made me feel very betrayed."

"You make it sound as though we are your enemies," Bennet said in surprise.

"At some point everyone is my enemy, including you," she said passionately.

"Do not shut me out, Rose," he whispered desperately, reaching his free hand toward her. "I thought it a harmless jest."

She ignored his hand. "I am not stupid, Bennet. No one persuades you to do anything you don't wish, not even your mama. You tricked me because it served your purpose and for no other reason."

Bennet gaped at her. "I'm—I'm shocked that you could so misinterpret—"

"No, you are surprised that I figured it out. That's all. Are you going to compound deceit with lies?"

"I think I dare not," he said humbly. "Have you also surmised what my purpose is?"

"To keep us here in London at all costs. You have already been put to considerable pain and expense to do so. A new mast! You had no idea yourself it was cracked until they pulled it out. And the house—"

"Very well, I concede it suited me to set your family up in London."

"But as to why, there I am mystified, a trio of country bumpkins…"

Bennet sent her a startled glance. "Has Harriet said anything to offend you?"

"No, as it happens, that was my appellation, not hers. Have you frequently to shield people from her tongue?"

"I have warned her that her wicked tongue will be her undoing. One day she will gossip about someone who can fight back—"

"Not to be led off the scent, your reason for keeping us here, sir," Rose demanded. "Tell me now or I promise you will never see me again."

Bennet halted, staring levelly at her, and stopping the horses in their tracks as though they, too, hung on his next words. "I suppose the time for dissembling is past. On Leighton's advice I was trying to avoid a public panic, but I feel sure now I can trust you not to tell anyone else."

"You are being rather dramatic. Tell anyone what?"

"Napoleon has escaped from Elba and is marching across Europe, attempting to gather his old armies about him again."

Even though she had already surmised as much, a profound chill went through Rose and tears sprang to her eyes, but she blinked them away and demanded, "When?"

"He landed at Cannes the first day of March. The last news we had he was heading north. Unless someone stops him he could be in Paris as soon as the twentieth. Now you see why I did not want you three innocents setting sail for Europe? You might never have gotten back again."

"Yes, oh yes. Bennet, this is horrible. I can scarcely believe it is possible, but I know in my heart that you are telling the truth."

"You have nothing to fear." Bennet dropped the reins of his horse and took Rose in his arms. "This news cannot affect anyone you know."

"But it does affect us most seriously." Rose looked up at him. "Stanley will certainly buy a commission now. Mother and I were able to prevent it before, but now he is master of his own fortune. If another army is raised he will be part of it."

"Surely not. Half of the army is still in Vienna. With any luck they will catch Boney again and lock him away."

"I wish I could be so optimistic as you. Vienna was spoken of as one of our destinations. The only difference is now Stanley will be going alone.'' She sniffed, knowing her eyes were red and not just from the cold.

''Even I cannot keep the news secret for long. By now Wellington and the Congress of Vienna know. Other informants must have arrived in London. Official dispatches will soon follow.''

''Informants?'' Rose took a step back from him, forcing him to release her. ''Spies, you mean. How did you come to know all this? For your efforts to keep us here began as soon as we arrived on the last day of February.'' She glanced about her, wondering who had seen the embrace and was startled to realize Martin had been providing a sort of cover to their private conversation. Such devotion should not go unrewarded.

''My business dealings put me in a position to hear rumors. I occasionally come into contact with…smugglers. I had some suspicions as early as January when we intercepted a shipment of china bound for Elba with gold coin packed in the straw.''

''The trunk of books in your office,'' Rose said, wanting so much to believe Bennet. ''It has a false bottom where gold could be secreted.''

''How did you know that? We discovered that shipment the very day you arrived.''

Rose reached into her pocket and produced the gold sovereign, her only evidence that he might have done something wrong. She placed it in his hand.

''Walters must have missed one. You are also very observant.''

''Have you had any luck tracing the shipment?''

''It should be the easiest thing in the world but this fellow has covered his tracks well. Unfortunately there are hosts of British citizens sympathetic to Napoleon.''

''And the books themselves?'' Rose prompted.

''What about them?''

"They are not all new. One or two of them had previously been inscribed. They must have come from somewhere, an estate auction or something. A list passed around to book dealers may give you some idea who has purchased all or some of those volumes. By carefully matching—"

"Why didn't I think of that?" Bennet said, smacking his fist into his palm.

Rose wondered if he could be faking his enthusiasm. If he was sending the shipment, there was nothing to investigate. Yet why leave it sitting about his office for any clerk to see? "You've had other things to deal with."

Rose fell silent, and Bennet watched her turning over the news in her mind, trying to find a way out of the trap he had shown her. Bennet personally thought that a short stint in a cavalry regiment would do Stanley a world of good, giving him the confidence he needed to be the head of his family, but he was perceptive enough to not voice this opinion to Rose.

Rose trembled visibly. "I suddenly feel quite cold. Perhaps we should go back."

As he helped her to mount he reflected that he had been in something like Stanley's position eight years ago, while his father still lived and could keep an impetuous only son from flinging himself into war for the sheer excitement of it. If only he had known he would force his heir to substitute far more dangerous, clandestine adventures.

Rose seemed quite composed when he helped her to dismount in front of Change House, but coldly distant as though she had to deal with the startling turn of events without his aid. She turned around on the bottom step and he went to her, carelessly tossing the reins of both horses to Martin.

"I forgot to thank you for the ride, and I was charged with a message from Alice."

"Oh?"

"You are invited to dine here tonight. I take it your mama and sister have already accepted but knew better than to speak for you. The party will be much what it was last night except that the charming Leighton will be replaced by that awful Dowd person. There, I have told you and given you a chance to escape. As news goes it is very nearly as bad as what you handed me."

"I shall be delighted to attend."

"You will attend," Rose said with a watery chuckle, "but you will not be delighted. It will be interesting to watch your pretense of pleasure. In your own way you are a far more accomplished actor than anyone I have seen on the stage. Leighton was wrong. You have seen many plays through to the end, without even knowing your lines. I congratulate you, sir, since I assume you rarely draw public applause."

Bennet watched her turn and go up the steps, still wondering what she was thinking. That he could not play the same tricks on her that worked with everyone else was certainly apparent. "Martin, would you take the horses back for me?" he asked, tossing the boy the gold coin. "I have an errand."

"Certainly, sir. Oh—I say. Thank you, sir."

Bennet strode toward his office at the western end of the banking district. It was a long walk but he had to clear his head or he would not be able to concentrate again today. These morning rides with Rose, though usually delightful, were distracting. She was right about him having other things on his mind lately. He generally could not get his senses together for business until noon, until he had done everything he could think of to ensure Rose's comfort and safety. But there was no way to turn back an army a continent away.

When he got to his office Walters said, "You have *a visitor*." That was his word for Gaspard.

Bennet went into his room and closed the door, shaking the Frenchman awake and handing him a whiskey in spite of his obvious fatigue. "What news from your smuggling friends?" Bennet asked in French.

"He has passed through Gras, Castellane and Digne."

"He's headed for Gap. What has been his reception?"

"Cool at first. He was never as well loved in those districts. He would never have dared to land on the west coast. But if even one contingent of the Royalist army goes over to him, they may all topple. Either that or civil war."

Bennet stared at Gaspard as though he could hardly believe his ears. At the end of the twenty-minute interview Bennet reminded the Frenchman that he could no longer use Change House and recommended he find a hotel. Fatigued and half-asleep from the whiskey, Gaspard left the office and headed toward Oxford Street.

When Rose returned home, Change House seemed empty. She went to her bedroom, which looked out on the backs of the neighboring street of town houses. It was a pleasing enough prospect for a city dweller, but for a country girl a daily ride in the park was just not enough. London might be pleasant a month from now, but she still found it rather chilling. Or perhaps it was the unsettled state of Europe, the ruin of all their plans. She did not know what she had expected from their tour. She half thought her mother expected her to catch a husband for herself in the next six months, perhaps a foreigner, someone who was not so particular about reputations. But she would never marry a man without telling him all, and once he heard it, would he suspect she had not divulged everything?

Cynthie came in to help her change. The girl was still nervous but had stopped begging her mistress to send her back to Wall.

"I think I shall take my bath soon, Cynthie. Alice and I are going to the theater tonight with Bennet's friend, Leighton. Would you and Martin—"

"Oh, please miss, don't make me go again. What if Lord Foy should appear?"

"Martin will threaten to shoot him again and Axel will go away. He may be valiant enough when wielding a saber himself, or when abusing a woman, but push the muzzle of a gun in his face and Axel Barton is quite the coward."

"Still, I think it best to avoid him, miss. If we call that night to mind for him, he may begin to remember what really happened."

"Yes, you are right, of course. The best thing would be to part company with him, but I do not know if this sea voyage will ever come off."

"Why not, miss, though I cannot say I'm sorry?"

Rose did not tell her that Boney was on the loose again, since the news had been given in confidence. That was the way rumors started. "Stanley seems more interested in getting on with his improvements at Wall than eager to look at paintings and statues. There is quite enough culture in London to satisfy him."

"But you was so looking forward to the trip, miss."

"For lack of anything better to do. We shall simply put forward our plans."

"Our plans?"

"Yes. I have decided to buy a farm as close to Bristol as may be possible. The three of us will live there. I may go to stay with Mother from time to time, but we will not have to give up our horses."

"Martin will like that."

"And what about you, Cynthie? There is never anything I can do to make up for what happened to you. What do you want?"

"To be anyplace Lord Foy is not."

"As soon as may be then, we will take the stagecoach to Bristol."

To Rose's surprise the dinner was not a complete disaster, owing to the servants having pretty much ignored all Alice's instructions about the menu and having cooked what they knew to be appropriate. Alice unflinchingly took credit for all these preparations and Stanley smiled fondly at her. She even accepted a compliment from Dowd on the decor of the dining room, which was royal blue and gold. But everyone in the room must have known Alice could have had nothing to do with it.

A new horror occurred to Rose. If Stanley were to go off to war, she would be the one expected to nursemaid Alice. The prospect of remaining at Wall, which she previously would have relished, was made ugly by the necessity to do so. Perhaps Bennet was right, and this fresh start of Napoleon's would amount to nothing more than a desperate last feint. But if Bennet really believed that, why had he been so intent on keeping them from embarking for Europe? Also she did not like the sound of "informants." What businessman kept paid informants? He might have told her the truth but only a very small part of it. She was staring at his jovial, boyish face with her fork suspended over her plate when an annoying voice interrupted her thoughts.

"You are not attending me."

"Did you say something, Mr. Dowd?"

"You should watch the performance with me tonight, not with Leighton."

"Why?" Rose asked, helping herself to another truffle.

"So that I can instruct you and Mrs. Wall." Dowd drained his wineglass.

"Tell us what to think, do you mean?" Rose laughed out loud. "I promise you, Mr. Dowd, that is not possible. No one has ever been able to influence me in the slightest."

"More's the pity," he said.

"Is that all?" Rose smiled sweetly. "Come now, you must have something further to say on that matter."

"It is very clear to me now that your mind has been corrupted by Leighton's views already." Dowd cast a dour look across the table at Bennet.

"Corrupted?" Rose chuckled. "You attach far too much importance to the theater and your opinions on it."

"My opinions are widely held," he said, glancing around the table for affirmation and getting nods from the other females present.

"Only by those who do not care to think for themselves," Rose said, ignoring that Alice was counted among this number.

"Gwen Rose!" Alice almost shouted. "Are you forgetting that if I choose to go to the theater with Mr. Dowd you cannot go with Leighton alone?"

"Do you not think that a bit rude, Alice? To excuse yourself from a prior invitation when you think you have a better offer?"

"Rose is right," Stanley said, putting a blush in the cheeks of his young wife.

"Termagant," Cassie muttered under her breath, then, remembering where she was, stuffed a bite of cherry tart into her mouth.

Axel was watching the lively exchange wearing an expression almost amounting to pleasure.

Stanley wiped his mouth and laid down his napkin with a sigh of defeat. "I suppose this means I must go with you, Rose, though I had promised to leave with Falmouth for the race meet tonight. I hope this play will be worth the bother.''

''It will not,'' Dowd said. ''I know the man's work, and he is never worth the bother.''

''Then why are you going?'' Stanley asked in some irritation.

''It is my duty to inform the public.''

Rose directed a menacing stare at Dowd. ''My mother always instructed us to either say something good or not say anything at all.''

''I wager she knew nothing of the theater,'' Dowd replied.

''It is a maxim that can be applied to all aspects of life, Mr. Dowd. Of course, with the views you hold, if you said only good things you would be left with little to say at all.''

Bennet let his knife clatter to his plate. ''I shall accompany Rose in Leighton's box and she will be as safe as if she were with her own brother.''

''Thank you, Bennet,'' Rose said skeptically. ''I look forward to the evening.''

Stanley had already left for his appointment and the ladies were about to rise from the table when a servant subtly slipped a note into Bennet's hand. He tore it open below the level of the table and groaned audibly, then excused himself. Rose came into the hall to see their footman receive a whispered instruction from Bennet and leave at a run. ''Have you sent Phipps for your carriage?''

''What? No—but perhaps I should.'' He came back to take her hands.

''I think Leighton will probably provide transport.''

''Of course, I was forgetting him,'' Bennet said distractedly.

''Sorry, if I gave you a bad turn in there, but I cannot

abide such nonsense as Dowd was spouting, even to be polite.''

"I know. If someone is being a fool you tell him so to his face. I like that about you.''

"Even if you are the one acting the fool.''

"Especially then.'' Bennet looked down as though he were afraid she might read something in his eyes. "I am so used to dealing with fools....''

"That the temptation to dupe them is overwhelming. Yes, I know.'' Rose withdrew her hands, reluctant to stop the banter but painfully aware that she was detaining Bennet. "I think perhaps I should get my pelisse and be ready when Leighton arrives.''

"If Leighton comes, see that he's welcomed, will you?'' Bennet asked with his hand on the door latch, as though he were the host rather than Stanley. "I will meet you at the theater.''

What he must think of their shabby manners! Rose didn't care very much what anyone else thought, but she did not want Bennet to think badly of her or Stanley.

"If? I do not think Dowd's presence will discourage Leighton,'' Rose said. "Leighton is too much like you.''

"If Leighton does not come,'' Bennet said, "I suppose you will have to endure the prosy Dowd.''

Rose stared at Bennet, realizing that what called him away might also involve Leighton. But she could not condemn him, not without proof that what they were doing was wrong. "Oh, well, then I shall continue to torture Dowd. Though with eight in his box there may not be enough room for much torturing.''

"I wish you were right about that,'' Bennet said uneasily. "Making sport of Dowd is not the safest game in the world, but there are far more dangerous predators about.''

"Yes, Lady Cat. I kept my distance. So long as she

thinks me and innocent country girl, she has no interest in me.''

''I hope you may be right.''

He was gone then at a run, and Rose did not know whether she should be upset or not. She thought she could have held him if she had tried, but to prevent what? She must know if Bennet and Leighton were involved in some conspiracy against the government, or she could not leave London with a quiet mind.

When Rose went to the green salon some minutes later to announce Bennet's defection, she had hoped one of the ladies would volunteer to keep her company in Leighton's box. If not Alice, either Harriet or Edith Varner would have been good candidates.

When they were silent, Axel said, ''I will occupy Leighton's box with you.'' This occasioned more than one sharp gasp and brought a leer to Axel's face.

''Thank you, Axel. That is very kind of you.'' Rose did not know why two men were thought to be a safer escort than one, especially if one of those men was Lord Foy, but this satisfied the proprieties, although it made Harriet as mad as fire.

To Rose's relief, Leighton did present himself at Change House. He was preoccupied, but present, which was more than she could say for Bennet. When they got to the theater Rose discovered that Leighton's box was on a lower tier and closer to the stage. It was not the sort of box where one could show off one's jewels or beaus to advantage, but it was an excellent vantage point for actually seeing the play. In spite of Axel's presence at her left side Rose was enjoying herself. She could see quite clearly Dowd's box across the way. They looked almost an armed camp with six of them crowded into it.

"I often wondered what would drive you to me," Axel whispered.

"Boredom or Magnus Dowd," Rose answered.

"They are one and the same," Axel replied, making Rose chuckle. "Where has Bennet gone?"

"The docks, I think," Rose replied. "Something has gone wrong with a shipment, I suppose. Bennet is rather a bore himself to be always flitting off."

"You did not seem to find him so in the park."

Rose could not disguise her start of surprise. "Were you there today? I was trying to buy one of his horses and he absolutely refused to sell even at an inflated price."

"That is why you are so out of charity with him," Axel concluded.

"I am very seldom in charity with him," Rose complained. "He never fails to make me angry within five minutes of opening his mouth." Since this was very true Rose had no qualms about misleading Axel. She did not go on to say that Bennet never failed to joke her back out of her ill humor with a skill that amazed her.

Partway through the first act, the curtains to the box opened and Bennet pulled up a chair behind Rose. "Sorry I was detained," he said to all three of them. If he was surprised to find Axel there, he did not show it. If he was at all jealous of Axel, that he did not show either. The whole evening was taking on a bizarre aspect, Rose decided, and she tried her best to concentrate on the actors and their lines rather than real life.

Bennet breathed a sigh of relief. He must have a word with Leighton, and although he did not mind Rose's presence, he could say nothing in front of Axel. At the first interval Bennet volunteered himself and Leighton to procure lemonade for the group, which surprised both Rose and Axel. Just to be perverse Axel insisted on going with Bennet himself.

"Do you ride often with Miss Wall?" Axel asked as soon as they had gained the corridor.

"As often as my business allows," Bennet said without missing a step. "But I have told the Walls to make themselves free of my stables."

"You have?"

"They are competent riders, as you are. You do know you can borrow a mount whenever you need one, don't you?"

"Why are you being so..."

"Foy, you are very nearly my brother-in-law. Whatever constraint was between us before should be forgotten."

"That's very big of you. How do you find Rosie's company?"

"Rosie? Oh, you mean Miss Wall. Frankly, she cares for nothing so much as a strong leg or a showy crest. I might as well be invisible as far as she is concerned when my horses are about."

Axel laughed. "Yes, that is Rosie."

"Was she always so...cold?" Bennet asked as he paid the vendor for four glasses of lemonade."

"No," Axel said, taking up two of the glasses. "When we were engaged she was quite passionate."

"You surprise me," Bennet said, making his way up the narrow stairs again. "She has informed me she will never marry."

"Who could follow me?" Axel asked.

"Indeed, even if I were on the lookout for such a wife, I do not believe I could persuade her to marriage if I offered her my entire stud farm."

"Though she might be tempted," Axel replied.

It was Bennet's turn to laugh. Both Leighton and Rose eyed the men strangely when they returned. Axel stayed no more than to the end of the interval. Then he left the box and indeed seemed to disappear from the theater entirely.

They actually watched the entire second act without interruption, though the tension between Leighton and Bennet enveloped Rose like a suffocating cloak. She knew that if she had not been there, they would have spoken all their concerns and totally ignored the actors. It was disquieting to think there was something going on that could divert Bennet's attention from her. She took herself mentally to task for this conceit. In the past she had never been uppermost in anyone's mind, not even her mother's. And she had rather enjoyed the freedom that anonymity provided. Even when she had been engaged to Axel, he had only looked upon her as a possession. He thought of her in terms of what she was to him. Bennet bothered to know her mind about things and he did care. But if he were working for the other side…

The act ended and Bennet sighed heavily, checking his watch.

"You have both been rather quiet," Rose said.

"Oh, I warned Leighton about the traps you set for Dowd at dinner, and he vowed to keep his mummer shut."

Leighton chuckled.

"Why do you keep company with me, Varner, when you are so ill-equipped to deal with me in my more volatile states?" Rose gibed.

"To keep me humble," Bennet replied. "And you never fail to succeed."

Rose smothered a laugh as a servant entered the box and handed Bennet another of those damned notes. She could not help but notice that it was one of the servants from Change House.

"Here it comes," Leighton said under his breath.

"Leighton is right, I'm afraid," Bennet said as he rose. "Fortunately, this does not require his presence. Understand, Rose, that only the gravest matters could tear me from your side."

Leighton half got up, and Rose grasped his forearm. "I swear if both of you go haring off at the same time, I shall scream. The least you can do is take turns playing your little games."

Leighton sat back down with a shrug. "I told you Varner never sees a performance through to the end."

"Is he coming back?"

"Probably," Leighton said, scrutinizing his watch in the dim light. "Don't worry. You are completely safe with me."

"Oh, I wasn't worried."

"That isn't exactly what a fellow likes to hear, even if it is true," Leighton said as he began to relax.

"Don't you like to be trusted? Bennet does."

"Only up to a point. Do you trust me more than Bennet?"

"By furlongs. You see, you never hide anything, at least not all that well, and he is the most deceitful man I have ever encountered."

"Well, that's why he—"

"Why he what?"

"Does so well in business. One never knows from his face what cards he is holding."

"Indeed. There's more to Bennet Varner than the boyish entrepreneur and henpecked son and brother. I do not know what all it is just yet, but I will find out."

Leighton cast a wary look in her direction as the curtain went up on the third act. They did not return to the topic even near the end of the play when Axel slid into the box and his vacated chair as smoothly as a snake, twisting his scabbard around to the side as he sat down with a flourish.

Rose turned to confront him as though she were expecting him to return. "You have missed the best part, Axel."

"I just came to warn you again to stay away from Bennet Varner. Those early-morning rides will become very dangerous from now on."

Rose drew back, feeling suddenly vulnerable. "What on earth can you mean?"

"When Varner is arrested in Hyde Park you do not want to be with him. I need only a bit more evidence."

"What are you babbling about?" Rose licked her dry lips.

"I have captured the French spy," Axel whispered dramatically.

"Captured? What are you saying? You have kidnapped a man?"

Leighton began to stare at them so Axel whispered in her ear. "When he confesses I will have all I need to show Bennet Varner up for what he really is, a man who has sold out his country."

"I don't believe it," Rose bluffed.

"Believe it. I have the Frenchman tied to my bedstead at this very moment."

"No, I mean I don't believe Bennet Varner has anything to do with spying," Rose hissed.

"You don't bluff well, Rosie. You've had doubts about him all along. Now I'm about to prove them true. As soon as this fellow wakes up I will have all the evidence I need."

"Why tell me this? You must think I care about you and Bennet, and the stupid games men play."

"You care about your country. There is nothing lower than a traitor."

"I can think of one thing."

Axel was gone then before she could protest further,

and Axel was right, damn him. She had never been able to lie very well and she had plenty of doubts about Bennet, but she had to do something. If Axel were to kill this man and he were innocent...

Without hesitation she thumped Leighton's shoulder and asked, "Do you know where we can find Bennet Varner at this hour?"

"Oh, no, not you, too," Leighton said in despair. "At his office, I suppose."

"We must go there at once. Give me that," she said impatiently, grabbing her wool pelisse and throwing it about her shoulders. She led Leighton by two strides the entire way down the hall and ran down the steps. "Which is quicker, walking or a carriage?"

"There's a hack right across the street," he said. "They wait for the theater crowd, you see, but most playgoers inexplicably stay to see the whole. Odd, isn't it?" he said as he helped her into the equipage and gave the man Bennet's direction.

"I am immensely sorry, Leighton, but this is extremely important."

"That's what Varner always says. I don't suppose you could just tell me."

"I could, but I need to speak to Bennet first."

"He's right about you. You are an unusual woman."

"Have you known Bennet long?"

"We were together at school. An upperclassman was twisting my arm out of its joint and Bennet threw himself into the fray without even knowing me."

"That sounds like something Axel would have done to you."

"Yes, it was Foy, but how did you know?"

"Just a guess. So their ill will goes back a very long way."

"Yes. After that Bennet and I looked out for each other."

"And you still do." Rose glanced at Leighton, his righteous profile showing up against the occasional street lamps. She could hardly quiz him on Bennet Varner's loyalties. "What do you think of Lord Foy?"

"He's a bully, but a soldier and one who is spoken well of. So I suppose he has some uses."

"You have no reason to suspect his...patriotism?"

"My dear girl, one does not endure the Peninsular campaign unless one is passionately loyal. Here we are then."

They descended from the hack and Leighton went up the front steps to thump the knocker, but no amount of pounding or shouting gained them admittance.

"That is his window," Rose said, pointing to the light on the second story.

"Yes. Hey, what are you doing?"

"Prying up this cobblestone."

"Is that a knife you have there? Where did you get a knife?"

"Never mind. Help me."

"That's too big. Here's a little one. Even so, you can never throw it that far."

"I shall have to in order to get his attention, if you are not willing to do so."

"Very well. Wouldn't surprise me at all if I ended up in the roundhouse after this night's work," Leighton said, heaving the stone, and catching it again as it rattled off the bricks. He took another throw.

"Don't be silly. The very worst we can do is break a window."

This reassurance was followed by the tinkle of glass and the appearance of a pistol thrust through the opening, then Bennet's head. "What the devil, Leighton? What are

you doing down there smashing windows and with my—
with Miss Gwen Rose Wall?''

"Do you think you could shout my name a little louder,
Bennet," Rose snapped. "I want everyone to hear."

"Are you at the bottom of this?"

"I must speak to you, now."

She stamped her foot and Bennet immediately withdrew his head and thundered down the stairs. "What is
so important?" he asked as he ran down the outside steps.

"Can Leighton be trusted?"

"I say, didn't I go and break that window for you?"

"Of course, he can," Bennet replied.

"Because I must trust you, both of you. Axel has abducted a Frenchman, knocked him out, I think, and means
to torture a confession out of him."

"Gaspard!" Bennet and Leighton both shouted.
"Where is he holding him?" Bennet demanded, taking
Rose by the arms.

"It must be at his lodgings. He said something about
tying him to the bedstead. You must hurry."

"I'm so glad you trusted me, Rose," Bennet said, giving her a hasty kiss on the mouth. "This could mean an
innocent man's life."

"I would not care if he was the most villainous of
French spies," Rose said, still clutching his arms. "I
could not leave anyone in Axel's power, if I could help
it."

Bennet stared at her strangely, reluctantly let her go,
then turned to Leighton. "Will you take Rose safely
home? Foy lives in those bachelor's quarters in Pall Mall.
I can get home and back there within the hour if I go
alone."

"But you should not go alone," Leighton protested.

"I shall get all the help I require at Varner House. And

Leighton, no one need know I was not with you the whole of the evening.''

"You mean you want us to lie for you?" Leighton asked with a grin.

"Oh, why not?" Rose said valiantly. "Bennet does it all the time."

Chapter Seven

Martin jumped and reached under his pillow when Rose shook him awake. "Hush, Martin. I need your help."

"Are we running away, miss?"

"Nothing so drastic. Get dressed and meet me at the kitchen door in five minutes. And Martin, be sure and bring that pistol."

"Yes, miss."

In less than ten minutes Rose was striding along the dark London streets in a buff walking dress and her gray cloak, apprising Martin of all that had occurred. Fortunately she now had some knowledge of these streets and knew how to get to Axel's lodgings in Pall Mall. "What do you think, Martin? Have I done the right thing by trusting Bennet Varner?"

"Of course, miss. Mr. Varner is a right one. Even I would trust him, and that's saying much."

"Let's hope you are right about your reading of his character. Thus far I have been getting ambiguous signals from him."

"He's just a bit awkward, but only around you, miss. Didn't you notice that?"

"No, I have not had leisure," Rose said, rubbing her

gloved hands together and glancing at Martin to make sure he was dressed warmly enough.

When they got to their destination, Rose backed a pace and gawked up at the three-story building, swearing under her breath. "I'm sure these are the lodgings Bennet referred to, but I just realized this block of rooms has a front and a courtyard, probably multiple entrances."

"What do you want me to do, miss?"

"I have prepared a note, asking Axel to meet me. No one will think anything of it if you deliver it to his servant. The doorman should be able to tell you which apartment is his. Do not try to go inside but try if you can to hear anything."

"Very well, miss, but are you sure—do you really wish to meet Foy?"

"I would as soon talk to the devil himself, but if I can delay the Frenchman's interrogation it is worth the pain."

"If he comes out, I will watch him close, but what if Lord Foy is not at home, miss?"

"Then take up your watch from the courtyard side. I will stay here, across the street from the front, and delay Axel should he return before Bennet arrives."

"How shall we delay him, miss? I mean to what extent…"

"Don't murder him, but raise a fuss. I'm sure you'll think of something."

While Martin carried the letter inside Rose had leisure to think of some devices whereby she might delay or distract Axelrod Barton, Lord Foy. He was always ready for dalliance, or argument. Argument it would be, for she was in no way practiced in the arts of flirtation, besides that being a singularly dangerous occupation where Axel was concerned. Rose also had leisure to regret her impetuous actions, all of them. This was just the sort of scrape she had got into when she had been a girl, but it was her curse that she could not stand to leave anything to chance.

Some movement on the rooftop caught her eye. She stared intently and made out a hunched figure in black skipping lightly between the chimney pots. Bennet to the rescue, perhaps? She paced the length of the building, her wool skirt chafing her knees and her riding boots sounding mannishly loud on the pavement. She paced back to the corner again and jumped when she heard a horse snort. There was a carriage waiting on the side street, and if she knew Bennet, he had risked his very best horses. Perhaps she was not even needed. Perhaps her interference would ruin everything, she thought, as she paced back along the building. After another ten minutes Rose began to fear for Martin's safety. What if Axel had answered the door and snatched the boy? So many uncertainties. A door banging shut interrupted her pacing.

"Rose? What is it?" Axel asked as he strode down the steps, shrugging on his uniform coat and clenching a cigar between his teeth.

Rose dashed across the street to keep Axel from seeing any activity on his own roof.

"I had to talk to you."

"I am all for clandestine meetings, but your character would never suffer being found in this rabbit warren of half-pay officers."

Martin slipped out behind Axel, and Rose motioned the boy toward the opposing corner to make him aware of the carriage. Of course, Axel would think she was getting rid of Martin for privacy.

"No thanks to you. What do you mean by telling me Varner is a spy, then disappearing as though you were dropping the latest society on-dit in my lap?"

"Can't this wait until morning? This fellow is about to come around. I must interrogate him."

"I think you would be better employed apologizing to him. No doubt you have, in your usual way, gotten it all wrong and have abducted a completely innocent trader."

"We'll see who's the fool, me or you, for trusting Bennet Varner."

"I don't trust him. I don't trust any man, thanks to you."

"Except that sniveling boy."

"Martin is like a son to me."

"Don't give me that. He is far too old to be anything of the sort. Why were the two of you meeting in the stable that night at Wall?"

"Meeting? We were trying to save his sister."

"No one should have been up and about that late at night. It could have been no accident—"

"Listen to yourself. You rape my maid, then stand there and accuse me of planning an assignation with a child. Five years ago Martin was but twelve."

"Well, he's not twelve anymore and you are far too friendly with him."

Rose raised her fist, but Axel was more wary this time and grabbed her arm.

"And Cynthie was fourteen, Axel," she said bitterly. "A child. How could you?"

"She was old enough."

"You're a monster."

"I'm a soldier. Besides, it was all your fault."

"My fault, for not stopping you in time?"

"No, for not satisfying my appetite. You should have expected the like when you refused to let me make love to you."

"So it was my fault for not giving myself to you before marriage?"

"What would three weeks have mattered?"

"You're insane, but getting back to the subject at

hand," Rose said, trying to calm her temper, "what possible evidence do you have that Bennet Varner is anything other than he appears?"

"I have the Frenchman and—" The smashing of a coping stone on the cobbles at their feet alerted Axel to the one means of escape he had not considered. "The roof!"

"Axel!" Rose tried to restrain him by grabbing his arm.

"Let go of me!" he shouted, pushing her from him and knocking her to her knees.

Martin sprinted across the street and caught Axel at the door. A boot to the midriff dispatched Martin, but by then Rose had caught up to them and grabbed Axel's sleeve again. The soldier escaped only by the expedient of wriggling out of his scarlet jacket and dashing into the building. They had not stopped him but they had delayed him. Who knew how precious those seconds were?

More scrabbling from the roof heralded the appearance of a heavy burden dangling by a rope. "Martin," Rose said to the boy, who was still gasping for air. "When you are able, try to help Bennet. He's lowering Gaspard on a rope. I'll get the carriage."

Martin managed to stand and grab the dangling end of the rope, valiantly braced to catch a man twice his weight while Rose ran across the way and into the side street toward the carriage. "Stilton?" she asked on a guess.

"Miss Wall! What are you doing here?"

"Never mind that now," she said, hopping into the open carriage. "Gaspard can't navigate. Bennet is lowering him by rope and needs help."

Stilton whipped up the horses and drove them expertly round to the front of the building opposite, masking at least some of the frantic activity of Martin, wrestling with the deadweight of the Frenchman.

"I'll take the reins," Rose commanded. "Go help him, man."

Whether by shock or necessity Stilton handed the reins of the restive pair over to Rose, who focused all her efforts on keeping them from bolting. Stilton produced a knife and cut Gaspard from the rope harness, taking the brunt of the man's weight and falling under him. It was all he and Martin could do to wrestle him toward the carriage, for Stilton was limping badly on his right ankle.

An unearthly wail of outrage drew Rose's attention to the roof, but from her vantage point she could see nothing. The clash of steel on stone told her that only Axel had a weapon. "Please, Bennet, don't get killed," she pleaded under her breath. "Please slide down the rope. I won't leave without you."

By now they had wrestled Gaspard onto one seat of the large equipage. Martin started up the rope like a monkey just as Bennet came pinwheeling over the edge of the roof. He saved himself only by grabbing the edge of it with one hand. Axel appeared triumphant above him, about to bring the saber down, when Rose screamed a most savage, defiant "No!"

The team froze as though they had been doing something wrong. Axel hesitated as well, and Rose thought he must be recalling the last time she had screamed that at him. He laughed, and his boot crushed Bennet's hand. Bennet twisted toward the rope, which Martin had walked along the wall in his direction. As his useless fingers slipped from the roof he caught the rope in his good hand and slid ten feet before Martin stopped his progress. Bennet wrapped the rope around his useless arm and let it take most of the burns as they slithered together to the paving stones.

They were no more in the carriage when Rose released the horses and set them on a gallop through the ill-lit streets, eager to do her part, now that the immediate danger was past. They were all alive, thank God. She had only to get them safely away without overturning them.

Bennet climbed up on the seat beside her, his right hand cradled in his left, which was not in much better shape. Rose gritted her teeth in sympathy at the pain he must be feeling. "Stilton can't drive," he informed her. "He can scarcely stand. What about Martin?"

"I think I can manage them if you tell me the way. Will Axel pursue us, do you think? I am going the wrong direction if you mean to take Gaspard home."

"Yes, we will have to get turned round. Axel will never expect me to take Gaspard to Varner House. Turn left at the next street."

Rose checked the horses as little as possible, and gauging the carriage to be a heavy brute, did not slow nearly as much as she would have for a light curricle. Bennet grunted as the nigh wheels touched the cobbles again, and glared at her.

"What?" she demanded.

"What lunatic taught you to drive like that?"

"No one taught me. I had to learn for myself."

"That explains much," he said, glancing over his shoulder. "I hear a carriage. Axel must have stolen a hackney. Turn left at the next alley and halt them."

Rose did as commanded, and in that split second between the time Bennet's team screeched to a halt and the harness stopped jingling, and before the beasts began stamping impatiently, the hackney with its solitary horse careened past the end of the alley.

"Go," Bennet commanded. "Straight for two blocks. Then we'll make a right."

"I just hope," Rose said, "that I'm doing the right thing."

"You know in your heart that I am no traitor."

"You don't give a girl much to go on but intuition."

"I am not a man who is accustomed to confiding in anyone."

"Least of all a woman," Rose supplied.

"I didn't say that," Bennet complained as he got out a handkerchief and managed to wrap it around his bloody left palm.

"You did not have to."

"Why did you come tonight?" He gasped. "No confidence in me?"

"Just my suspicious nature. If I really was aiding and abetting a spy ring, as Axel claims, then I wanted to see for myself."

"Is that why you and Martin interfered?"

"Yes. Who is Gaspard anyway?"

"An old friend. He saved my life once when I was trapped in Paris. But for him I would not have made it out alive."

"I thought you said you had never been to Paris," Rose chided.

"So far as anyone knows, Bennet Varner has never been there."

Rose chuckled. "If you ever did tell the truth, I think the heavens would split and the world would end."

"I love you, Miss Gwen Rose Wall, and that is the truth." He waited for her to glance at him. "See, no cataclysm. It is quite normal for a man to love a woman."

"Not a woman like me."

Rose slowed the team to a trot when they reached South Audley Street. As they approached Varner House she drove the carriage into the cobbled stable yard as sedately as though they were all just returning from an amusing evening at the theater.

Stilton perked up to say, "Take them straight into the

stable, miss, that's right. You are a wonder, miss. That was something like the adventures we used to have in the old days, eh, Mr. Varner?''

Bennet glared at his groom. "Could you hold your praise down a bit, man? We are not safe yet.''

Martin jumped down to go to the horses' heads.

"Where can we take Gaspard?" Rose asked.

"My quarters are just in here, miss." Stilton limped to the end of the block of stalls to unlock a door. Rose got a shoulder under the Frenchman's arm and Bennet did his best to help him from the other side.

They deposited Gaspard on the small bed, and Stilton limped to the single chair.

"I'll send Martin for a doctor as soon as we cool these horses," Rose said.

"I should be the one giving the orders," Bennet reminded her peevishly as he slid down against the wall to sit on a stool.

"So what are your orders?" Rose demanded, tapping her booted foot impatiently.

After a short struggle with himself Bennet said, "I'll write out the address of a doctor. Martin can go for him once you've cooled the team.''

"Oh, that's so much better than my idea," Rose said as she shut the door behind her.

Stilton chuckled, causing Bennet to send him a warning look. "If anyone ever hears of this night's work, I'll know who to blame.''

"If those fingers of yours are broken, as I expect, everyone in London will know about tonight. What a game lass. If you don't marry that one, I don't know what you may be waiting for.''

Less than ten minutes later Martin came for the address, painfully scrawled with Bennet's left hand and the broken stub of a pencil. Rose let herself in with a pail of water.

"What are the damages, gentlemen?" she asked as she turned Gaspard enough to observe that he was breathing.

"The Frenchie looks drugged to me," Stilton volunteered. "I've got nobbut a sprain. I've had worse. See to Mr. Varner's hands."

Rose put the pail on the wooden floor where Bennet was slumped and warned him it would hurt as she plunged his right hand into the icy liquid.

"Agggh! I believe you enjoyed that. In fact, I believe you enjoyed this whole imbroglio. A normal woman would be thrown into spasms of shock."

"At least I was doing something useful rather than sitting home worrying."

"Think on, Mr. Varner, what would we ha' done without the lass and lad? We would not have got him away."

"No, I suppose not," Bennet said grudgingly.

"Are you going to have Axel arrested?" Rose asked, as she examined the rope burn on his left palm and plunged that, too, into the pail of water, causing Bennet to hiss between his teeth.

"I'd rather deal with him myself," Bennet said when he was able to talk again.

"More to the point, I suppose, will Axel be able to have you arrested?"

"No, not with my connections at the Foreign Office, but he could destroy my effectiveness if anyone believes the nonsense he talks."

"So, you are a spy?" Rose stood.

Stilton guffawed. "Not one of the best, miss."

Rose stared angrily at Bennet. "Well, I think you might have told me that in the first place." She knelt beside him again to examine the burn mark on his right sleeve, which had gone clear to the skin.

"Oh, yes, that's always how I introduce myself to

young ladies. How do you do. By the way, I perform secret services for the government.''

Rose burst out laughing. "Finally, Bennet, I believe you.''

When Martin escorted the doctor into the room, Rose found employment rubbing down the team again and checking their legs for bruises. The great creatures ate up the praises she heaped on them and would gladly have made another treacherous run through the city for her. The doctor mumbled endless instructions, and Rose was really quite chilled by the time he took his departure and she was able to sneak back into Stilton's room and warm herself at the small stove.

"He's taped me ankle and given the Frenchie somethin' for his head but there's naught he can do for Mr. Varner beyond a bit of salve," Stilton said. "I'm goin' to sleep in the lads' loft up the stairs. That will keep them from intrudin' here when they get back in the morning.''

If anything, Bennet was looking more bedraggled than before the doctor had arrived. Rose bent to scrutinize his eye while Martin helped Stilton up. Bennet jerked his head as she touched a tender spot on his brow. Ruthlessly she grasped his jaw and held the candle up to assess the damage. "Even if you wear gloves," she said kindly, "there's no way we can hide that eye.''

"And Axel will boast of the thrashing he gave me,'' Bennet said morosely.

Martin returned a few minutes later carrying a narrow mattress and an armful of blankets. Bennet watched with disfavor as the boy made up a bed over a mound of fresh hay. Martin put a bottle between Bennet's hands and removed the cork. By clasping it between the heels of his bandaged hands Bennet was able to get a portion of the fiery contents down his throat.

"I may as well go to the house," Bennet said, "if Martin can take you home, then return to keep an eye on Gaspard.''

"What will your valet say to all of this? Can he be trusted?''

"I don't have a personal valet.''

Rose shook her head. "Now that I think of it, he would be a hindrance to your activities. But how will you undress yourself? Those fingers are already swollen beyond movement.''

Bennet raised the bottle for another drink.

Martin stared at Bennet's obviously throbbing fingers and brought Rose a slip of paper. "The doctor recommended an application of leeches. See, he even gave me the direction of an apothecary I could rouse in the middle of the night.''

"Why didn't I think of that?'' Rose asked. "They prevent bruising. Of course they would work in this case.''

"I don't want to hear any more talk of leeches.'' Bennet's speech was already beginning to slur.

"Bennet Varner, you are the outside of enough. You engineer a foolishly daring rescue, risk falling off a building, not to mention decapitation, and you cavil at the mention of a few leeches.''

Bennet laughed hoarsely and Rose decided he was one of those men who got silly when he drank, rather than dangerous.

"Put that way, by all means, bring on the leeches. It will be on your head, Gwen Rose Wall, if they gnaw my fingers off.''

"They are not going to chew your fingers off. They have no teeth.'' Rose pulled some coins from her pocket. "Here's money. Go for them, Martin, before he changes his mind.''

"I suppose after all the human bloodsuckers I've dealt with, this should not turn my stomach in the slightest.''

"I should not be ranting at you, in your condition."
Rose stepped close and hugged him to her, his head resting against her stomach. It was a very wifely caress and Bennet was in no condition to spurn it. "You are in pain, no matter how well you may disguise it."

"I did not think I had disguised it at all," he said tiredly.

"I do think you might feel better if you lie down." Rose tried to help him, but he drew back from her and slowly got to his feet. He walked the few steps to the mattress with more dignity than she thought possible and stretched out on it with a groan.

"I'm going to lay a cold compress on your eye until Martin gets back."

"You should not be attending to me."

"I will leave Martin with you for the night. By morning you should be able to move your fingers."

"What a brave lad," Bennet said sleepily.

Rose drew a blanket over Bennet, then piled another on top of that. With the heat from two dozen horses, the stable block stayed much warmer than the outside air, but Bennet might not be used to sleeping rough, or was he? "I have always found Martin so," Rose answered.

"Not to mention your role in the whole affair."

"That indeed, is best not mentioned. As soon as we have you comfortably settled I shall slip back home."

"I hardly think I would describe having leeches hanging off one as comfortable."

"You will see some immediate relief, I promise you. They will drain the excess blood and relieve the pressure in your fingers. Also they will prevent much of the bruising by slowing the stagnation of blood and keeping the circulation going. I believe the application of a leech by your eye would stop it from blackening so much."

"On my eye? The creature would suck it out."

"It will not suck your eye out," Rose said, like a mother reassuring a frightened child. "You are such an alarmist. Many is the time Mama used them—well, never mind. Leeches are perfectly safe. Had they only better features themselves…"

"Such as faces, you mean?"

"Yes, they might be quite likable creatures. We used to keep a dozen in a brandy decanter in the back parlor and feed them on raw liver."

Bennet shuddered under the pile of blankets and turned his face to the wall. Rose added coal to the banked fire in the small stove and checked Gaspard's breathing, which was strong and regular. She touched her hand to Bennet's cheek, but he was asleep or feigning sleep. So Rose pulled the creaky chair up to the stove and sat to wait for Martin with relief flowing through her as the heat warmed her. To her amazement they were all alive, and except for some bruises and rope burns, not even hurt much. There would be talk, of course, but she found that if she ever cared what people said of her, she cared less and less now. This was what was important—survival and doing the right thing, the courageous thing, no matter what it cost.

Martin returned in good time with what Rose proclaimed to be a capital batch of leeches, but Bennet insisted Martin escort Rose home before it got any later. Rose suspected he either did not wish her to see him look ridiculous, or did not want her to see him shudder again. Once safely in her chamber she lay awake for those few hours left of the night, wondering what the morrow would bring. To expect Axel not to talk of the events of the evening would be like expecting the tide to cease. How Bennet meant to counter that gossip she did not know, but if he could appear fairly normal, when Axel would have told everyone he had a broken hand, that would discredit the soldier's tales of French spies.

And Bennet's qualms over having Axel arrested for abduction, Rose thought, derived from pride on Bennet's part, not because he was doing anything underhanded. He wanted to beat Axel himself, not with the help of the magistrates or anyone else. Rose wondered just how much Bennet minded her own interference in the night's adventure. She rather thought that Stilton was right, that she and Martin had been indispensable to the success of the rescue. So this time her impulse had been the correct one. Never leave anything to chance.

As to how Axel would savage her character after this night's work, she did not even want to think about it. For she had no defense. She had been at his lodgings, had been involved in a brawl in the street, had driven a carriage at a reckless pace through the dark streets of the city. They could have been killed a dozen times over, but they had not been. So what was the point of regret? Whatever anyone said of them now, she had shared something with Bennet she would treasure always. He had trusted her, reluctantly at first, but he had trusted her. Now she must trust him to do what he could to save the shreds of her reputation.

Chapter Eight

*T*he team was fresh and eager to run. Rose snapped the whip in the air to excite them. Where on earth had she gotten a whip? Bennet sat beside her, laughing. The din of pounding hooves increased and Rose glanced over her shoulder. It was Axel after them, of course, twirling his saber over his head as he rode his foam-flecked mount to catch them. Where were Martin, Gaspard and Stilton? To her surprise she was not driving the carriage, but a light sporting curricle, pulled by Bennet's team. Axel could never catch them. She twisted and turned through the streets and circuses of a dark, still London, encountering absolutely no one. The buildings and storefronts flew past on the sides as the cobbles disappeared beneath their wheels. Time and again, Rose feathered a corner, or skillfully evaded a hole on the road. When they reached the mail road to Bristol Rose relaxed her grip, and the team tore along in good earnest, leaving Axel shouting after them in frustration. It was as though they were the only three people in the world and the horses would be able to run on forever.

Rose jerked awake. Of course they were the only three people in the world of her dream. She did not know whether to label it dream or nightmare, for she and Bennet had been laughing victoriously as they had the night before, but Axel had been shouting the most acrimonious threats. Rose pushed the covers off. Yes, they would pay today for last's night victory.

She washed her face, noting her eyes looked clear and bright after no more than an hour's sleep. The excitement was still with her, humming warm and confidently in her breast. There was a conspiracy but she was part of it now. She excitedly donned a vivid green walking dress, raked a comb through her hair and skipped down the stairs.

From the first morning she had awakened at Change House she had taken an early breakfast of tea and toast in the small book room. The staff seemed to look more approvingly on her for this than on Stanley and Alice whom they had to wait on in bed. Therefore, when she invaded the kitchen at the crack of dawn with a request for a hamper to carry to the stable at Varner House, they hopped to aid her without question. "Martin has been sitting up with a sick horse there all night," she lied, without so much as blinking, "and I thought it would be a nice surprise for him and Stilton to have something hot right away."

Cook nodded in complete acceptance if not complete belief as she laced a pot of tea with brandy and began to load a basket with hot rolls and fried ham. "I can have the boot boy carry this basket up for you. You should not be going about alone."

"Nonsense, the hamper is not heavy, and that steaming pot of tea in there will keep me warm. Besides I can see Varner House from here."

In no more than twenty minutes she set off, but did not, to her disappointment, find anyone but Martin and Gaspard in Stilton's room. However, these two were so grateful for the hot mugs of tea she presented to them, laced with cream and sugar besides the brandy, that she felt the trip was not wasted. The wedges of bread and cheese and slices of fried ham were devoured with eagerness. Belatedly Martin thought he should share their bounty with Stilton and carried the remains of the meal to the long loft room over the stalls.

"Mademoiselle, you have my most sincere thanks," Gaspard said in French, reaching to take her hand and carry it to his lips. "Not only for the victuals but for aiding Varner in saving my life. He has told me your drive through the city was most dangerous."

"It was a small matter to me. At the time, truly, I did not know if I was doing my country a favor or a disservice. I am happy that I chose correctly."

"You thought, perhaps, that all Frenchmen had run mad after Bonaparte, but I assure you the royalist faction has never given up the struggle to put a king back on the throne."

"A king who would owe his people a great many favors and be easily managed."

"*Oui*, but why, mademoiselle, did you come to our aid if you did not believe us innocent?"

"An irresistible championing of the underdog. I did not care at that moment what you or Bennet were guilty of. I only knew that I still liked you better than Axel."

"What would he have done to me had I awakened?"

"I do not know, and it is pointless to speculate, but have a care never to fall into his hands again. He is a dangerous man, drunk or sober."

The door was thrust open. "There you are," Bennet said. "I was just coming to take you for a drive. That is, if I can find anyone to help me harness my team. The stable boys will all be still snoring after their night on the town."

"I can do it," Rose said as she stood up and brushed the hay from her dress.

"That you shall not. Bad enough you had to unharness them last night. Gaspard, Walters is finding you some safe accommodations."

"Why can he not stay at Change House?" Rose demanded.

"I can think of no place he would be more likely to encounter Foy unless it be Varner House."

"Oh, I had forgotten. But Gaspard should not be alone for a while."

"I will assign a burly seaman to watch over you until you're recovered. Now that I think of it, the *Celestine* is probably the safest place for you. Tell Walters to take you there."

"Oui, mon ami."

As Rose watched Martin and Bennet's groggy tiger harness the bays, she thought that Gaspard and Bennet had worked together a long time. Probably Bennet had been intriguing against Napoleon ever since the emperor had come to power. Someday she would make him tell her all about it. Bennet was a generous man with everything but the truth. Perhaps that was why he was so good at what he did.

The heavy carriage had been pushed out of the way by Martin and the tiger. Now they led the team out and hooked them to the light curricle.

"We won't need you today, Basset. We do not mean to stop anywhere," Bennet said as he helped Rose to the high seat. Then he got in and took the reins himself.

"Your fingers, you can move them!" Rose cried with delight as she watched him feather the corner out of the stable yard.

"I confess I am amazed, as well."

"Give me the reins and take off your gloves." Rose

steadied the team and set them straight up South Audley Street as she gazed at his right hand. "It is red and sore surely, but it looks only as though it had been chafed by the cold. So long as no one sees the burn mark in the palm of your left hand no one will know. Your eye, too, amazes me. Had I not seen it last night it would never occur to me someone had punched you."

"What say we drive toward Richmond Park today? You can drive, Rose."

"So, you trust me now?" she goaded.

"I thought I should return the favor."

Rose smiled. "Gaspard seems to be recovering nicely, but I did not get to see Stilton. How is he?"

"He is hungover, as they both are—Gaspard from whatever they drugged him with and Stilton from whatever he drugged himself with after he left us."

"They will make good companions for each other today," she said confidently. "Am I headed in the right direction?"

"Make a right at the end of the street. How comes it that you drive like a veritable fiend from hell?"

"It's quite simple. At Wall the young horses not sold as hunters by the age of five are broken to harness and sold as carriage horses. Someone has to train them. I can drive a team of four," she said proudly.

"I don't doubt it. Besides being a natural healer, what other talents do you number among your accomplishments?" He pulled the lap robe a little tighter about her.

"That's about it, except for…my facility with languages." She shot him a sidelong look that drew a chuckle from him.

"I was afraid of that from the beginning. Tell me, if you suspected I was involved in something nefarious from the night I found you in my library, why did you not tell someone?"

"I suppose because I am used to keeping things to myself. If someone were shredding my character, I would say nothing, pretend they had not been talking about me and feign ignorance. It was always my only defense. You cannot walk up to someone and say, 'No, I didn't do it,' when you do not even know the accusation or the accusers."

Bennet stared at her with an awed mixture of compassion and admiration. The more she knew him, the less she saw of that foolish smile and she almost missed it. But this was a serious business. "I tried to convince myself there could be an innocent explanation for Gaspard," Rose continued, "the talk of Napoleon's escape, the trunk with the false bottom—and there was. I simply did not peg you for a spy."

A mail coach rumbled past them then, but Rose held the team steady and praised the horses when they did not shy.

Bennet did smile then, and it was genuine this time, a smile she thought very few people got to see. "You could have gone to the authorities." He flexed his hands, shook his head in disbelief, then put his gloves back on.

"And you with a ringer in the Foreign Office? I would have looked a proper fool."

"Whatever your reason, I'm glad you did not tell on me."

"My discretion buys you nothing. Axel will tell everyone what happened last night, and your effectiveness will be at an end. But I suppose that does not matter anymore. Was there ever a point at which Napoleon could have been stopped?"

"Only if he had been assassinated on Elba," Bennet said gravely.

His reply had been so swift and sure that Rose realized

it had been considered by someone as a permanent solution to the problem. "But you would not permit it."

"It was Gaspard's idea, and he would willingly have given his life to carry out the plan, but…"

"It seems not quite gentlemanly."

"I had hoped such extreme measures would be unnecessary. Now I wish I had pulled the trigger myself. I do not know how many will die, compared to the thousands of lives Bonaparte has already destroyed. But if even one more man dies, then we should have stopped him at any price."

"Do not bludgeon yourself with that thought. If anyone dies it will not be your fault. It will be Bonaparte's."

"Even if it is your brother?"

Rose caught her lip between her teeth. "I will never blame you. You know that."

"Well, we must see what we can do now to aid the war effort, and I have some ideas along those lines that should keep Stanley out of the thick of it."

They drove through the gates of the park just then, so Rose could not spare more than a glance to see if Bennet was serious.

"Is it true what Mother told me, that you neither play nor sing?" Bennet asked.

"Not a note, though I appreciate good music when I hear it. I never had the time or patience to study."

Bennet pointed out a tree-lined drive and Rose took the team down it.

"Good, there is no danger in taking you to Lady Catherine's musical this afternoon."

"Afraid I was going to torture you with a pianoforte?"

"No, I was afraid Lady Catherine would prevail on you to entertain without preparation."

"Why would she do that? She doesn't even like me."

"Simply to embarrass you."

Rose stared at him. "Don't you know any kind people besides Leighton, Gaspard and your servants?"

"Of course I do, but they are mostly in business or politics. You will meet them at my dinner tomorrow night."

Rose glanced at the so confident Bennet and thought she preferred him a little more desperate. "Thank you for such a gracious invitation. Won't that be a sore trial to your mother and sister?"

"Mother will go to bed directly after the meal with a headache. Harriet would normally arrange to be elsewhere, but if I invite Axel I may persuade her to play hostess."

"Invite Axel to dine? I still do not see why you don't just have him arrested."

"It's not just myself I am thinking of. Gaspard is useful as an agent only so long as his identity remains secret. A trial would require him to take the stand as a witness."

The answer seemed rehearsed to Rose. "Is that your only reason?"

Bennet stared ahead for a moment. "I should prefer to best Axel myself rather than calling for help," he said finally.

"In some ways, Bennet, you are as naive as Stanley."

He grinned at her. "Not the same ways, I hope."

"This is some sort of duel with Axel, a feud of long standing."

"Yes, the stakes used to be Harriet. Now I have come to think they involve you, no matter how much I have tried to allay Axel's suspicions about us."

"Is that supposed to please me, to be fought over like a bone between two dogs?"

"A rather pretty piece of blood and bone," Bennet said, glancing at the sleek backs of the bays. "Being a horse fancier, that should not offend you."

"You are fortunate I need both hands for driving. How

do you mean to keep last night a secret? Axel will certainly speak of it. I would not be surprised if half the town knew of it by now. You must show Axel up publicly for the villain he is, or even your reputation may be ruined."

"That's what I plan to do today. Axel will be at this musical soiree. He dotes on Cassie just to make Harriet jealous."

"And Lady Catherine dotes on him. That is where the real attraction lies."

"Oh?" Bennet said, staring at her, and then shrugging. "Either way he had better stop showing such marked attention to other women, if he wants to marry my sister."

"My dear Bennet, Axel is the sort of man who would not see his marriage to Harriet as an impediment to his relationship with Cassie, Lady Catherine or even me."

"I see, or all three of you together," Bennet concluded angrily. "Has he made such an offer to you?"

"Not yet. But if you think marriage to Harriet will solve the problem of Axel you are wrong. And that is the way in which you are naive. One woman will never be enough for a soldier like him."

"Not all soldiers are like that, always looking for conquests, taking what they fancy."

"The few I have known are, but I do not think it has anything to do with being a soldier. Axel cannot see another man have a woman without wanting her for himself."

"Still, it mystifies me why he has been trying to prove a crime against me. If I am soon to be his brother-in-law, one would think he would be trying to make peace."

"But you are not going to be his brother-in-law. Harriet has turned him down, at least for now."

One of the bays tugged at the bit, begging for a canter, but unlike in her dream, Rose wanted to keep a tight rein on everything today.

"Good for her. I did not think she had so much sense. Still, I see no advantage for him in disgracing me—not if he still entertains hopes of courting Harriet."

"He feels you still hold too much influence over her. If you were knocked from your pedestal, or even off a roof," Rose suggested, "would Harriet turn to Axel for support?"

Bennet's brows wrinkled in concentration. "She might. So that was his plan? How do you know his mind so well?"

"Necessity. I know a lot about leeches, too, but not by choice."

"There is more at stake here than my private quarrel with him. Let us hope he did not recognize you."

Rose shrugged and focused on the bobbing heads of the horses, for Axel most assuredly knew she had been there last night and had certainly leaped to the conclusion that she was a decoy sent by Bennet. What revenge Axel would wreak she could well imagine. A day from now she would be the talk of the town, her character in shreds, and even Bennet might not wish to associate with her. She was amazed that this thought did not frighten her more. From the beginning of this mad jaunt to London she seemed predestined to embarrass her family. It would be an interesting test of Bennet's character to see how he received the news that she really was infamous.

If he failed this test, if he snubbed her, or showed embarrassment in her presence she would retreat to Bristol until she could set up a horse farm. Eventually Martin and Cynthie would find mates and she would have a family of sorts. But she desperately wanted Bennet to prove to be as courageous as she suspected he was.

When they returned to Change House more than two hours later, Bennet drove gaily off, promising to return to escort Rose to the musical in good time. Rose went to

examine her wardrobe. This latest flurry of invitations
would use up the last of the new dresses she had bought.
The violet cambric would do well for this afternoon and
the bronze silk for Bennet's dinner, if she was not disgraced by then. She smiled at the matter-of-fact way she
now weighed the contingencies of her apparel.

"Rose," Alice said from the doorway. "Did we bring
any sheet music with us?"

"I am quite sure we did not." Rose turned from her
scrutiny of the deep purple ribbons, which reminded her
of the lilacs at Wall. "Have we a piano I don't know
about?"

"No, Lady Catherine has asked me to play something
at her musical this afternoon and the only thing I know
well enough by heart is my favorite adagio."

"Then play that."

"I'm bored with that," Alice complained.

"I thought you had mastered that Beethoven sonata. I
know. Send one of the servants into the city to get the
music. They are Bennet's people, which means they are
resourceful enough to know where to find it."

"I wish you had been invited. I would not feel so nervous then."

"Oh, I am going with Bennet." At the silence this pro-
voked Rose looked at Alice, who was blushing. "How
did you know I had not been invited?"

"Cassie and Harriet told me while we were shopping
today. It's just that they have only enough room for their
particular friends."

"I'm sure Bennet would gladly surrender his seat to
me. His mother is compelling him to attend, though he
would rather not."

"I shall be going with Mr. Dowd."

"Dowd? Oh, I had forgotten Stanley went to that race
meet."

"The last word I heard from him is that he will not be back until Sunday night."

"Do you think he would be content not to go to Europe?" Rose asked, thinking to prepare Alice for the news about Napoleon that would probably be public knowledge soon.

"Oh, I hope so, for I have made such friends in London. I should dislike being torn away now just to suffer the inconveniences of travel."

Rose nodded. Alice might change her mind about London after the scandal broke.

The Wall women were ready and had their pelisses tossed over a chair by the front window a good hour before the recital was to begin. Rose sat writing her mother another letter full of excuses for their delayed departure, including now, the rumor printed in the paper of Napoleon's escape. Perhaps the next letter would have to confess her disgrace. It was provoking of Bennet to be so late, but at least the letter was finished. Alice's agitated pacing did nothing to soothe Rose's nerves.

"Do not be distressed over not having a chance to practice," Rose said soothingly. "You have your music and will breeze through the piece."

"It's not that. Mr. Dowd is very late."

"Forget Dowd. Here is Bennet coming up the steps now. Walk up with us. To be sure, Dowd has been delayed someplace where they need his opinions."

Since Alice walked on Bennet's other side, Rose could not express her concern about his tardiness. She thought they should have tried to arrive early to gain a social foothold, so to speak, before Axel appeared to embarrass them. But then, Axel was always horribly late.

Lady Catherine's residence was only two doors away from Varner House. It was the typical town house with two windows to the left of the door, and scarcely more than a room wide throughout. The footman who opened the door was wearing black livery with scarlet facings, the same as the groom who had accompanied Axel. The man directed them up the stairs to the first floor. The music salon was decorated in black, white and gold, with fake pilasters and large urns of flowers everywhere. Rose was startled to see the back of Axel's scarlet uniform and pondered whether the color was part of Cassie's attraction to him. He did not clash with her complexion.

Cassie, in her cream and scarlet day dress, stared at Bennet savagely, as did Harriet and Lady Catherine. Edith Varner sat holding a vinaigrette to her nose.

"Here is Varner now," Lady Catherine said in a sharp voice, "and he does not look as though he has been falling off a roof."

"You are looking as lovely as always," Bennet said as he grasped the lady's hand and kissed it, showing off the dexterity of his fingers.

Axel turned deliberately and Rose gasped. "Axel, what happened to your face? You look as though you have been thrown from your horse."

"You know very well what happened. I was fighting Bennet Varner last night."

"Indeed?" Bennet said, scrutinizing Axel's bruised cheekbone and split lip. "I have no recollection of it."

There was a satisfying titter from the people talking in small clusters around the room, and sending speculative glances toward Bennet.

"Then you must have a very bad memory or a twin brother," Axel replied.

"Axel," Rose whispered loudly. "Have you been drinking again?"

Axel gaped at her. "You know what happened. You were there."

"Where?" Rose demanded.

"At my lodgings last night."

"I was at the theater with Mr. Leighton," Rose said as though she were offended and had every right to be. "And Varner was with us."

Hearing his name, Leighton wandered over to lend his support. "Marvelous play. I knew Dowd would not like it. But we all enjoyed it immensely."

"No one gives a damn about the play!" Axel almost yelled.

"Really, Axel," Bennet said. "Wine or brandy are no great matter, but that blue ruin you drink is like to fog your mind."

By now half the people in the room were looking at Axel as though he were insane, but he had not the sense to accept defeat graciously. "I crushed your hand with my boot. I've told everyone so."

"I assure you my hand is perfectly all right. They both are." Bennet waggled his fingers to demonstrate. "Perhaps you should sit down."

"I don't know how you managed this recovery, but it was you I fought last night."

"Perhaps someone who looked like me," Bennet said, as though he were humoring a lunatic.

"I very nearly killed you, Bennet Varner," Axel growled. "Now I wish I had."

"But Axel, that is illegal, like so many other things."

"I knew it was a sham," Harriet said. "Bennet is too much a milk toast to engage in anything shady or even a fistfight."

"I tell you it was your brother," Axel growled.

"Well, look at him. His eye, his hands are fine. I think perhaps you did fall off your horse, Axel, and hit your head." With that condemnation Harriet flounced away and took up a seat at the pianoforte, her stiff white gown settling jaggedly over her limbs. The dress complemented the room better than it did her.

Lady Catherine gripped Axel's arm so tightly that even the seasoned soldier winced. "Sit down, Axel. It is time to begin."

Harriet played first, a spirited piece, with all of Cassie's precision, but much more passion.

"She is very good," whispered Rose to Bennet when the girl had finished.

"Harriet always plays best when she's angry," Bennet said. "And Axel seems to have set her back up."

"A righteous indignation at his accusation toward you," Rose whispered charitably.

"Or disappointment that Axel's tale was all a hum. Did you notice that Dowd was already here when we arrived? He must have been instructed to ditch Alice. I wonder why?"

"What do you mean? Perhaps he just forgot he was to stop for her," Rose said worriedly as she glanced toward Alice, who was sitting between a pouting Cassie and a stone-faced Lady Cat. Alice noticed Dowd in the audience, as well, and sent a puzzled frown in his direction.

"She seems suddenly to have fallen out of favor with the Gravely women," Bennet said. "And she hasn't even played yet."

"Was she ever in their favor?"

"For an observant woman you miss many nuances."

"Hush."

Alice lost herself in the piece as she usually did when playing. It was the one thing she did really well. Rose's only regret was that Stanley was not present to witness her triumph.

The applause from Bennet and everyone else was genuine. "Very prettily done. Let us hope that she does not

completely outshine Cassie, or she will make some enemies indeed.''

"Enemies? For playing well?'' Rose stared at Bennet.

"Her superiority in any way would be enough to turn
them against her. Trust me, I know women.''

"You make me almost glad I never took up music.''

"Ah, but you ride well. And Cassie does not ride at
all. That is enough to cause your downfall.''

"Do be serious, Bennet. I thought Alice's piece went
well too, but why have Lady Catherine and Cassie been
making faces at each other the whole way through it, and
now they are arguing. You would think they would have
chosen the music by now.''

"Ah, this is perfect,'' Bennet whispered gleefully.
"Without knowing it, Alice has copped one of Cassie's
pieces. Cassie can't play that now. She'll have to choose
something else.''

"What are the chances of that?''

"This is wonderful.'' Bennet rubbed his hands together.
"One does not often see the Gravelys get their comeup-
pance.''

"I think you are enjoying their discomfort too much.''

Lady Catherine finally arose. "Perhaps we can prevail
on Miss Wall to play for us.''

"I fear you have been misinformed,'' Rose said clearly.
"I do not play.''

"Every young lady plays the pianoforte.''

"We cannot all be as talented as Harriet or Alice. Now
if you want a fox harried or a stag run to ground, I am
your person, but I have never touched a keyboard in my
life.''

Lady Catherine's hissed "I see'' was lost amidst the
amused laughter of the audience.

Cassie finally embarked on a piece unfamiliar to Rose,
but she was quite sure it should not have had so many

long rests in it. She looked toward Bennet, and he grimaced.

"Are you in pain? If you are not, I wish you would stop wincing."

"I did not."

"Yes, you did," she whispered. "I definitely saw you."

"Well, my ears are killing me. Let us go."

"We cannot," she said desperately. "You do not need to be so blatant about it. Her playing is not that bad."

"Not if you are tone deaf," he said in an under voice.

Dowd swiveled in his chair and stared them down.

"Quiet," Rose whispered to Bennet. "You are disturbing everyone."

Chairs creaked resignedly as the two dozen guests arranged themselves for Cassie's final onslaught, rehearsing perhaps in their minds, Rose thought, suitable comments to murmur about the piece over the refreshments. *How rare for a player to be so overcome with emotion by a piece.* Yes, that would do. Bennet would have to think of his own. The music came to a merciful end and a unanimous sigh of relief went up. Women adjusted their silk skirts and men tugged at their cravats, regretting the overheated room.

The patter of genuine applause that the music was at last put to rest was cut short by Lady Catherine handing Cassie, who was nearly in tears, another piece of music. Bennet groaned and Rose kicked him in the ankle so skillfully only he noticed. The eagle-eyed Lady Catherine searched the audience for the author of this sound, but not even the redoubtable Bennet would own to it. He stared straight ahead through the entire piece. It was obvious this music had been better practiced, but Cassie was in no state to render justice to any work now. Rose thought Bennet's intent gaze was fixed on the flower arrangement on the pedestal column next to the pianoforte, but he accidentally caught the attention of Cassie, who flushed and lost her place again. Bennet glanced apologetically at Rose and surprised a smile upon her lips.

As soon as the piece was over, a smattering of applause was delivered, and the press of people had moved into the refreshment salon. There, Dowd's high praises for Cassie's performance drummed into the heads of the others whose wine they would be consuming. Meanwhile Bennet dragged Rose toward the door.

"God, did we hear the same music as Dowd?" Bennet asked.

"We have to wait for Alice," Rose said, "for it does not look as though she is staying."

Alice, looking downcast, was making her way to the door against the tide flowing into the adjacent room. "Did you hear what Dowd said? That I would improve with practice. I thought my playing much superior to Cassie's, though Harriet's was quite good."

Leighton came up to take Alice's hand. "Yours was the very best and so I shall tell everyone, but not here. I am desperately in need of a drink."

Rose smiled at Leighton's kindness as he took Alice's arm.

They retrieved their wraps from the anteroom at the bottom of the stairs. Bennet helped Rose with her pelisse and Leighton performed this service for Alice.

"Shall we repair to Varner House and see what is in the cellar?" Bennet suggested.

As Leighton and Alice walked ahead of them, Leighton still assuring the girl of the superiority of her performance, Rose turned to Bennet. "There is one thing I do not understand about Dowd."

"Only one thing?"

"You say he is wealthy. I accept that he tears people

down for spite. But such a man does not have true friends. He has no reason to praise Cassie or Harriet.''

"I have often noticed a similarity in taste between Dowd and Lady Cat. She uses him to promote anyone she means to show a preference for. She certainly used him to bring Harriet into fashion."

"That's no reason. There must be more to it."

"Yes, I have often wondered about it. To be sure Lady Cat has something on Dowd, but what I cannot venture to guess."

"Where is Cassie?" Axel demanded of his hostess after the last of the guests had left the refreshment salon.

"Upstairs, crying her eyes out. You made a right mess of things today," Lady Catherine accused, ignoring the servants who were beginning to clear away the leftovers.

"You did not exactly help the day along, insisting the girl play when she did not wish to."

"Why did you invent that stupid story about Varner? You might have guessed he could prove you wrong. I don't want to hear your excuses. And Bennet Varner is not to be harmed, not so much as damaged, do you understand?"

"You have no right to interfere between me and Varner," Axel said, tossing another glass of champagne down his throat.

"I want him as a husband for Cassie. If she does not marry this year her looks will be completely gone and I will wash my hands of her."

"Then she should have caught Varner when she had her looks."

"Edith Varner told me he was a sure thing, a dutiful boy who always obeyed his mother. Now he is going about with the Wall strumpet on his arm. How do you think that makes Cassie feel?"

"Not as bad as your remarks," Axel vowed.

"I was promised Varner for my daughter and I will have him and his fortune. Why do you think I bothered with Edith and Harriet? My bringing them into society was my part of the bargain." She shook her finger in Axel's face. "Now Varner had better marry Cassie or I will destroy them just as surely as I made them."

"You have a pretty high opinion of your powers." Axel leaned against a table and held a bottle of wine up to the light to see if it was worth finishing.

"All it takes is a word in the right ear. I could destroy you if I wished." Lady Catherine's tiny shoes punched at the oak floor as she paced back and forth.

Axel laughed out loud. "I have no reputation, or only what people expect of a hardened soldier."

"But you have creditors precariously kept at bay until they see if you will manage to attach Harriet Varner. If I let them know you haven't a prayer they'll hound you the whole way to your ruined estate in Yorkshire."

Axel stared at her. "You would, wouldn't you, just for spite?"

"We are agreed then. You will help me attach Cassie to Varner and I will persuade Harriet to accept you. I have influence with her."

Axel carefully poured the wine into his glass and sniffed it. "And if your influence won't work, I fancy you are not above threatening her."

"My word, do I detect a spark of caring? Of chivalry, perhaps?"

"Nothing so noble." Axel tossed off the wine and wiped the back of his hand across his mouth. "I need Harriet and I don't mind her. She won't hold my interest forever, not even for long, for she's a cold sort of girl unless she's attacking a pianoforte. I hardly think she will be demanding. She simply wants her independence."

"How could God have been so foolish as to make men so necessary?" Lady Catherine asked with her hands on her hips.

"God is a man," Axel said with a silly grin.

"Yes, that explains it, I suppose."

"You once found me pretty necessary." He reached a drunken arm toward her and she evaded the grope.

"That was when you were a young man, a virgin almost—now I find you merely dangerous. Do you know Robin Coates has the pox?"

Axel's head jerked up as though she had slapped him. "I've heard."

"From you?"

"Don't be absurd. I have always been extremely careful of the company I keep. In Spain and Portugal I took only virgins to my bed." He attempted to straighten his stock.

"Then you are completely safe."

"Unless one of them slits your throat with a knife."

Axel flushed with anger. "I never had to force a woman, except…"

"Except who, that Wall strumpet? You're as close as thieves with her."

"Rose? Now she is the type who would slit your throat. She has threatened my life as often as she has said goodmorning to me."

"Another cold one?"

Axel regarded Catherine with smoldering eyes. "Yes, now she is."

"Did you ruin her?" The woman paced toward him again. "For if you did I see a way we can use that against Varner."

"No, I did not, though not for lack of trying." Axel glanced at the table but the wine was all gone.

"Well, we have only to say you did and people will believe it."

"You really have no conscience!" He grasped her by the arms. "Here I am a murderer of innocents, despoiler of maidens, and I have more feeling in my little finger than you have in your whole icy body."

"You know nothing of it."

He attempted to pull her closer but she went rigid in his arms. "I remember that it was icy," he hissed. "For all your seductive looks, all your suggestive love talk, you were as cold as stone every time I had you."

Lady Catherine glanced about her and discovered the room to be empty of servants. "That was your fault. You did not set me on fire."

"I think a witch's pyre is the only thing that would set your cold heart on fire."

Axel released her and strode from the room, his bruised hand resting on the hilt of his saber. As he walked to his lodgings he went over the previous night in his mind again. He had not been dreaming or drunk, not that drunk, anyway. And he had the evidence of the fight on his face. How had Bennet Varner managed to heal himself overnight? Perhaps that witch Rosie had worked a spell on Bennet. She had a way of enchanting men. Axel remembered their courtship with perfect clarity, how happy he had felt, how...virtuous.

One drunken night had ended all that. He remembered the maid, Cynthie, in the barn. Martin was there as well. And now he remembered Rose had hit him. She had screamed "*Axel, no!*" in that same anguished voice she used last night. Then she had knocked him out. What had happened then? He would remember.

He had awakened two days later to a thumping headache and the news that Rose's father was dead and their engagement was off. When he had been well enough to leave his bed he had attempted a reconciliation, and Rose had vehemently returned his ring, with the resulting scar.

He stroked his cheek again. That pain had stayed with him longer than the hurt from any other wound. And that was where his life had started its downward spiral. Superstitiously he felt that he somehow must go back and put that right before fortune would smile upon him again.

Chapter Nine

Rose spent the evening at the opera with Bennet and Leighton. She had the feeling Leighton was there as an alternate in case Bennet was called away again, but no such thing happened. Boney's escape was common knowledge now and was causing no more of a stir than the latest fashion in hats among the women. Young men tended to stand about in groups and discuss the possibility of another conflict with what Rose thought was joyful excitement.

That was another thing she would never understand about men, how they could look forward to war, especially where their own lives might be at stake. Were they too stupid to realize they might be killed? Or had nature always intended that spare men would be disposed of in such a wasteful fashion? That would be fine if they were men like Axel, who were no good to anyone, but perversely, men of courage and honor were the ones who did not return. She sighed with the knowledge that women were so powerless to keep men from the folly of their baser instincts. Even Bennet, an intelligent man, would rather battle Axel on his own than take the sensible path and have him incarcerated.

These ruminations would not have distracted her from her enjoyment of the performance or from the banter of Bennet and Leighton, except that there was something subtle going on among the audience. People were staring at her who had never given her a second glance before. She was being pointed out and mumbled over. So it was starting, just at it had in Bristol. No doubt Axel had broken his end of the bargain and his malicious tongue had been at work again. That neither Bennet nor Leighton thought it strange was a measure of their complacency. But she, who had never felt secure in society at the best of times, imagined snubs perhaps where there were none and gossip where none—no, there was no mistaking the matter. They were talking about her and she would lay odds they were not saying anything good.

She turned from her scrutiny of the crowd to laugh artificially at Leighton's comments, to smile sweetly at Bennet's rejoinders. She had said she was no good at lying, but perhaps she was. She could walk into a room and have everyone she approached snub her and she could manage not to blush. It was not pleasant but she could do it. In fact, she cared little what people thought of her; she simply hated a scene. But she had come to care in this case what one man thought of her.

"The world is not run by thought but by opinion," Leighton said.

"And not always well-founded opinion," Bennet agreed.

Rose looked across at the Gravely box, where Magnus Dowd was talking his head off. "When people are too lazy to think for themselves, a Magnus Dowd will come along to relieve them of the bother," Rose said.

"Actually we had moved on to Parliament, but the same thing applies in society," Leighton said, following her glance. "Men and women such as Dowd strive to conceal their own deficiencies by attributing them to others.''

"Next time I see Mr. Dowd and argue with him I think I will challenge him to write a play himself, if he is such an expert.''

Bennet chuckled. "You always argue with Dowd, Rose. He'll find a good excuse to slither out of it. I'm sure you would not be the first to challenge him.''

"Has he no employment but to cause trouble?'' Rose asked as she watched the people mixing in the boxes opposite. She wondered if Bennet thought it singular that no one came to visit their box.

"He has more money than is good for him,'' Bennet said. "Inherited from some great-uncle whom he worried to death. Dowd dabbles in trade, but knows almost nothing about it.''

Leighton rested his chin on his fist. "Mr. Dowd has set out to be a maker of fashion. It was the only cover he could think of for being so ineptly rude.''

Rose laughed but wondered if Dowd had a hand in her personal downfall, adding his mite to the flame of gossip lit by Axel. It really didn't matter. She could see no benefit to not arguing with Dowd.

After the performance the men delivered her to Change House and then went on their way to see if the news about Boney's escape had reached the gaming houses yet.

In spite of the lateness of the hour Rose began packing her books and letters. She had accumulated an amazing number in less than a fortnight. They could take the stagecoach from Oxford Street and be home in less than two days. She had promised to carry Cynthie away from Axel and that took precedence over her own inclination. Though she had to admit to an impulse to flee London. She could leave Bennet a note excusing herself on the basis of her mother's needs. But she had never done anything so cowardly in her life.

She did not mind the agony of suspense she would have to go through the next few days, if only Bennet would not cast her off utterly. If he would stand her friend it was worth staying firm. It was also a challenge, to see how long she could carry off her pose of not knowing she was the object of so much scandal. It would be useful to know what was being said of her, but hurtful as well. Whatever it was she had no means of defending herself, so perhaps it was just as well not to know.

The faces were all around her, leering at her. Perhaps it was a masquerade and they were all wearing exceedingly ugly masks. But they were not masks, just faces distorted by viciousness. Some were from Bristol, some from London. Lady Catherine with her strident tones led the condemnation, talking about Rose as though she were not in the room. Cassie was smug, Harriet angry and Edith Varner's face withered with disgust. Even Alice and Stanley were shocked and believed the awful stories. Leighton was bereft, and Bennet, Bennet looked as cold as stone. She was tensely waiting for some reaction from him when Martin ran into the room with a pistol and fired.

The bang sat her up in bed, wondering what had happened and how her sleeping mind could work a sound that it had not even heard yet into a dream in progress. She heard a broom sweeping fragments of crockery and assumed a teapot had met its end on the back stairs. She threw off the covers, washed herself and was dressing in her green riding habit when Cynthie came into the room.

"Have the rest of my trunks brought up and begin to pack some of these things that I have already worn several times."

"Are we going to go on the ship?" Cynthie asked in trepidation.

"No, that is out of the question now. I was thinking of going back to Wall as soon as Stanley gets home Sunday. I'll talk to him about it then. Is Martin up?"

"He's waiting for you, miss."

"Ask him to saddle Bright Valor for me today and bring the horses down directly."

"It's very early, miss," Martin said a short time later in that flat way that was just an observation of some new behavior of hers.

Rose mounted as usual without his assistance. "I'm not hungry for breakfast yet. I thought we would ride early, just the two of us."

"But why are you avoiding Mr. Varner?" Martin persisted as they walked the restless animals toward the park.

Rose looked away from his sharp brown eyes. "I'm not, I simply need to think. I plan to leave for Wall on Monday if Stanley persists in staying in London."

"Has something happened, miss?"

"What could possibly have happened?" Rose asked lightly. She thought she had better practice a little more discretion with her emotions if Martin could detect that she was bothered. But he was sensitive to her moods. Someone like Harriet would never be able to tell that she was hurting. At least Rose hoped not.

As on most days that Bennet did not ride with her it seemed sadly flat in spite of the willows starting to bud into leaf. She would be glad to get away from London, but would miss Bennet's gay bantering. A rider did appear at a distance, but his coat was scarlet, not black. Rose stared at him for only a moment before she subtly changed their path so as to avoid the soldier. It was Axel; it had to be. He drew out his saber and saluted her. Rose gave no sign that she saw him. He could have been stalking her and Bennet on any of their rides and she would never have noticed him. Certainly it had never occurred to Bennet to worry about his nemesis here, where they had spent so many joyous hours. She ran over in her mind all they had done: much talking, besides riding. They had embraced once, but she did not think she had been so lost to reason as to have kissed Bennet Varner here.

Martin stiffened in the saddle.

"Don't panic," Rose warned. "Keep the horses to a walk."

"Is it him?"

"I'm pretty sure it is Axel, but I do not think he will do anything so long as we do not run from him."

"Like a vicious dog?" Martin asked.

"Something like that. I feel sure that galloping would provoke him to follow and try to catch us."

"I wish Mr. Varner were here."

"I do not."

Martin turned his head to stare at her. "But after all that has happened…I mean, I thought that you and he…"

"Nothing has changed between us that I know of, but I will never presume too much. They were gossiping about me at the opera last night, and if that bothers Bennet, then I will not force my company on him."

"He is not like that, miss, I feel sure."

"I hope you are right about him, Martin. You will have to excuse me today. A very old wound is hurting and there is nothing I can do about it."

"None of the things that happened five years ago was your fault. And you could not have prevented any of the disasters that have befallen us since we came to London."

"Except by not being here. We remove to Wall on Monday unless my brother feels he has something to say in that matter. If Bennet cares he will say so before then."

"Yes, miss, but he is powerful busy just now. Left the house at the crack of dawn by what Stilton says."

"Yes, of course you are right. He has a war to help run. Bennet has no time to think of me right now."

When Alice declined to embark on a shopping expedition so early in the morning, Rose took Martin and Cynthie with her to pick out new clothes for them and some bolts of silk for her mother. As always their lively chatter cheered her. London had been some bizarre dream. She would be glad to get back to Wall for a little. Bristol would be another matter. While they were out she stopped at a land agent's office. He knew of no properties for sale around Bristol, but gave her the name of a colleague there. Her life was beginning to move forward again, but every step she took left Bennet farther behind.

It suddenly occurred to her that she had seen nothing of London except for the shops and the parks where they rode. So she set out with the two youngsters to tour the city.

"Is this your idea of fun?" Bennet asked five hours later as he caught up with them at Montagu House. Rose was in the Italian gallery, giving each painting a quick scrutiny as she paced along the wooden floor. Martin and Cynthie sat quietly on a bench, the girl covertly sneaking one shoe off at a time to massage a foot.

"Well I have not much time, Bennet. If I guess aright I may be on my way back to Wall on Monday. If I don't see something of London now I may never get the chance. There is certainly no prospect of Europe now, and that is the only reason I came."

"I had thought you might by now have a reason to stay that has nothing to do with paintings or dead statues."

"Of course. I mean to see all the churches and public buildings as well."

Bennet gave a snort of frustration. "London in three days? It cannot be done!" he shouted with upraised arms as he trailed after her. "Rose, you must stay."

"I should like to stay," she replied, giving a Caravaggio a quick glance. "But that would be unwise. Besides, we have already done St. Paul's, the Royal Academy, the Society of Painters in Watercolors..."

"What can you possibly retain at this pace?" he demanded, grabbing her hand to arrest her progress.

"Bennet, you will put us off schedule."

"Rose, I want you to stay in London. I simply need more time."

"What you and I want does not matter. Once these latest rumors get about, you will be glad to see me gone."

"What rumors?"

"You will hear them soon enough."

"If you must persist in this madcap tour at least send your maid home with Martin. The child looks faint."

Rose glanced at Cynthie and had a sudden attack of common sense. "You are right, of course. Martin, find a hack and take Cynthie home."

The alacrity with which the children left made Rose smile. Martin trusted Bennet Varner perhaps more than she did.

"Now what is all this frantic activity in aid of?"

"If you must know, I need activity, frantic activity, to keep me from thinking about what they are saying."

"And what are they saying, thanks to Lord Foy?"

She hesitated. "I'm not precisely sure, but if my suspicions are correct, it will be even worse than Bristol."

"Well what do you suspect they may be saying?"

"Well, it is not so much a matter of what I suspect, but of what I fear. For Axel has been remembering more and more of what happened at Wall."

"Very well, then, Rose, what do you fear is being said of you?"

Rose stared at him and decided against all her fears to tell Bennet the truth. "That I murdered my father."

Bennet gaped and she fixed him with a penetrating gaze, then said, "Are you not going to ask me if it is true?"

Bennet gave a sigh. "Of course it is not true. Only an idiot or a simpleton would believe such nonsense."

"Well, we are in London."

"Come, I will take you home. You will be too tired for the party at the Quintens' tonight."

"I had forgotten about that."

"After Mother went to such lengths to obtain the invitations?"

"You mean after you forced your mother to go to such lengths to obtain the invitations."

"It comes to the same thing."

"Will you be there?"

"Of course."

In spite of what Bennet had said, it was Leighton who turned up to escort Rose and Alice to the Quintens'. Alice was in the downstairs hall adjusting her pink silk gown and deciding that a shawl would be enough of a covering for the evening.

Rose came down the stairs in dove-gray, a color she thought highly suitable for someone who wished to blend into the background. "I hate to make you come round here for nothing, Leighton, but I'm not sure I want to go tonight," Rose said.

"Not go?" Alice piped up. "But I have been planning on it. Why is it when I want to go somewhere you are too tired, but when you—"

"Very well, we will go, but we do not even know these

people. What if there is no one there who will talk to us?''

"Do not be absurd," Alice said. "I know lots of people in London. I will have a wonderful time even if Stanley is not with us."

As Rose had already guessed, their greeting on arrival was less than warm. The concerned set to Leighton's face increased to downright worry when he went to get Rose some punch. Alice had attached herself to the wife of one of Stanley's cronies. Rose could see from her vantage point by the doorway that the lady was trying to evade Alice, was in fact trying to snub her. But Alice had never been snubbed before, and did not know it for what it was.

"Spit it out, Leighton. What are they saying of me?" Rose scanned the brightly lit salon, like so many other rooms in so many other town houses, with all the people talking about her. She took a sip, but the sweet drink clawed at her throat, for she had just seen Lady Catherine and Harriet whispering together.

"To me, nothing. But from what I can overhear it is something to do with your affair with Foy."

"I was engaged to him, but that was five years ago. Old news, in fact."

"The wildest thing I heard was that the clandestine affair produced an illegitimate child."

"Who is?"

"Who is Martin, your groom."

Rose burst out laughing, nearing choking on the sugared wine. "This all happened when I was what? Six years old?"

Leighton grinned sadly. "It is amazing what people will repeat, even if they don't believe a word of it. I just want you to know that if worse comes to worst…"

"You will stand my friend? Thank you, Leighton."

"I will offer you the protection of my name," Leighton said like a man about to face a firing squad.

"Leighton!" She whispered, the tears springing to her eyes. "That is the most gallant, courageous thing anyone has ever done for me. I admire you exceedingly for making the offer, but I cannot accept."

Leighton looked somewhat relieved, but said, "My offer stands no matter what they may say of you."

"Again, I thank you but I refuse, and not just to keep from ruining your life. You see, I am in love with Bennet Varner."

"I know. A man would have to be blind not to see that."

"And since both of us have decided never to marry, nothing can ever come of that. I do hope that we shall always be friends, the three of us."

Leighton stared at her. "Never marry? But when did Varner decide this?"

"Years ago. Is that not why you offered yourself as the sacrificial lamb, so to speak?"

"No! I mean, yes, of course."

"Anyway, it was very noble of you."

"I hope so. Do you mind if I leave you for a moment to rescue Alice? She is looking lost."

"No, go to her. I am used to being alone at these affairs. See if you can convince her to go home early."

Rose took her glass and wandered toward a row of seats away from the fireplace. It was a vantage point from which she could watch the dancing like the duenna she was supposed to be. She knew better than to approach anyone, and ignored the departure of two dowagers, who hunched off whispering together. She had lived on the fringes of society for years, like a strange mare, just permitted to eat at the edge of the herd. She was recognized as being of the same species, but any attempt on her part to join in a conversation would be summarily snubbed, the way her mares would show their teeth or heels to a newcomer. But mares were eventually assimilated; people like her were not.

She saw Axel make his entrance, almost as though he had been called to attention. In spite of the recent marks of conflict on his face, he looked crisp and dashing in his scarlet coat and white pantaloons. How much grief that scarlet coat had given her years ago, for she did not look well in scarlet or any color she could think of that went with scarlet. It was Axel who had caused her predilection for gray and cream.

He saw her then, and his tanned handsome face split into a grin. Half a dozen people followed his gaze across the room. This was not helping her cause any, she decided, but at that moment she would no more have rejected his overtures than she would have turned her back on Bennet Varner. For Axel did share one thing with her. He was infamous, and he did not give a damn what anyone thought of him.

When he came to her she rose to meet him with a smile. It bothered her that she would be so desperately bored for conversation as to welcome this villain to sit with her, but she greeted him with the sort of relief a condemned prisoner feels when confronted by a kindly executioner. If nothing else he would make a quick end to her character and she could shake the dust of London from her feet forever.

"What the hell is going on?" Axel demanded, pushing his saber hilt out of the way to cross his legs as he sat down beside her. He motioned to a waiter and procured two glasses of champagne for them.

"You must know. I assumed, since I had been cut by the entire audience at the opera, half the people in the shops, and everyone in this room that word of our *scandalous affair* must have made the rounds by now.''

''Not unless someone else spoke of it. We had a bargain, and I have said nothing.''

''Perhaps while you were drinking,'' Rose said, her brows drawn together in puzzlement.

''If there is one thing I know how to handle it is drink.''

''You perceive I have no qualms about talking to you now that the damage is done. It was only a matter of time until the Bristol rumors reached London. But if not by you, then who spread the tale?''

Axel grinned. ''You have ripened since you were that green girl. You were desirable enough then, but now...''

''Cut line, Axel,'' she demanded with a sweet smile pasted to her lips. ''If you did not tell anyone, who did?''

''I would hardly repeat a tale knowing that you could do just as much damage to me.''

Rose scrutinized his laughing open face.

''Come now,'' he said with a grin. ''I may be a wastrel and a brigand, but I am not a liar, at least not in this case.''

''What are they saying, then?''

Axel downed his champagne and signed for the waiter to bring him another. ''Sorry, I did not mean to keep you in suspense. The talk is that you are a woman of experience, that you know all there is to know of men and women without the benefit of the marriage bed.''

''That's very vague. How was I to have attained this experience?''

''No names have been named.''

''Not even yours?'' she asked skeptically.

''I have let it be known that my siege of your fortress is still in progress.''

''Only a soldier—''

''Would have defended your reputation in the teeth of

the entire town,'' he supplied. "You don't give me enough credit.''

"I credit you for ruining my character in Bristol. You owe me something.''

"The only name I have heard in connection with the rumors is Cassie's. Perhaps she or her mother are the agents of your downfall.''

"They have never made any secret of their contempt for me, but why bother?''

"You stand in the way of Bennet's marriage to Cassie.''

Rose bubbled over with laughter at this picture and caused quite a few heads to turn in her direction. "Bennet Varner and Cassie? You must be joking.''

"It has been spoken of by the family for years,'' Axel quoted.

"Not by Bennet, I take it. No wonder he is a confirmed bachelor.''

"Yes, I would have a qualm or two myself, if the match were proposed to me.'' Axel cast a critical glance at Cassie.

"Does Lady Catherine really believe she can compel Bennet to marry Cassie by getting rid of me? He will more likely hate her for it, especially if it was Cassie's idea. Harriet has been too deeply influenced by both of them and Bennet knows that.''

Axel appropriated one of Rose's hands. "Lady Catherine is a powerful woman, who franked the Varners into society on the strength of that promised alliance. If I can persuade Varner to marry Cassie, she will aid my suit with Harriet.''

"And Harriet would listen to Cassie. Look what they got her to do to her hair. But you make Lady Catherine sound so malicious.''

"She will stop at nothing. If your death would aid her

purpose she would dispatch you with no more thought than shooting a dog.''

"But being the woman she is, she can get rid of me more easily than that," Rose continued.

"And make you suffer. But if you were to persuade Harriet to marry me…"

"I don't hate Harriet enough to wish you on her." Rose tried to slip her hand out of his grip but he held fast. So that was what he wanted.

"There is only one thing to do then."

"What?" Rose demanded impatiently.

"Marry me."

"You?" Rose went into another peal of laughter and Axel waited, smiling until she had finished.

"It solves everything. I need money, you need a husband. We don't need any of them and we are well suited."

"What a gracious proposal," Rose said, wiping tears of mirth from the corners of her eyes. "Still, I do not think I will accept it." She did snatch her hand back this time. "I have my own fortune. Why should I put myself under the rule of any man?"

"I would not expect anything of you except an heir. We could go our own ways."

"Don't be absurd. Were we to wed, you would be murdered within a fortnight."

"You are not serious."

"Deadly serious. For I would not brook my husband leaping from another woman's bed into mine, and that is exactly how long it would take you to become bored with me."

"I think you do not give yourself enough credit." Axel grasped her hand again with both of his and drew it to his cheek. "Remember the night you did that?" he asked as he ran her knuckles over the scar.

"Vividly."

"Everyone thinks it is a war wound."

"It is. Men and women will always be at war. Perhaps we are not a species destined to survive."

"Then do your part and marry me. I am a jolly enough fellow when I am not forever worrying about money."

"I am not your kind of woman," she assured him.

"And who is my kind of woman?" he asked in his most caressing voice.

Rose glanced around the room but hesitated to name either Harriet or Cassie, though they both leaped to mind. "Someone who is destined to be a victim."

"Someone who perhaps even prefers to be a victim?" he suggested.

"Don't be absurd. No woman would prefer to be a victim."

"You do not know women as I do."

"Apparently not." She sent him a puzzled frown.

"Marry me, Rose. I loved you once."

"No, you only wanted me. It's not the same thing at all."

The buzz of talk seemed to grow louder, and Rose wondered if it actually had or she had just now let it penetrate.

Axel smiled. "How does it feel to know that every woman in the room is talking about you, and every man as well?"

She spared a glance for the crowded room. "Lonely. It feels very lonely. But I'm sure you think it the most famous lark."

"That is the difference between men and women."

"No, that is the difference between you and me." She recaptured her hand and pulled her shawl about her to try to end the interview. "When I am a singularity I feel the hurt. You feel only exhilaration."

"I did once feel the hurt. But they can only hurt you

if you care for their opinion. Get over caring and you will have no problem with them.''

''Become as cold and callous as you? Impossible.''

Heads turned at that moment and Rose was drawn irresistibly to look toward the door. Bennet stood there smiling his benign smile, greeting acquaintances, until his questing gaze fell on Rose and Axel. Then his brows drew down as black as thunder, and he disengaged himself abruptly to stride across the room. Rose could not read his face except to know that he was extremely angry. For the moment he looked far more dangerous then Axel, who grinned at his effect on Bennet.

Rose stood and drew her shawl closer, feeling she had somehow betrayed Bennet. ''I had thought you were not coming tonight,'' she said defensively.

''Obviously,'' Bennet said harshly as he grasped her arm possessively. ''I came to escort you home.''

Axel stood up slowly, unbending his lean frame and stretching to his full height. Rose thought that if he were a dog she would see his hackles rising.

''Perhaps Rosie does not want to go home.''

Rose had instinctively resisted the pull on her arm but realized she must defuse the situation. ''I was getting rather bored.''

Axel looked shocked for a split second, then his sly smile spread slowly across his face and he laid his hand over his heart. ''You always knew how best to wound me, Rosie.''

Bennet's grip tightened. ''If you have taken advantage of my absence to insult Rose…''

''Insult her? I have offered her marriage, since your sister will have none of me. Are you insulted, Rose?''

''No, under the circumstances I am—'' she glanced around the room at the people who had been snubbing her ''—I am touched, but the answer is still no.''

"I still have the ring," Axel called after her as Bennet nearly dragged her from the room.

"Touched indeed! How could you fraternize with that man?" Bennet demanded his carriage from a passing footman so gruffly the man almost snapped to attention before striding toward the back stairs.

"Because he was the only one in all that glittering throng with the courage to speak to me," Rose said, her shawl trailing behind her on the stairs as she hurried to keep up with Bennet.

"But he is the cause of all this gossip."

"Axel was not the one who set the stories about," Rose said as they gained the front foyer.

"How do you know?" he demanded, almost thrusting the butler aside when the man opened the door for them.

"I accused him and he denied it."

"You believed Axel?" Bennet hauled her impatiently down the outside steps.

"I can tell when he is lying, which is more than I can say for you." Finally she pulled her arm out of his grasp and gathered up her errant wrap against the night chill.

Bennet's head snapped around and in the gaslight his angry face looked very like a stranger's. "I have no reason to lie to you."

"And yet you do, sometimes. How do you account for it?"

"If it was not Axel, who then put these stories about?" he asked, brushing aside her accusation.

"Axel traces them back to Lady Catherine." Rose could see the muscles of Bennet's jaw work and she detected a weary sigh.

"That means she made use of Cassie and Harriet in spreading this filth," he concluded.

Rose was glad his anger was abating, for he had almost

frightened her when he was so beyond reason. "Don't you want to know why?"

The carriage arrived and Bennet held his answer until he had helped Rose in and relaxed heavily into the seat opposite her. "Rose, Lady Catherine doesn't need a reason to destroy someone. It may only be that you ride better than Cassie. I have seen her ravage a young girl's reputation for no better reason than the child was not enough in awe of her. She is drunk on her power. Everyone fears her tongue may be turned against them. Now Cassie and Harriet are becoming equally dreaded."

"But if everyone fears them, why do people pretend to like them?" Rose stared out the window at the gaslit facade of the Quintens' town house before Bennet's carriage whisked her into the darkness of London.

"Society will turn on them one day," Bennet predicted. "They will lie so often and to so many people that their credulity will suffer from the sheer weight of the poison they spit out. But for the time being they can cut you out of society and Alice and Stanley with you."

"There is nothing either one of us can do to stop them. Why did you take your anger out on me?"

"Axel always cuts me out with women. To see you responding to him…"

"But I did not. And you might have shown a little more self-possession."

"Yes, I am a sad disappointment to myself." Bennet rubbed his forehead tiredly. "I had not thought he could still get at me. What is worse, he now knows how much you mean to me."

"It does not matter. I will be going back to Wall on Monday."

"Running away?" he chided.

"I had already decided to go back where I belong,"

Rose replied angrily. "If I'm going to be shunned by people, they may as well be people I know."

Bennet sighed and reached across to take her hand firmly in his grip. "Perhaps the situation is not past mending."

"Bennet, I really do not care. You do see now why I wanted to pass through London as quickly as possible. If not for you and your damned interference we might be in Paris by now." Rose dashed the tears away from her eyes with her free hand.

"Ah…Napoleon is in Paris," Bennet said, like a schoolboy hesitantly offering an objection to his professor.

"Damn, I was forgetting about him." Rose sniffed. "What a bother the man is. Perhaps we should send Lady Catherine out to deal with him."

Bennet chuckled and Rose gave a watery laugh.

"Do not lose faith yet. Perhaps my esteemed mama can do something to repair the damage."

"But Bennet, if your mother draws her social position from Lady Catherine she will not dare do anything to help me, even if she were willing."

"I do not think that can be the case, for she has gotten you invitations."

"Perhaps you were too young to remember how the Varners came into society, or mayhap you did not even notice. It was all part of the scheme to marry you to Cassie. Getting rid of me would be a step in that direction. Or at least Lady Catherine thinks so."

"What are you babbling about? I never had any real intention of marrying Cassie. I was only joking about being entrapped by her."

"Oh, then ten to one Axel has got it all wrong. In that case perhaps your mama can help. I do not care so much for myself, but Stanley and Alice will never forgive me if I ruin their connections in London.''

By the time they arrived at Change House and he escorted her to the door they were both fully composed.

''Do not lose sleep over this, Rose. Mother will mend this if she wants to remain at Varner House.'' He left her then, for she was too tired to argue with him. Let him see for himself, Rose thought, that the situation was hopeless. Perhaps by the time Stanley returned they would all decide to go back to the country.

Rose went to bed, but not to sleep. She heard Alice stomp up the stairs talking to herself a half hour later. Rose slipped out of bed and locked her door, then turned a deaf ear to the knocking. Some things were better left dealt with on the morrow. And with any luck Alice would sleep late and Rose could be gone before she had to confront her condemnation. Would Bennet ride with her anymore? He had been angry when he had confronted her at the Quintens'. She had almost thought she was to witness just such a scene as she tried to avoid. But his last words to her in the carriage had been words of hope.

Chapter Ten

The question of riding the next day was settled by the drenching downpour that settled over the area—not a fitful winter storm of sleet and rain, but an earth-soaking spring rain that would call the bulbs forth from the ground and the buds from the trees. As she let the curtain fall back into place at her bedroom window Rose thought of her home at Wall, which she would have to give up no matter what happened in London. But Wall did not have the only bulbs or trees in the country, certainly not the only pastures and barns. She would find a place for herself, and had already in her own mind given up on London. With all the disappointments in her life she had not expected much from the city, and it had not given her anything except, perhaps, a friend. Hanging on here had some importance only because it was what Bennet wanted. And Rose thought that if he had been a key figure in supplying the army during the past war, he would very soon be too busy to bother with her problems.

Instead of her riding habit Rose donned her sturdy buff walking suit and asked to have her tea and toast in the book room. The room reminded her of Bennet and the outfit reminded her of the night she had perhaps saved

Bennet's life. No matter where she was she would always think of that. It was a dress meant for crawling about antique ruins, climbing mountains or driving a spirited team through the middle of a dark night. In a few years when they were settled on their farm and Martin was old enough to be her courier, they would go to Europe, just Martin, Cynthie and herself. That is, if the troublesome Bonaparte had been locked up again.

A footman brought in the post and Rose was just beginning to slit open her few letters when Alice burst into the room, teary-eyed and red-faced, with a frilly dressing gown thrown over her nightdress. "Is it true what Leighton told me last night?"

"What?"

"That I was being cut because of some gossip about you."

"Yes, it appears Lady Catherine has put me on her list of people to destroy."

"But why? Because you refused to play at her musical?"

"I have it on good authority that there need not be a reason for her to take a personal dislike to someone."

"I cannot credit that she would gossip about you for no reason."

"The other possibility is that she feels I'm stealing Bennet away from Cassie, when really he is only my friend. In fact, Bennet has repeatedly said he has no more interest in marriage than I do."

"Perhaps if someone were to tell Lady Catherine this, make it plain that you are no competition for Cassie..."

"Not me. I intend to stay as far away from her as possible. Bennet is going to see what his mama can do to help us."

Alice left, somewhat mollified, and the first letter Rose opened was from Edith Varner. But the contents were like a knife to the heart. It was a long letter, full of accusations couched in polite terms, and it took Rose much time to master it. The upshot was that the Varners would have nothing further to do with the Walls, and no attempt should be made at communication. Moreover, it said, a similar letter had been sent to Rose's mother apprising her of the situation. This last was the cruelest blow and Rose knew she must leave for Wall as soon as Stanley returned to support Alice.

She sat down to try to write her mother an encouraging note but it was difficult. She held Edith's letter up to the candle again, hoping that on second reading the rejection would not resound quite so blatantly, but the words seemed expressly designed to wound. It was not a letter written in an angry moment, but a formal declaration of war composed, if Rose guessed aright, by not one mind but three or four. Her impulse was to burn it, but she could not. Destroying the letter would not change the hatred that had produced it. For the first time in her life she felt unable to act, and stood staring blankly at the piece of paper.

When the footman told Bennet Miss Wall was in the book room he said he would announce himself. He rapped lightly on the door and opened it to find Rose standing indecisively at the small desk. She looked up, those dewy blue-green eyes full of incomprehension. When she finally perceived it was he, she sat down abruptly in the chair and carefully laid a letter facedown on the desk.

"Whatever is the matter?" he asked, stepping to her side at this unprecedented show of weakness.

She stared at him in confusion for a moment, her face still white with some shock, then forced a tremulous smile to her lips. "Just lost in thought."

"You're so pale, I thought someone had died. Is it bad news?"

"No, I am fine. Was I—have I forgotten an engagement?"

"No, I just dropped by. I know it is still misting a bit but I thought you might like to go for a drive."

"I don't think—" She stared at the blotter for a moment. "Yes, a drive would do me a world of good." As she rose she deftly picked up the letter and tossed it into the wastebasket. "I'll go get my cloak."

"I'll wait for you in the hall," he said as he followed her from the room. As soon as her steps had disappeared up the stairs he strode back to the book room and nipped the letter out of the trash. He knew he should not read it. He was a spy, after all, but this was no matter of national security. This was only the matter of his beloved's happiness. The more he stared at the folded letter the more the image of Lady Catherine came to him, and he realized it was her scent, her stationery. But when he opened it, the thing was written in Harriet's hand, with his mother's drunken signature affixed at the bottom. He had read it thrice before he heard steps and was about to discard it when it occurred to him his mother was not above denying such vile actions. He folded it carefully and tucked it in his pocket.

Rose thought Bennet looked older than he had just yesterday, and she realized it was because he was being serious. Without that impish smile he looked like what he was, a successful businessman, a political figure. Perhaps even a spy. He let her drive again, and she put all else from her mind as she guided the team expertly toward Hyde Park. Obviously his mother would not help the Walls and they must leave London in disgrace. Poor Bennet was only searching for a way to tell her. He had enough worries without having a social scandal thrown on his plate as well. He was not saying anything, just looking grimly ahead, with the raindrops beading on his greatcoat.

Rose shivered inside her wool cloak. She told herself that nothing would have come of their relationship anyway. She would never have let it get that far. But she had lost her dearest friend. He simply could not bear to tell her so. Somehow she must make it easy for him. As soon as they were within the confines of the nearly deserted park she said, "I thought I had better thank you now for all you have done for us."

"You have thanked me more profusely than I deserve."

"I will be leaving on the Bristol stagecoach Monday, no matter what Stanley decides to do. I think…I suspect Mother is not well, and I should be with her."

"What about me?" He turned his serious face toward her.

"What do you mean? We can still be friends. I can write to you."

Bennet was silent, angry almost, from what she could see of his profile.

"Rose, just because things are said of you does not mean people will believe those things, or even that they care if those things are true or not."

"What things?" she asked suspiciously.

"Do not ask me to repeat such nonsense."

"That bad, is it? At least during the inquisition you could confront your accusers, hear the charges. You could not win, but at least you could defend yourself. I am surprised that they have managed to convince you."

"Do not be absurd. No one has convinced me of anything."

"Then why make the point that you do not care if the rumors are true?"

"I did not say I do not care."

"Then you do care if they are true."

"Yes—no! You are confusing me on purpose."

"I had hoped that one good thing would come out of

this whole disaster, that I would have at least one friend in the world, but now I find myself wishing I had never run into you on the steps of your house.''

''Don't say that, Rose. I love you.''

''What was that, friend?'' Rose looked straight ahead over the bobbing ears of the horses. ''You throw 'love' around a bit loosely. Don't you mean you feel sorry for me?''

''Never. I admire you. I want—''

''No, let me tell you the right of it. The war was over, or so you thought. You were simply a stray Galahad, looking for a cause to champion, a knight errant suddenly without employment. Well, you have another war to run, Bennet Varner. You scarcely need my tawdry affairs to occupy you now that Napoleon is on the loose again. So go back to your shipping office, your secret meetings, your spying and your maps. This may surprise you but I don't need you either, not you or your dour-faced mother, or your spiteful sister.''

Bennet was silent for a moment, and Rose clamped her mouth shut, afraid to look at him after her outburst.

''Stop mincing matters, Rose. Why don't you tell me what you really think?''

Rose gasped and then burst into tears, a thing she scarcely ever did, especially while driving a touchy team and curricle through even a moderately empty park. Bennet removed the reins from her hands and said, ''I think you should pretend you have something in your eye.''

She sniffed and brushed the tears away impatiently with her knuckles. ''This is all my fault for wanting to be like everyone else. I am not like anyone else, and I cannot change that.''

''Don't. I like you as you are. And this is all my fault for throwing you into society without preparing the ground first.''

"What is the matter? Did you not manage to bribe enough people?"

Bennet glanced at her and she sighed and gave him a misty smile. "I used to be better at hiding things."

"And I used to be better at managing things."

"One cannot manage lies, Bennet. It's like trying to get hold of a snake. Seriously, may I write to you or would you rather I did not?"

"I would rather you did not go away at all. I have only a few people I regard as true friends, and none of them is a coward."

Rose bit her lip and stared at him with that hunted-deer look. Bennet watched her but could not divine what she was thinking. She was right. She was like no one else. She could not be comforted like an ordinary woman. But had he been right to challenge her? He glanced again and her chin was set, her eyes determined. The unprecedented silence lasted until he returned the team to the front of Change House.

"Thank you for letting me drive them again," Rose said formally, as she hopped down without any assistance.

"I mean to escort you to the theater tonight," Bennet stated.

"I do not think that would be wise."

"Perhaps not, but it is necessary. You cannot turn tail and run. If I cannot come, Leighton will be here."

Rose nodded vaguely and he whipped up the horses and drove away before she could say any more. The anger against his family that he had kept so tightly leashed in Rose's presence was beginning to boil. Truth to tell he had always ignored most of their foolish persecutions, with the result that never having clamped down on them, they thought they could go their length to destroy an innocent and pay no price. They would learn differently today. It might be too late to repair the damage they had done, but it was never too late for revenge.

Bennet Varner found his mother and sister sitting together over a late breakfast with the society pages spread about the table like the picked carcasses of turkeys. When Hardy brought a pot of hot tea Bennet told the butler they were not to be disturbed. He closed the double doors into the room himself with a resounding slam.

"Bennet, my head!" his mother complained, flinging a black scarf about with her hand. He watched her dourly as she poured a dollop of brandy into her cup and warmed it with a spot of tea.

"Perhaps if you quit drinking quite so much you would not have such a headache in the morning," he suggested as he served himself tea.

"I need this to settle my nerves, especially after what we have been through. I do not know if I can stand to show my face outside the house again."

"And what exactly have you been through?" Bennet asked through gritted teeth as he pulled out a chair and sat down between them.

"The nasty shock of having that Wall woman shown for what she is."

"Do be quiet, Mother," Harriet said warily, pulling her lacy negligee tighter about her.

"Were you too drunk to know what you were signing then?" Bennet demanded, laying the letter in front of her.

"My God. Where did you get this? Did she give this to you?" Edith pressed her vinaigrette to her nose.

"A shocking piece, isn't it, Mother? But you have answered my question. You were not so drunk that you do not remember it. You sat here, the three of you, or was Cassie involved, too? You composed this tirade expressly to cause Miss Wall the maximum amount of pain."

"I'm surprised that she showed it to you," Harriet said coldly. "If she had any regard for your feelings—"

"She did not. She did her very best to hide it from me, but I stole it from her wastebasket."

"Bennet!" his mother said in shocked tones.

"So, you have decided to sever all connection with the Walls, have you? It is unfortunate you have taken such a dislike to my future bride."

Harriet choked on her tea.

"I expect you both to repair the damage you have done to her reputation."

"Impossible!" his mother shrieked.

"That is indeed unfortunate. Since Varner House is my permanent residence in London I will expect you both to vacate it within the week."

"What?" they shrieked in unison.

"Your presence here will be 'unduly painful' to Rose as it is already painful to myself, to quote your letter." He held this missive up. "'Therefore I feel sure you will not hesitate to remove a presence that has been both an embarrassment and a burden.' I see here you give her only two days, knowing full well she can do nothing until her brother returns to town. I think a week is generous on my part."

"You cannot be serious," Harriet reasoned. "Where are we to go?"

"A hotel. There are many in town that would have you, Mother, assuming you have not spent your quarter's allowance."

"But I have," Edith said, looking frightened now rather than outraged.

"Then throw yourself on the mercy of your partner in crime. I'm sure Harriet will support you."

"But what am I supposed to do?" Harriet jumped up and paced to the window.

"If I were you I would accept Axel's offer. It is the only one you are likely to get after the way you have behaved. You cannot deal in lies and deception without getting your skirts dirty."

"It is not my behavior that should be held up for censure. Miss Wall is the one who has seduced both you and Axel." Harriet wrung her hands in agitation.

"Rose did no such thing. Only a demented mind would concoct such nonsense."

"This is a sham, Bennet," his mother shouted. "You have said you would not marry. That is the only consideration that has kept Lady Catherine—"

"Yes, go on."

Harriet jumped into the breach. "You must know Cassie has been expecting an offer from you these seven years. It has been talked of in the family all this time. Everyone expects you to marry her."

"Cassie is a damn fool to pin her hopes on me when she has engaged in every form of vituperation and gossip-mongering one can imagine. It matters not to me that she was raised that way. She is an adult and could have modified her behavior. As for you two, there is no excuse. Harriet, you could have married any one of the eligible men I have been associated with these seven years."

"Cits!" Harriet hissed.

"Respectable men, good and honest men. The men who will run this country. And I am one of them."

Edith gave a wail of despair equal to the entire chorus of a Greek tragedy. "To think that a son of mine would treat his own flesh and blood this way and take up with some whore."

"Watch your tongue, madam. I had always entertained the hope that I was not your flesh and blood but adopted out of an orphanage. Thank God I have my father's nature, but then I recall he could not abide your backbiting and recriminations either, hence his removal to Change House. Well, I will not be put to rout. Varner House is mine and I mean to claim it. You both may remain on condition that you accept and recognize the Walls. I shall give a ball here in three days' time. You have that long to consider your crimes and their consequences.''

"Is that it, then?" Harriet demanded.

"Not quite. You will both of you, in your own hand, and without any advice from Lady Cat, write an apology to Miss Wall."

"Never!" they both shouted.

"I think you had better reconsider. Never is a long time to be cut off from everything you know and hold dear."

"We will always be accepted by our friends." Harriet stood staunchly to face him.

"I think you underestimate my influence. Those you call friends—how many of them have you victimized with your wicked tongue? You talk about this one to that one without realizing the two of them may talk to each other."

Harriet had the conscience to blush at this.

"Your only alternative is to marry Axel and hope he does not find out what a shrew he is getting for a mother-in-law."

Bennet exited amid a tirade of threats and walked briskly to his office.

Rose had finished packing, but was too depressed to do any more shopping or touring. Bennet had been right about not being a coward. But she could not dawdle in London forever just to prove that the gossip did not hurt her. She would go to the theater tonight. Until then she had just one more errand to perform before leaving London. She had decided she could not in good conscience let Bennet's sister make the misalliance of marrying Lord Foy. In spite of Edith Varner's warning to the contrary

she presented herself at Varner House to warn Harriet
about Axel.

Hardy admitted her to Varner House, but then returned
to say neither lady was in.

"I'll wait," Rose said, "but it is only Harriet to whom
I must speak."

"Please wait in the gold salon, then, Miss Wall,"
Hardy said kindly. He went away and in a few moments
angry steps approached the room.

"When a lady says she is not in to company, a polite
guest would take her leave," Harriet stated flatly as she
entered and closed the door. Her white muslin looked too
young for her, just as her evening dresses frequently
looked too old for her. Now that she knew something of
fashion Rose was rather amazed that Harriet so often got
bad advice about her wardrobe.

"I know," Rose said, rising from her chair, "but this
is important."

"If you have come to beg us to reconsider…"

"Of course not. My trunks were packed days ago. I
came to warn you about Axel."

"Warn me—of all the nerve. You try to steal him away
from me and you—"

"If I did not want Axel five years ago why should I
want him now? I don't really care about you, and God
knows I don't owe you anything, but you are Bennet's
sister."

"What makes you think I would believe anything you
say?" Harriet walked to the sofa and seated herself
primly.

Rose resumed her chair. "Because I have no reason to
lie. Axel is a violent man, either because he is a soldier,
or perhaps he became a soldier because he enjoys vio-
lence. It does not matter. If you wed him he will beat you,
I am certain of it." Rose got up and paced to the window

and back as she delivered her much rehearsed speech. "You may think you can charm him but he will find excuses, he will trap you into arguments. He will pick at you until you strike back, then he will beat you until he feels like a man."

Harriet's lips had parted in fascination and Rose began to wonder if her warning was having the proper effect.

"I shall be able to handle Axel. Did he beat you?"

"He struck me once and I never gave him the chance again. That scar he carries on his left cheek—that was not done by Toledo steel, but by my engagement ring."

"Axel will deny all this."

"Of course he will. He lies charmingly. He is charming and probably does not realize what a brute he is, but the consequences are the same for you whether he feels guilty about it or not. He will feel guilty, try to charm you, buy you presents. And you will forgive him. But he will hit you again. If you marry him you will be trapped in a vicious relationship." Rose ceased her pacing in front of Harriet.

Harriet's bosom heaved and she squirmed in her seat. "I do not care. I can control him."

"You don't—surely you don't love him?" Rose faltered.

"What does love have to do with marriage?"

"You won't listen to me, I suppose, but I had to try. You know it is possible for a wife to be raped by her husband. And you can never bring him to justice for it. He can do anything he wants with your body and you will be powerless to stop him."

Rose saw the surge of craving go through Harriet and it startled her. Why would a woman be sexually aroused by such information?

"I think I know Axel better than you," Harriet said, licking her lips.

"But I know the kind of man he is. I know what your life will be like," Rose persisted.

"How do you know?"

Rose vacillated between the truth and a lie as she took a turn to the window and back. Even if she told a lie it could cause more gossip. What was another mite of scandal compared to what had been said already? "Because that is what my mother's life was like."

Harriet looked at her, then dropped her eyelids as though she were replaying some secret fantasy.

"Harriet? Are you unwell?"

"No, I am fine. Now that you are going, I will marry Axel and it will all be as though you had never come to London."

"If only that were true. I am not leaving because of your ultimatum. I cannot promise to carry Alice and Stanley with me, for I will never reveal to anyone your cruelty. No one would believe it."

After Rose left Harriet walked to the fireplace and hugged herself, picturing Axel naked. She had some idea from talking to Robin what he might do to her on her wedding night, and the vague knowledge left her breathless and roiling inside. Rose must be a cold fish to turn her back on a man like Axel just to get a milksop like Bennet. She decided then and there to offer Axel the power over her money that he demanded in exchange for marriage. For she would have all the other power. The very idea of that stupid Rose warning her that Axel was dangerous. Of course he was dangerous, that was his appeal. But where Rose had cringed and run from him, Harriet Varner would be equal to the task of taming him. She had a fantastic vision of them both naked, locked together in an animal struggle to mate, her writhing under him, her hands locked in his hair, his lips crushing hers…. She felt suddenly faint and had to sit down and fan herself with a copy of *La Belle Assembliée*.

Rose returned to Change House to be greeted by the news that Alice had gone out. The confrontation with Harriet, though it had been easier than Rose had expected, had not gone as she had anticipated. It was almost as though the girl was entranced with Axel *because* he was dangerous. Perhaps it was that scarlet uniform. At any rate the interview represented her last obligation and had not taken very long at all. She must be feeling more herself, for she now thought of one or two more errands to occupy the time before the theater engagement.

Rose left Cynthie at home to pack the rest of her things and took Martin with her to visit the bookshops and buy some presents for her mother. Breaking the news that she meant to set up for herself would not be easy. Perhaps she would go to Bristol for a few months until her mother had gotten settled in. A companion was what Mrs. Wall needed, but rack her brain as she might, Rose could not think of one. If she found a pretty enough place in the country perhaps her mother would come to live with her. After all it wasn't the country her mother disliked, only Wall, and that was only because of all that had happened there.

Magnus Dowd wasn't the last person Rose expected to see in Hatchard's, eagerly scanning the newspapers, but she did not relish meeting him. She tried to escape the poetry section without his noticing her, and since he was chanting "Wonderful! Eight thousand troops. Wonderful!" to himself, she thought she had almost pulled it off. She could not imagine what he found so wonderful in a newspaper full of reports of Boney's successes.

"Oh—Miss Wall! What are you doing here?"

"This is a bookshop. I am buying books," Rose said,

carrying her purchases to the counter and gaining the attention of a clerk. "What are you doing here?"

"Just…just selecting a newspaper."

"Did they print your review of *The Exile?*" Rose asked as she counted out her money.

"What? Oh, yes, they always print my reviews. It was a wonderful play, wasn't it? I have seen it three nights in a row now."

"It was acceptable entertainment for an evening. But I have seen many better plays that you disliked entirely. Our tastes must be opposite."

"That is because your taste is uninformed."

"By you."

"What?" he asked.

"Uninformed by you. In fact, now that I know we are opposites I can read your reviews and know that if you dislike a play I will love it."

"That is not what reviews are for," Dowd said angrily. "They are to guide the taste of the public."

"I think most of the public would prefer to taste plays for themselves."

"I have many readers," he boasted.

"You can only assume that. I wager that if you asked a hundred people off the street if they read your reviews you might find one."

"People off the street can barely read. If you asked a hundred of the ton—"

"The ton represent a very small part of the population, even of London, and most people can read. Where the devil have you been the past two decades?"

"Lady Catherine was right about you," Dowd said in disgust. "You are of the lower orders yourself."

"Bennet Varner was right about you."

"What did he say?"

"Even a lady from the lower orders would not repeat his opinion of you."

"Well...well, good day to you, madame."

"Yes, it is a good day," Rose said, collecting her parcel of books with satisfaction. She was glad she had got to trounce Dowd one more time before she left town, and to have talked him speechless was wonderful.

"I brought you to see a fairly bad play tonight," Leighton said, "just so you have some basis for comparison."

Rose forced herself to turn her head away from the staring audience and smile at him. "I thought only Dowd intentionally went to bad plays," she said, smoothing the cream silk of her evening gown.

"In his opinion that applies to many of them. It could be a perfectly fine production, but if the playwright or actors are not favored by his particular set, or if they have not sent him any expensive gifts or invited him to dinner, he will fasten on just one line and unravel the whole play based on that. It really is as though he doesn't listen to the rest of it."

"And if someone has sent him an expensive gift...?"

"Such as tonight, you mean. He will give high praise in such generalities that he could be talking about any play."

"You are saying it is possible to buy a good review for your own play?" Rose stared at him in blank astonishment.

"My dear, not only is it possible to buy a good review for yourself, it is possible to buy a bad review for someone else."

"But that's despicable. If everyone else likes a play, or if Dowd never gives a reason for his dislike, won't he eventually be discredited?"

"He will fool many people for a while, those too stupid

or lazy to think for themselves. But there are many argumentative and acute persons in London, such as yourself, dear Rose. Eventually Dowd's pronouncements will fall out of fashion. And yes, people do notice when a person has nothing good to say about anyone. Makes them wonder what the person is saying behind their back.''

''So Lady Catherine and her set, if they go too far...''

''Will be brought down by their own lies.''

''Bennet said some such thing to me once—that Harriet had got in with the wrong set and was riding for a fall.''

''Harriet is not trusted by many already. In less polite circles...''

''You mean the men's clubs.'' Rose grinned knowingly at him.

''Yes. Lady Catherine is known as the Lady Cat. That is the pet name for a scourge used by an unsavory set of characters. I suppose Harriet is seen as some sort of she-cat in training.''

''I am not unhappy to be leaving London.''

''Are you leaving?''

''Just as soon as Stanley gets back.''

''I would not advise it,'' Leighton said staunchly.

''You think I should stay and fight, too?''

''Yes. To leave now admits the truth of the gossip.''

''But I cannot defend myself. I cannot just walk up to people and say, 'No, I am not Foy's mistress and never have been.'''

''You can face them down.''

''You do not understand, Leighton. Aside from your opinion and Bennet's I do not care what these people think of me.''

''Bennet cares what they think of you.''

''Perhaps too much.''

''What do you mean?''

''He is a man of business, moreover a man who must

retain his involvement in politics for the good of the country. He cannot afford to be alienated from society. He must drop my acquaintance.''

Leighton seemed dumbfounded by this, but as the curtain went up he needed to give no reply.

Rose was shocked when Dowd visited their box during the interval. She rather thought she had polished him off that afternoon and would not be subjected to his pompous prosing again.

''How are you enjoying this one?'' Dowd demanded.

''I'll not say until I know your opinion,'' Rose replied. ''I do not want to influence you.''

''Impossible. Your opinion cannot matter.''

''Then why did you ask if not to disagree with me? I meant I do not want to make you think the opposite.''

''The last scene in the act is flawed,'' he stated. ''If Pino knows Bette has been unfaithful to him he will not still desire her.''

''That's not a flaw. You are imposing your own motivation on Pino. Just because you would drop a woman who has been weak, does not mean that a hero would.''

''Most people will agree with me,'' Dowd replied, missing the cut.

Leighton laughed. ''What did I tell you? He has teased out what he thinks is a loose thread and will unravel the whole play in his review such that the author himself will not even recognize the work, nor will anyone else who has seen it.''

''At least I have the courage to voice my opinions to the public.''

Rose stared at him. ''But not the courage to write plays. If you are so knowledgeable, then produce an excellent play. Only then will I take any notice of your opinions.''

Dowd thought for a moment, then said in French, '' 'It

is the glory and the merit of some men to write well, and of others not to write at all.'"

"Who said that?" Leighton demanded.

Dowd scratched his head. "La Rochefoucauld."

"No, it was Jean de la Bruyère," Rose corrected, "but I do not think it means what you think it means."

Leighton began to laugh as Dowd colored from his ear tops down.

"It doesn't mean you have no need to write, Dowd," Leighton said, as Rose concentrated to remember what work the quote had come from. "It means the world would be a better place if you did not write at all."

"You have completely misinterpreted—"

"I have it." Rose gloried in being able to demonstrate her own French accent. "'The pleasure of criticism takes away from us the pleasure of being moved by very fine things.' So there. Since you enjoy tearing pieces down so much you cannot possibly appreciate them."

"I should have known it was useless to talk to a woman."

"Last time I checked better than half the world was composed of women," Rose said as Dowd got up. "If you're not careful you will severely limit your audience."

Dowd whisked out of the box with an incoherent grumble that set Leighton to laughing again. "I shall have to remember that one. Was it from Bruyère, also?"

"Yes. I was just reading a collection, but I can't seem to remember where. One of the bookshops, I suppose. Odd that Dowd would quote such an obscure author."

"Doubly odd that you should be able to retort in kind. You caught him off guard, Rose, and I think your reputation will pay for it."

"Oh, we were destined to cross swords from the first, him being a sycophant of Lady Catherine. I would be tempted to stay and fight it out with Dowd, could even derive a guilty pleasure from his discomfiture. But he's too stupid to realize when he's been bested. I wonder why that paper prints his drivel?''

''Oh, didn't you know? He owns part of the *Chronicle*.''

''Now that is absurd.''

''The whole town is absurd, Rose. Let us contrive to enjoy the rest of the play just to spite Magnus Dowd.''

Rose's concentration was somewhat bothered by trying to place the quote. It was odd that she had known the source. She could remember seeing it lately, but she read so much she could not call to mind where.

Bennet never did put in an appearance that night. That should mean nothing, or only that he was extremely busy trying to provision an army to meet Napoleon. But it seemed to her that every hour she was without the reassurance of his smile meant he was that much farther away from her. She tossed and turned the night through, thinking how to tell him they must end their relationship, if that's what it was. Perhaps they could correspond. Over that pitiful thought she cried herself to sleep.

Chapter Eleven

Rose sat, heavy-eyed, over her tea in the book room, feeling sure now that Bennet had abandoned her, wondering how she would face him when it was time to part. Perhaps it would all be very simple. He would not come to say goodbye and she would never have to hear him pretend to still care.

Rose heard a clatter of hooves in the street, and Cynthie poked her head in to say Martin had brought the horses. Rose had no intention of riding today, but had forgotten to tell Martin. Now she went to the sitting room window with the intention of telling him to take the horses back when Gallant nodded his head eagerly at sight of her.

She threw open the window and called, "I shall be changed in five minutes. Please walk them, Martin."

As good as her word, Rose reappeared in a very few minutes and mounted the horse held by Martin as easily as Varner could have tossed her up onto it.

"Stilton said Mr. Varner went out early to the docks. According to Hardy that usually means he won't be back until noon."

"This business over Napoleon, I suppose. He really has not time to bother with my problems."

Martin looked a question at her. "Lord Foy?"

"Actually not. From what I have been able to discover it is a bunch of gossipy women who are harrying my character."

"Oh, well, they are easily ignored."

Rose smiled at the boy. "Still, I think we have overstayed our welcome. I will be journeying back to Wall as soon as I can speak to Stanley. We'll get to Europe someday."

When they reached Hyde Park Rose let her horse open up into an easy canter. Only in the outdoors could she find a measure of serenity. The grass, trees and horses cared not if she was in disgrace. What did her reputation matter in the grand scheme of things? It was too bad about Stanley and Alice, though. She might dodge Alice, but she would have to face Stanley's condemnation.

The letter she had posted to her mother could neither undo nor soften whatever venom had been dispatched by Edith Varner. What was the point of hurting Mother? Rose wondered. Perhaps they thought she would recall Rose in disgrace. If she could have ridden back to Wall at that moment she thought she would have, even if it meant never seeing Bennet again.

They had nearly come to the end of their run when she heard hoofbeats other than theirs. She forced herself not to look. She wanted so much for it to be Bennet that she was afraid it was not. She slowed Gallant to a trot.

"Sorry I was late," Bennet said in his apologetic way.

When Rose looked around she saw the boyishness was all gone from his face and Martin had dropped back to a discreet distance.

"I thought you had business to attend to," Rose said with relief. "I have been thinking I should return home if for no other reason than to remove myself as a distraction. You have, after all, a war to get ready for."

"And I have a multitude of people to help me. The *Celestine* had to be unloaded and reloaded with supplies to go to Ostend."

"Compared to the possibility of another decade of war, my problems seem so trivial." Rose let Gallant walk.

"Not to me. I have spoken to Mother and Harriet."

Since he left the statement suspended in the air, she completed it. "And they refused to undo the damage. Frankly, Bennet, I do not think it is in their power to take back what they have said."

"They are considering their positions."

"You make them sound like opponents in a war."

"They are. Do you not understand what happened to you that night at the Quintens'?"

"I was snubbed, probably the most thoroughly anyone has even been snubbed in this town, if that is a distinction."

"During the war we would have called it a cutting-out operation."

"That is a military term," she said as she let Gallant drop his head to munch grass. She knew she should not let the horse graze while mounted, and it spoke much for Bennet's absorption that he did not regard it.

"More of a naval term. If you can distract a ship away and get between it and the rest of the convoy you can pretty often capture her."

She looked surprised. "Or destroy her if you cannot capture her. So Axel was not there by accident." Rose urged Gallant to walk on.

"No, and Stanley is not out of town by accident. I was not called to the docks by accident that night. Had the plan worked you might have accepted Axel. That was not what Lady Cat—Catherine wanted, but Axel is not one to miss the main chance."

"And he's not smart enough to know that I can see

beyond his charms. I cannot like him as a husband for Harriet no matter what she has done.'' Rose tensed, and Gallant took it as a signal to trot.

"You have spoken of your fears of Axel before. Witness your own dangerous rescue operation for Gaspard, a man you had never met.''

"And for you.'' Rose sent him a haunted look.

"What exactly is Axel capable of?''

Her head came up and she stared at him with such a look of pain he regretted the question.

"Are you asking me if the rumors are true?'' she whispered.

Bennet could see her gathering the horse's reins in her gloved hands as though she were ready to bolt. "Hold up, Rose, I have lost a stirrup.''

"Well, find it again,'' she said impatiently, causing Gallant to dance under her.

"I shall have to dismount and tighten my cinch,'' Bennet shouted after her. Rose spun Gallant to watch Bennet make a running dismount from the bucking Chaos that left her amazed that he was still on his feet, rather than dragged behind the beast. But Chaos quieted as soon as Rose walked her horse back to them.

"And no, I do not believe the rumors,'' he said as he fiddled ineptly with the cinch, "or you would have told me all about it long ago…friend.''

Rose gave a sigh, calmed the horse and slid to the ground with such grace Bennet realized she never needed his help where horses were concerned. It was more difficult to keep Rose from bolting than one of his overfed beasts, but somehow he had managed it.

"I should have told you there was a cloud over my head in Bristol, but it seemed unnecessary. I did not mean to stay in London.''

"Detaining you here was my fault. Why did you break your engagement with Axel?"

Rose began to walk, leading the horse. "He came home wounded with Father on leave, a very dashing young officer. My father proposed the match, and I had no reason to object. As you know, Axel can study to be pleasing. We were to be married in three weeks. As far as it went it was a peaceful visit from Father, not like his usual…"

"How was Colonel Wall usually?"

"There are some men for whom it is not enough for a wife to be compliant. They will always suspect, as he used to say, that another stallion had been in the paddock. He always, when he came, would accuse Mother of infidelity. Frequently he beat her. That is why we saw to it that Stanley stayed away at school."

"And how you acquired your expertise with leeches."

"Yes. But this time he seemed not even interested in Mother anymore. He did not take her to his bed, at any rate. I truly believed that Axel was a mellowing influence on him. Can you imagine that? Axel, a noble influence." Rose looked down at her gloved hands as though gathering her strength.

"He is not the person I abhor most in the world," Bennet said. "Are you going to change that?"

"He raped my maid, Cynthie," Rose whispered desperately. The tears sprang to her eyes.

"Martin's sister?"

"Sorry, I thought I had cried all these tears years ago." She cleared her throat. "They caught her coming back from the little house late one night—"

"They?"

Rose's lips trembled and she licked them. "Axel and my father overcame her and dragged her into the barn."

"If you don't want to continue…"

"No, I want you to know." She dashed a hand across

her eyes. "They didn't realize Martin was sleeping in the loft, looking after a new foal. I had heard Cynthie scream and ran as fast as I could from the house. Axel had already done with her and Father had her down while Axel was grappling with Martin. The boy was outmatched, of course. Axel was about to smash his fist into Martin's face when I yelled at him. Then I brought the shovel down on Axel's head. They were drunk, both of them. Father staggered to his feet with the girl. When Martin tore Cynthie out of Father's grasp he gave my father a shove. Father staggered and fell against an anvil."

"That's how he died?"

"Do you understand, Bennet, if this were even known, Martin would be put on trial? He could face hanging or deportation. That is how much I trust you."

"Your trust is not misplaced. Axel has no memory of it?"

"Some, up to the part where I knocked him out. I let one of the stallions loose and gave it out that in their drunkenness both soldiers had been trampled while trying to saddle the beast. When he awoke Axel was too groggy to contradict the story. He was angry at my breaking the engagement, though. So he spread a lot of stories around Bristol about having had me and finding me not to his taste."

"Damn him!" Bennet swore under his breath.

Rose looked at him fearfully with that hunted-doe look. Bennet dropped Chaos's reins and took her in his arms. He wanted to reach back in time and comfort the hurting child within her.

"You are not shocked?" she asked.

"I am surprised that you could think so clearly after such a terrible event."

"Not disgusted? I as good as murdered my own father." She pulled away from him and turned her back.

He laid a gentle hand on her shoulder. "I know of no other woman who would have thought of her groom and maid at such a time. But then, look at the fortitude with which you faced the gauntlet of London society and the single-minded rescue in Pall Mall."

She turned to face him. "I know they were soldiers and they probably did that sort of thing all the time during the war, but this is England."

"Yes, and they were less than soldiers. They were animals. Apparently Axel has fallen very far since the last time I dealt with him. I will be careful I don't take any chances with him in future."

"So you see that I must leave."

"No, retreat is not an option."

"The only reason I told you is that I wanted you to see my position."

"And I tell you we must face down this scandal or it will be that much more difficult for you to be accepted in London as my…"

"As your what?" she asked with a puzzled frown, the tears still wet on her cheeks.

"As my wife."

Rose gasped, speechless for a moment. "Your wife? Are you mad? You told me you would never marry."

"That was before I knew you."

"Another one of your lies? You said I was your friend. Can you not see that is what I need, rather than a husband?"

"Can I not be your husband, as well as your friend?" Bennet reached for her but she pulled away from him.

"But you tricked me again." Her horse was becoming as agitated as Rose.

"I already told you I love you. What did you think I meant by that if not that I wanted to marry you?"

"But everyone will think I trapped you."

"You said you did not care what people thought," Bennet argued.

"Bennet, I shall never forgive you for this betrayal!" Rose scrambled onto Gallant's back as best she could and thought to leave Bennet in the dust, but when she turned her head she saw him leap onto Chaos, finding his stirrups without the slightest difficulty—that, too, had been a sham. He caught up with her by the time she reached the edge of the park.

"Do you mean to run my horse to death?" he shouted.

"You are right. I should not take my anger out on this innocent beast. I will never ride with you again, Bennet Varner. You are the most deceitful man I have ever met. It would serve you right if I did marry Axel."

"I thought you said you would never marry," he taunted.

"I have changed my mind."

"So have I."

"Leave me be!"

Rose looked over her shoulder to see that Bennet had stopped pursuing her and was turning in at Varner House. She trotted the horse straight to Change House, with Martin following in despondent silence. Rose halted Gallant in the street and dismounted without waiting for any assistance. This unusual arrival attracted the attention of two smarts, an elderly couple and a nursery maid out airing her charge. Rose threw the tail of her gray riding habit over her wrist and tramped up the steps to encounter a locked door. She pounded the knocker against the back-plate as though she were pounding sense into Bennet Varner's head.

He could not possibly marry an infamous woman. What about his position? Beyond the deceitfulness of it, how did he think it made her feel to be offered for only because she was ruined? Because he was sorry for her. He was a trickster, little better than Axel when you came right down to it. When had she ever trusted a man, any man, not to play her false? Her repeated pounding brought only Alice's face to the side window.

"Unlock the door and let me in."

By now two more people had stopped to observe how her difficulty would resolve itself. Martin had dismounted and was holding the reins of both horses, trying to appear nonchalant. Poor Martin. Rose had put his fate in Bennet Varner's hands. Surely he would never say anything. He had a fondness for the boy. And an equal fondness for an awkward country girl, Rose's calmer self reminded her. Why had she not simply refused his offer graciously as she had done to Leighton?

The door opened a crack but no more. A junior pimply-faced footman Rose had never seen before said, "Mrs. Wall is not home to you."

"Not home? Don't be an idiot. I just saw her face in the window."

"You are not to be admitted."

"I live here!" She made as if to push past him, but he slammed the door in her face again and locked it. She kicked it so forcefully the oak shuddered, but it did not give way.

"Perhaps if you was to hold the horses, miss," Martin suggested. "I could see what I could do."

Rose turned to discover that their audience now numbered twelve assorted people, two of whom had ogled her at the theater the previous night. "Very well, Martin. Try your luck."

Martin talked to the footman, actually got his foot in the door, and only because he was outweighed by the brutish lad inside, was thrust out again. The front parlor window was pushed up and a much heated Alice stuck her head out. "You may as well go away. I am breaking my connection with you. It is your fault we are shunned by everyone. Harriet told me so.''

Rose gaped at her. "My God, Alice. What have you done to your hair?'' Tossing the reins to Martin, Rose ran up the steps for a closer scrutiny.

"It's a new look,'' Alice said, clapping her hands over her ears.

"You've hacked it off just like Harriet. Stanley will hate it.''

Martin breathed an exasperated sigh and Rose brought herself back to the matter at hand.

"Stop playing the fool and let me in. I have had quite enough of fools for today,'' Rose said, gazing at the still gathering crowd.

"No. This is my house and I don't have to admit you. Give me the direction of your hotel and I will have your things sent there.''

"I cannot walk into a respectable hotel in a riding habit with no baggage and expect to be given a room.''

"You should have thought of that before you alienated everyone.''

"It wasn't me who did it. It was sweet Harriet and Cassie, your friends, and Lady Catherine. Do you think discarding me makes you acceptable to them? I realize they put you up to this, but I would have thought you would have more sense than to listen to them.''

"Just wait until Stanley gets back.''

"But he won't be back until tomorrow night.''

"He will be so angry he will pack you off to Bristol.''

"Which is where I intend to go as soon as I collect my baggage.''

Alice let the window fall shut and drew the curtains closed as well.

"Martin, did you see her hair? Stanley will be livid,''

Rose said, still gazing in disbelief at the closed window and the memory of Alice with her shorn locks.

"Miss, perhaps we had better cool the horses."

"Yes, how unthinking of me," Rose said as she descended the steps to take Gallant's reins.

"Miss Wall, is it?" One of the dandies approached with a simper. "I should admire to give you lodgings for the night."

"Martin, have you got your pistol by you?"

"Always," Martin said, drawing the small, but lethal-looking weapon.

"No offense. Just joking." The dandy backed off and crabbed across the street, looking over his shoulder. The crowd seemed inclined to disperse after this, but Rose paid them no attention. She led Gallant toward the Varner stables, wondering what on earth she was going to do now that she was no longer welcome in either house. She had some thought of looking for Leighton, but she had not his address. The only other residence in London she knew was Axel's, and she would not turn to him for assistance if she were starving.

"What do you think we should do, miss?"

Rose looked at Martin and smiled, knowing the boy would stand her friend no matter who else betrayed her. "I don't precisely know, Martin. The hell of it is I left the house so quickly this morning I did not even think to throw a few coins in my pocket. We could not afford a hotel even if they would let us have rooms. And I am not well-known enough at my bank to be able to get funds on my signature."

"That footman was new, not part of Mr. Varner's staff. Once we stable the horses I must find a place for you to wait until I can get Cynthie to let me in."

"Good, tell her to give you my reticule from the bureau. She knows where it is. In the meantime I will talk to Stilton.''

''I was thinking you could wait in the house…'' Martin faltered.

''And risk running into—Edith or Harriet? Not likely.''

While Rose led Gallant into his box, Martin had a quick word with Stilton, then made off down the alley. Rose distractedly listened to Stilton's praises again about their nocturnal adventure. He was still walking with a limp but it did not seem to incommode him in his work.

In a few minutes quick footsteps on the back stairs that led down into the stable block announced the arrival of Bennet, who was wearing his usual foolish expression, but Rose was too tired to do more than look up at him.

''Rose, what a surprise. My housekeeper, Mrs. Marshall, is writing out those recipes you wanted. Since I knew you were planning on leaving I thought you might like to step into her room for a moment. Also she would admire to have your recipe for that soup you brought Gaspard.''

''Soup?'' Rose gaped at him and he nodded toward the stairway that led down into the kitchen. ''Oh, yes, the soup,'' she said, and walked numbly with him toward the back door. After he had shown her into the housekeeper's sitting room, Mrs. Marshall entered with a tea tray with some scrawled recipe on it.

''I'll just leave you two to enjoy my scones.''

''But…''

''Her scones are the best,'' Bennet said as he bit into one and plopped down onto the sofa. ''Will you pour or shall I?''

''This is absurd,'' Rose said, but she sat down and poured them both a cup of tea and she did have a scone. ''Do you often take tea with Mrs. Marshall?''

''Actually I do. When I was a boy I used to take refuge

here. Whatever Harriet or Mother had found to torture me with seemed not quite so awful once I had wrapped myself around a few of these treats.''

"You are a favorite of Mrs. Marshall, aren't you?''

"Yes, she is very motherly and I was always cute,'' Bennet said boyishly.

Rose smiled reluctantly, shaking her head. No matter what had happened Bennet Varner was always able to make her laugh. "I take it Martin did not go to Change House as I told him, but went to you instead.''

"A boy of excellent sense. On the off chance that your brother really does get angry enough to discharge him, there will always be a place for Martin with me.''

"Martin works for me,'' Rose said stubbornly.

"There would always be a place for you with me, as well—no, that's no good either. Help me out, Rose. I have never proposed to a woman before and I have no idea how to go about it.''

"I do not know much about it myself,'' she said, staring at him in fascination, "but horseback does not seem to work all that well.''

"Yes, and I sensed myself that the stable was probably not the best of settings.''

Rose smiled and set down her teacup. "Do be serious, Bennet. You cannot expect me to marry.''

"Marriage is an honorable estate.''

"Marriage, that social institution that barters women like cattle and sets men up as studs?''

"Yes, that one,'' Bennet answered brightly.

Rose chuckled. "I have been needing you. You can make me laugh in the face of disaster.''

"Women are only bartered if they marry unwillingly,'' he said, ridding himself of cup and saucer and sliding closer to her.

"But your marriage to me would be a sacrifice whether

it was willing or not. You would alienate your entire family."

"Actually, in my case, that would be an advantage." Bennet possessed himself of one of her hands.

"I don't fit in here."

"You don't have to. I spend as much time as I can in the country or in Portsmouth. I have a house there as well. Frequently I go to Europe—"

"Yes, you lied about that as well."

"Except for Paris. That might be dangerous. But I spend most of my time in the ports. We can see Europe together, Rose."

"You would have to give up all your friends."

He took her hand. "My friends, my real friends, do not listen to gossip or fribbles or vindictive matrons. They are business people with jovial wives and enterprising children. And they would all love to see me comfortably settled." He held her hand between his two, warming the coldness out of it. "What is the matter? Can you think of no more impediments to throw in my path?"

"There is one." Rose wet her pale lips. "When I told you about Father and Axel I did not do it to make you feel sorry for me. I wanted you to understand—"

"Is that what you think? That I am taking you out of pity?"

"The thought had occurred to me that you might be as gallant as your friend, Leighton," Rose said with a rueful smile.

"Whom you turned down. I was as mad as fire when he told me he offered for you. No, I want to marry you because I love you, and for no other reason. We have become more than friends in spite of ourselves. What's the matter, Rose? Don't you trust me?"

"That's the problem with you, Bennet. You are so often not serious, that it is difficult to accept your sincerity without looking behind it for a joke.''

''Well, look behind this, Miss Gwen Rose Wall.'' He extracted a document from his coat pocket and handed it to her. ''Do you know what that is?''

''It's a special license.''

''Do you know how long it takes to get one of those?''

''Not very long if you know a bishop,'' Rose quipped.

''But look at the date.'' He pointed to the paper.

''It says the eighth of March.''

''That was three days ago, before all this nonsense started. I knew that if I ever found the right moment to ask you, I would have to rush my fences and get you to a church straightaway. None of this business of waiting three weeks.''

''Why, no, anything could happen in three weeks,'' Rose replied. ''I might come to my senses.'' She held one hand to her forehead, wondering if this was really happening or if she was only dreaming.

''Don't ever do that,'' Bennet said, leaning over to tuck a lock of hair behind her ear. ''Don't ever be anything but the mad girl you are now.''

''Still, I need time to think.''

''Take all the time you need. There is a whole pile of scones left.'' To demonstrate he grabbed one and took a bite.

''Bennet, you are insane, but I do love you.'' Rose turned to him, letting the paper fall to her lap.

''In spite of my insanity?'' he asked, leaning back into the sofa.

''No, I think because of it.''

''Say yes, Rose,'' he begged.

''Bennet, you are impossible.''

''Definitely. Someone needs to take me in hand. Say yes, Rose.''

"Yes…thank you, I will have another cup of tea." Rose took mercy on his bereft face as she picked up the teapot. "And your hand in marriage."

"That's my girl." Bennet jumped to his feet. "I'll have the horses hitched. We can be at St. Giles's in less than an hour."

"Bennet, wait," she said as he plunged toward the door.

"You prefer St. Stephen's? I could probably get you St. Paul's but on such short notice it will cost an arm and a leg."

"No," she said, standing and holding out her dress. "I prefer not to be married in my riding habit."

"Oh, are you sure you would not as soon saddle a couple of horses and trot over there?"

"Bennet!"

"Well if you insist on a wedding dress…"

"Not a wedding dress, just a dress."

"I'll nip upstairs and see if I can borrow something from Harriet."

"Don't you dare." Rose stamped her foot. "That would curse us, for certain. I want one of my own dresses and I mean to get one. Alice cannot legally hang on to my baggage."

"If you promise to stay right here for twenty minutes I will go myself and get your trunks."

"Yourself?" Rose asked, coming toward the door.

"Well, I may take a few stout footmen with me."

"Are you going to kick the door down? I should like to see that."

"Well, I suppose I could, but it seems a waste of time when I have a key."

Rose gave a gurgle of laughter. "And don't forget Cynthie."

Bennet was gone then, and Rose did pour herself another cup of tea. She felt as though she had just taken a stunning fall. Her head was buzzing and she wanted nothing more than to be left alone for some time to regain her equilibrium. Yet she felt this uncontrollable gurgle of mirth building inside her. She jumped up and strode about the room. Bennet Varner's wife! It was beyond anything she had ever imagined. Such things she could do. And she would be a help to him in his work, with his horses and certainly in bringing some sobriety to his madcap existence. She never even considered that she might be making a mistake. This felt so right.

As good as his word, Bennet returned victorious with all the baggage. Cynthie and Mrs. Marshall dressed Rose in her gray silk evening gown, which shone like silver in the afternoon sun. Bennet must have sent servants running ahead of them in all directions, for their carriage paused on the way and a shopkeeper came out with a bouquet of roses. In Oxford Street they stopped in front of a jeweler's shop and the proprietor himself came out with a selection of his best rings. They were attracting a bit of a crowd by the time Rose made up her mind. Bennet complained that she could have the whole tray if she wished, but she finally chose a blue diamond because it was unusual. When they got to St. Giles's, Leighton was waiting for them, looking enormously relieved.

The wedding supper was at Varner House with only Leighton, Gaspard and Captain Cooley attending. Mrs. Marshall said that Mrs. Varner was under the hatches, whatever that meant. Rose said they had enough food for fifty.

"Don't fear it will go to waste," Bennet said. "Our bounty will overflow into the servants' hall. They have much to celebrate."

"But they scarcely know me," Rose replied.

"When they have been under the thumb of my wicked

mother and sister all these years, I promise my marriage to a cross-eyed imbecile would be met with well wishes of the highest order.''

Rose had to translate ''cross-eyed imbecile'' for Gaspard and then convince the incensed and slightly drunk Frenchman that Bennet was only joking.

Gaspard was only mollified by being allowed to recount a story to Bennet's discredit. This led to other war stories, particularly from Captain Cooley, which Rose encouraged in the face of Bennet's growing impatience. Finally all three guests were too drunk to do much of anything coherently except disparage Bonaparte.

''I know it is customary for the blissful couple to depart on a protracted series of visits,'' Bennet said finally, as he took Rose's hand and pulled her from her chair.

''Nonsense, you have work to do and so have I.''

''Work?''

''You are in some part responsible for supplying the army, are you not?''

''Yes, but I don't see—''

''You will have to contract for blankets and uniforms as well as foodstuffs and ammunition. I shall begin making lists in the morning.''

''Somehow I suspected you would not be content to sit home and train horses or sew samplers,'' he said as he lifted her off her feet.

Rose curled her arm around his neck. ''I will train your horses, but there will be no time for that until we have vanquished Napoleon.''

Cooley, Leighton and Gaspard all drank to Bonaparte's ill health as Bennet carried Rose up the stairs.

''So this is your room,'' Rose said as he put her down.

''Yes. Mother never would vacate the old master bedroom so I had this suite redecorated for myself. I suppose it is a bit on the masculine side and there is no bed in the adjoining room, so you will have to sleep with me to-night,'' he said, shutting the door.

"Bennet, there is a point at which you can stop joking.'' Rose bounced on the edge of the bed.

He came to unhook her pearl necklace, and she stood up to let him undo the fastenings on her dress. "The devil of it is I have played the fool for so long I'm not at all good at being ardent.''

"Well, we have all night to experiment.''

"Experiment? I should rather think—'' Rose spun and stopped his retort with a kiss. She thrust her arms around his waist under his coat. He shrugged this garment off and let her undo his waistcoat buttons.

"I see I will never need a valet with you around. My turn.'' He knelt and ran his hands up under the silk dress, pulling it over her head, then paused to plant impassioned kisses on whatever skin was revealed by each layer he removed. He spent the most time over her breasts, which he proclaimed the finest he had ever seen either in or out of a gown.

"I should be careful about drawing comparisons,'' Rose warned. "You have no idea what I have seen.''

"No, I know for a fact that as a temptress you are a sham. While I was recovering your trunks I finally got out of Alice what started all this gossip.'' He stripped off the rest of his clothes and took delight in the gasp of surprise she gave as he unleashed his aroused member.

"I forgot what you were saying,'' she said as she came blushingly to embrace him.

"Your bride's lecture to Alice.''

"Was there ever anything more absurd? You would have thought her mother would have prepared her. When she asked me what to expect I could only draw parallels from livestock.''

"And do I compare favorably?" he asked as he thrust himself against her flat stomach.

"Very favorably. I am happy to see there is more to you than that foolish grin." She looked down at him and started to kneel, but he stopped her.

"No time for that." He pulled her toward the bed and laid her down upon it, resuming his kisses and running his hands over her slender limbs in a passion of wanting. "Sweet Alice confided your expertise to Harriet, who spilled the beans to Cassie." He drank of her lips again, then suckled at her breasts until this news penetrated.

"But then...it is Alice who is the author of our downfall. I had nothing to do with it."

"Ironic, isn't it?" Bennet asked from the nether regions. He ran his tongue along her thighs, then demanded a taste of her secret treasures. And Rose opened to him just as she had opened her heart to him. There was no guilt of any kind. It had not been her fault, any of it. When his member demanded entrance she raised her hips, reveling for once in her vulnerability. Bennet entered slowly, sending shivers though her body, and suspending time with his coming and going. Had they truly only been married a few hours? This felt so real, as though they had made love a hundred times before. She knew the impatience of wanting him inside her, wholly hers. One sharp thrust, part his, part hers, and he was rubbing back and forth inside her, like long warm waves on a friendly shore. She wanted him to go on like this forever. To think that she had almost missed this.

"I have been waiting for this..." Bennet said in a measured way through gritted teeth "...all my life." His thrusts grew more urgent and sent Rose into paroxysms of ecstasy until his seed burst inside her. She hugged him to her. She wanted him and his children. Bennet fell on top of her, breathing as though he had been running for miles.

Rose waited until he had gathered some strength. "If it takes this much out of you, Bennet, I promise I won't be a demanding wife."

"Oh, you won't?" he said, gasping. "I suppose once or twice a week will do you."

"Oh, no, keeping in mind the rigorous breeding schedule I set up for my horses, I was thinking more like once or twice a day."

"You wretch."

Rose kissed him and sighed contentedly as she ran her hands through his hair and down his neck. "Stanley is going to be very angry."

Bennet raised himself to look down at her smiling face and make sure she was joking. "About you marrying me? Then it's a good thing I have been currying his favor."

"Oh, no. He won't regard that. Did you see what Harriet did to Alice's hair?"

Bennet went off into a gale of laughter.

Chapter Twelve

The wheels of the Gravely carriage clattered along the dark streets of London, and for once Lady Catherine was silent. Cassie gave a noisy yawn and Harriet stared at her friend. When had Cassie gone from voluptuous to purely heavy? It was a fine line, Harriet decided, but discarded it as a problem since it would certainly never happen to her. Harriet reflected instead on the odd coolness among the guests at the party she had just attended. She had gone with Lady Catherine and Cassie, but they had spent the whole evening talking among themselves. Nothing was as interesting as the harrying of the Walls anyway. There were only a bunch of dull people there tonight. But it was odd that no one had asked either her or Cassie to dance.

And Lady Catherine's reaction when Harriet had told her of Bennet's ultimatum was rather odd. When she had confided to Cassie her doubts about convincing Bennet to marry her rather than Rose, Cassie had turned absolutely huffy and Lady Catherine had called for the carriage. Really, Harriet didn't see why they would blame her for her brother's irrational starts. Lady Catherine had said Bennet Varner had better come to his senses with a viciousness that boded no good for any man. Harriet wondered what possible lever Catherine could use on Bennet and hoped it would not be something that would discomfit her.

Then the subject of Cassie's marriage to Bennet had been dropped, and just when Harriet needed advice on her own dilemma. But she knew it would appear selfish to be flaunting Axel's offer when Cassie had never had one. Above all, Harriet must decide if she should finally accept Axel. She had always intended to marry him, but not until she had tortured him an appropriate length of time. There was no one else she wanted to marry. If Bennet went so far as to marry the Wall chit she supposed Axel would lose interest in Rose, and that had been Harriet's chief objection to him—that Axel still pursued Rose Wall. What did the girl have anyway?

After being left on the doorstep of Varner House, Harriet used her key and was disgruntled to find no candle lit and waiting for her on the hall table. She made her way up the dark stairs, still ranting in her own mind about Bennet's unfairness and the lack of any sounding board for her thoughts. She supposed she would never be able to wake Mother if she had been left alone with the brandy all evening. Well, she needed to talk to someone, so she knocked on Bennet's door.

Harriet listened at the panel and was sure she heard some movement within. And she knew her brother did not employ a personal valet. She flung the door open and in the light of the single candle on the side table she saw Gwen Rose Wall snuggled comfortably in her brother's embrace. And most horrid of all, under the single sheet that covered their entwined bodies she was quite sure they were both naked.

"How dare you, Bennet Varner? And in our own house," she proclaimed from the doorway.

Bennet raised his head to stare at her groggily. "What are you talking about? This is my house."

"And I will not stay in this den of iniquity another moment. I shall send for my trunks in the morning." She slammed the door with such force that Rose was jolted awake.

"What was that, Bennet? It sounded like an explosion."

"It was. Don't worry. Just Harriet venting her wrath."

"Harriet was here?" Rose pulled the sheet up to her chin.

"Don't worry. My body shielded yours."

"Bennet? Again?" Rose asked with a chuckle as he devoured her with kisses.

"You are too appetizing. I cannot help myself. When I think of how close we came to not marrying it scares me."

"It frightens me as well," Rose said as she ran her hands though his long dark hair. "I was being a prideful fool. But Bennet?"

"What?" He gasped as his manhood plunged between her thighs again.

"Does Harriet even know we are married?"

His peal of laughter nearly drove Rose crazy with desire as he jostled inside her. "Possibly not. No wonder she was so shocked."

Rose started laughing too, and their combined mirth made the whole of the lovemaking more enjoyable for being something of a guilty pleasure, at least, where Harriet was concerned. It was a private joke between her and Bennet, the first of many she planned to share with him over the years.

When they had completed their intercourse with hot passion and cooled each other with loving kisses, Rose said, "You don't think she will tell anyone, do you?"

"That her brother has turned his house into a brothel? Not even Harriet would be so stupid, since this touches

on her reputation as well. Besides, whom would she tell
in the middle of the night?''

Rose turned in his arms and went back to sleep in complete contentment.

''And she did not even wake up, the hussy,'' Harriet
said as Cassie stared at her, the pale flesh of the older
girl's bosom heaving above the edge of her scarlet robe
at her little gasps of outrage.

In spite of her anger, Harriet had not left Varner House
immediately but had awakened her maid to pack a valise
for her. Since this ungrateful wench refused to quit the
premises with her, Harriet had to carry her own baggage
to the Gravelys' more than an hour after she had parted
company from them. After repeated knocks, Cassie herself
had come to open the front door.

''She has bewitched him,'' Cassie hissed finally, one
plump bare foot smacking the parqueted floor in the cold
front parlor ''just as she seduced Axel. We must drive her
from town.''

''But how? If those rumors about her and Axel did not
do it, I don't see how revealing this affair with Bennet
will get rid of her.''

''But this is so much worse. Axel is a soldier. People
expect such behavior of him.'' Cassie took her single candle and used it to light a candelabra. ''They will be much
more scandalized that she has seduced a respectable citizen such as Bennet Varner and driven you from your
home. When word of this gets out, Bennet will have to
marry me, for no other girl will have him.''

Harriet looked dubiously toward her friend and shivered, wondering why Cassie had not welcomed her to her
bedchamber rather than holding this conference in a fire-
less room. ''Don't you understand? This is my family we

are speaking of. If this came out I could never go back to that house."

"You will stay here, of course. I shall have Williams prepare a room for you and my maid will bring you a nightdress."

"If I stay in your room we can talk."

"Harriet, I must sleep some time. We both must if we are to do anything tomorrow."

"But what can we do?"

"Mother will know."

As Cassie led her up the stairs Harriet had, for the first time, a deep sense of foreboding about the morrow.

"What was all the row about?" Axel asked as he pulled on his other boot and stood up from the bed.

Cassie looked longingly at him. "Why did you bother to dress? We have all night."

"Because I cannot afford to fall asleep here, my pretty." He lifted her chin and stared into her still child-like face. "Your mother would not like it." He went to the window and threw it open, scrutinizing the street below. "Who was that anyway? It almost sounded like Harriet Varner."

"It was. She came to report that your precious Rose is at this very moment in bed with Bennet Varner."

"Damn his soul to hell!" Axel whirled on her.

"Close the window. It is freezing in here."

"You see what you witches have done. You've driven her into his arms. You women know nothing about these matters and should not meddle in men's affairs."

"Why do you care? You don't love her. I don't think you love anyone."

"Love is just a word for this," he said, grasping one of her ample breasts and rubbing his thigh along hers. "What more do you want from a man?"

"I want Bennet Varner and you had better fix it."

"Or what? You are in no position to be giving ultimatums, my girl, not after your checkered career. If I told what I know of you and your mother you would both be whipped out of town at the cart's tail."

"You wouldn't dare!"

"A soldier, such as myself, will dare anything. I shall need more money to get her away from him."

"I have no more. I told you that."

"Then I'll take these."

"My rubies? What will I tell Mother?"

"Don't worry. I'm only going to pawn them. You'll get them back as soon as I marry Rose."

"But—but what about Harriet?"

"That cold witch. She sets too high a price on herself. You have given me the information I need to get Rose. That's all I care about. You'll have to seduce Bennet Varner. You've had enough practice."

"I'll tell—I'll tell…"

"You'll tell what?" he asked, taking her throat in his hand. "One squeeze and the bruises will keep you in the house for a week."

"Don't," she pleaded.

"Beg me," he commanded.

"Please don't hurt me," she whispered.

He kissed her brutally, then strode to the window, stuffing the rubies into his pocket. He threw one booted leg over the sill, then turned to regard her with a harsh laugh. He disappeared then, along the ledge, and she heard him slide down the drainpipe at the corner. She closed the window, feeling cheated in every way possible.

Rose dressed herself, as usual, though she made slow progress with Bennet helping her, and sometimes undoing what she had just done. He was insatiable, but then, so was she. If he had, at any point, said "Take off that riding habit and come back to bed," she would have leapt at the suggestion. But they did eventually make their way down the stairs, though it was not easy with him trying to pinch her behind. They sobered themselves as they came into the breakfast parlor. Edith Varner was there, presiding over the teapot and looking pasty-faced and grim.

"What do you think you are doing, both of you?"

"Taking my wife to breakfast, Mother. What does it look like?"

"Then it's true what Mrs. Marshall says? You have married the girl."

"Yes, of course. Were you too drunk to notice?"

"But what am I to do?"

"You are perfectly welcome to stay, but it will look odd to people if you do so without supporting your new daughter-in-law."

Edith Varner chewed this over in her mind as she masticated a bite of toast. "What will you expect of me?"

"You need only put in a short appearance at any social function. Say nothing disparaging and you may retire when you wish."

"And what do you expect of me?" She turned to Rose, who sensed this was no time to be weak.

"That you conduct yourself like a respectable dowager," Rose replied. "I am quite willing to forgive what you did to try to destroy me, but I will not tolerate any more gossip...and no association with the Gravelys."

"But they are our lifelong friends."

"Supposedly so was my mother your friend, but you sent her that letter all the same."

"Those damnable letters!"

"There is a Mrs. Wall in the hallway," Hardy announced. "Shall I show her in?"

"Mother!" Rose shouted. She ran into the woman's

arms and they embraced and kissed each other. "Let me introduce my husband, Bennet Varner. And you already know Edith Varner."

"So, you are married," the pert brunette said as she removed her gloves a finger at a time. "Does this have anything to do with that bizarre letter I received and the nearly incoherent one of yours in the very same post?"

"Axel is in town," Rose said, as though that explained everything.

Bennet pulled a chair out for Mrs. Wall, and she sat down, arranging her brown traveling dress to her satisfaction. "I see. I had entertained some hope that he would get himself fatally shot in the Peninsular campaign. But I suppose there is no crying over spilled milk. Edith, I think you might offer me some of that tea," she said, fixing her blue eyes on her reluctant hostess.

Bennet laughed and took the cup from his mother's trembling hand. "Some rolls and bacon, perhaps?"

"Yes, I am starving," said this slightly older version of Rose. "Most certainly let us eat now and straighten out the muddle later."

Rose filled her mother in excitedly on all that had happened since their arrival in London, kindly glossing over the part Edith and Harriet Varner had played in her difficulties.

"That explains why that silly Alice would not let me in. Locking you out, indeed. Stanley is going to have to give her a talking to. So, I have come all the way from Bristol for nothing?" Maryanne Varner said, regarding her daughter with amusement as she finished her tea.

"Oh, Mother, if I had known you were coming we would have waited a day for the wedding."

"We would?" Bennet asked, grabbing a fresh scone and passing the plate to Mrs. Wall.

"I would never have wanted to delay such an urgent

event," she replied. "You are perfect for each other. I can see that. I simply wish it had not been done in a havey-cavey fashion."

"But it was not," Rose insisted. "I had a gray silk gown, a bouquet of primroses, and just look at my ring. Bennet's friend stood up with us."

"But where did the ceremony take place?" her mother asked, taking a bite of scone.

"At St. Giles's," Bennet supplied. "I know a bishop who owed me a favor."

"I see. You certainly seem to be an enterprising young man."

"Mother, Bennet is responsible in part for supplying the army. He has much work ahead of him these next few months."

"And that is the other thing," Maryanne complained. "We are to have Bonaparte visited upon us again? That on top of everything else. What are we going to do about that?"

Maryanne struck her small fist on the table and Bennet hastened to respond with all his plans for equipping the army as though he owed this country matron an explanation. As the conversation turned political, Edith rose to leave them.

"Just a moment, Edith," Maryanne said as she got up. "I want to have a talk with you."

She took the older woman's arm in hers and only looked back when Rose spoke up. "Mother, she did not write that letter."

"I did not suppose she had, Rose."

After they had left Bennet said, "That was kind of you."

"Kindness costs so little."

There was a loud rapping at the front door, followed

by the entrance, without benefit of announcement, of Mr. Stanley Wall.

"Rose, what the devil is going on?" Stanley demanded, flinging his hat onto a chair. "I return to find Alice in bed with a very bad haircut and saying she has no idea where you are and that Mother is in town. If Cassie and Harriet had not stopped by, I would not have had any idea where…" Stanley faltered and blushed when he saw Bennet. "But you cannot stay here."

"We are married." Rose said, guessing the reason for her brother's embarrassment and wishing to relieve his mind of its chief worry.

Stanley sat down abruptly in the chair vacated by Mrs. Wall. "Leave it to Alice to get it all wrong and for Cassie and Harriet to embroider the truth with the worst possible lies. But, you know, I think you might have waited until I returned. Congratulations, anyway. And, Bennet, old man, good luck to you." Stanley reached across the table to shake Bennet's hand. "You don't know what a relief this is."

"Thank you, Wall. I always knew you were a fellow of good sense."

"But what happened to Alice's hair?" Stanley asked, returning to his second cause for distress.

"I don't know," Rose replied. "Isn't it awful?"

"I hate to drag you two away from such weighty matters," Bennet said, pouring Stanley a bracing cup of coffee, "but we have plans to lay."

"What do you mean?" Stanley asked, not at all curious about the sudden change in his sister's status as he helped himself to eggs and ham.

"Tomorrow I hold a formal reception in this house to introduce my bride to society. You and Alice must attend."

"Of course, we will, hair or no," Stanley said with his

mouth full. "I shall buy Alice a wig if she refuses to go out."

Mrs. Wall came back into the room to retrieve her reticule. "Stanley, so you're finally back."

"Mother?" Stanley rose to peck her cheek. "You're here?"

"Of course, where else would I be? Stanley, you need a haircut."

"You wouldn't say that, Mother, if you could see Alice."

"I have seen Alice, at your town house window. That is what put the thought into my head. Her hair is shorter than yours."

"I had better go with Mother," Rose said, pulling her hand out of Bennet's with a squeeze.

It said much to him. It said, above all, be kind to silly Alice and smooth over the difficulties with Stanley. Bennet vowed to do his best to shield Alice, no matter how much blame he laid at the door of the Gravelys and no matter how he sacrificed Harriet's character.

When Rose and Mrs. Wall had gone, Stanley said, "I cannot believe my wife locked my sister out of the house. The only excuse would be insanity."

"Alice has been under a great deal of strain."

"I cannot thank you enough for coming to Rose's rescue. As brother and sister we have not always been close. God knows there is very little we agree on, but I would not have her hurt for the world. I love Rose."

"So do I. I had always intended to marry her. This emergency merely pushed our happiness forward a few months. Why did you return early?"

"Have you not heard? Napoleon is unleashed again. I must see if I can come by a commission. Can you help me?"

"If you like, and if you think that is where you can do the most good."

"What do you mean?"

"What the army needs right now is armaments and supplies. Artillery is in particularly short supply. I had hoped, with your connections around Bristol, you could be my envoy where shipping is concerned. It will, no doubt, mean many expeditions to the Continent. I can get you a commission as well, but the pay won't be much."

"Who cares about that? Something useful to do. That is what I crave. When do we start?"

"Now. Come to my office with me."

"But, I say, it's Sunday. Can we get in?"

"Of course. I have a key. And there isn't a moment to lose."

Rose evinced no surprise when Hardy, the butler, informed her that Varner and her brother had gone to "the city," his euphemism for Bennet's office. Rose and her mother enjoyed being introduced to the staff and settling in. Her mother exclaimed over all Rose's presents and demanded to go shopping with her the very next day. Rose contemplated the expedition with joy, listing all the best places she would take her to. When she had said she did not belong in London she had been wrong. She liked the city fine and knew it rather well by now. She thought it could do without some of its more malicious inhabitants. And now that she was Bennet's wife she would not retreat.

She approved Armand's choices for dinner, addressing him in French, and making him her devoted slave in the space of a few short minutes. Speaking French brought back her conversation with Dowd and those so bothersome quotes. She related the experience to her mother and together they spent an enchanting afternoon in the library prowling through Bennet's whole collection, which as it happened, did contain many volumes in French, but not one by Jean de la Bruyère.

"I suppose I must have read it in the book room at Change House," Rose said. "Perhaps we will call round there tomorrow, assuming Stanley will have been able to mollify Alice by then."

Her mother looked again around the magnificent room. "I must admit, Rose, when I sent you along with your brother all I had in mind was keeping him out of any really serious difficulty on the Continent. I never expected you would do so well for yourself."

"Actually I have Napoleon to thank for Bennet's interest in me. Had he not been trying to keep us from taking ship for France, he probably would never have noticed me."

"I like Bennet. He has such an open innocent face. He is a man you can always trust to tell you the truth."

Rose pursed her lips in a prim smile. "Yes, Mother."

"Trust is very important in a marriage."

"I know, Mother. But what of you living in Bristol alone?"

"Oh, don't worry about me. Now that I am free I do not care where I live, but I really feel that no house should have two mistresses."

"The other reason you dislodged me from Wall. I would have been forever tramping on Alice's toes. I must say I am impressed with how reasonable Stanley has been about all our adventures."

"I did worry that you two might argue the whole way across Europe."

"Fortunately it did not come to that. I am agreeably surprised in my brother's maturity. He has not said one word about a pair of colors."

The front door slammed and murmurings in the hall

were followed by the gentlemen entering, still discussing the weight of armament they could reasonably ship on the *Celestine*.

"Have you ladies been enjoying yourselves?" Bennet asked as he poked at the fire in the grate. Stanley obligingly threw on another log while Bennet poured them all a small glass of wine.

"We were just inspecting your library," Mrs. Wall said.

Stanley chuckled. "Any other two women would be inventorying the linen or counting the silver. The Wall women always were bookish."

"Find anything of interest?" Bennet asked.

"I was looking for a volume by Jean de la Bruyère. I must have been reading it at Change House."

"I don't recall owning him, though I have run across him lately—I know, the trunk of books our spy was using to hide the gold. There was a volume by Bruyère in there. You may have it if you like." Bennet turned to pour more wine so he did not see the look of excitement that passed over Rose's face.

"We did try tracing the inscriptions, but—what is it, Rose?" Bennet asked as he turned around. "You have nearly overturned your glass."

"Dowd!"

"What?"

"Magnus Dowd was quoting Bruyère to me at the theater the other night. Don't you see, Bennet?"

"Dowd? He seems such a fribble. I can't credit he would be involved in an international intrigue."

"What reason would an Englishman have for betraying his country?" Stanley demanded.

"Not money. Dowd is as rich as me, and I say that in all modesty," Bennet bowed in the direction of Rose's mother.

"Rich enough to fill a trunk with gold and ship it to Napoleon?" Rose asked.

"Yes, that rich," Bennet said thoughtfully. "What would be the one thing Dowd might want from Boney?"

"Would he want a title?" Rose asked.

"Possibly. But it's not much to hang a case on, and whoever our traitor is he has covered his tracks too well to be traced."

Stanley stood up and paced to the mantel. "Could you perhaps trap him? You are by nature of your business in possession of information such a man might think useful to Napoleon."

"Good idea, Stanley. You will all have to help me lay the trap. Dowd will not think it odd that I invite him to my reception tomorrow night, but he might become suspicious if I mention secret papers."

"Reception? I had forgotten." Rose gasped, almost choking on her wine.

"Did I omit to tell you? Don't worry. Everything has been arranged. You need do nothing, except perhaps drop a hint in Dowd's ear about the secret conference in the library. You will be able to do that with a straight face."

"I can manage it, but why me?" Rose asked.

"Not to offend you, dear, for I have the utmost respect for your intelligence…"

"I know, but Dowd does not. He will not be the least bit suspicious if a woman lets that valuable bit of information slip."

"I must inform Leighton and Gaspard," Bennet said almost to himself. "They will wish to be in on the kill."

Hardy came to announce dinner, putting an end to their plotting. Bennet and Stanley were like two boys, Rose thought, but this was not a child's game. She had trouble herself picturing the incompetent Dowd as an intriguer, but if he was not, no harm done. If he was guilty, then they would have caught at least one of England's enemies.

After an entire dinner and evening of business talk that caught up Rose and her mother on all the war preparations, Stanley seemed rather reluctant to go home to a pouting wife. But he promised to call at first light the next day to help Bennet draft some specifications for cannon, which he would deliver to the foundries on his way to Bristol.

Cynthie was just leaving Bennet and Rose's suite of rooms after turning down the bed and laying out their nightclothes. She giggled and fled up the hall toward the servants' stairs. Bennet smiled after her as he held the door for Rose.

He undid her necklace and buttons and watched in fascination as Rose let her dress slide to the carpeted floor.

"Was Cynthie...was she badly hurt by Axel's attack?"

"The doctor says no, but I will not push her to do anything. So long as she remains with me, she is fine, but as for ever marrying...we must wait and see. She trusts some men—Martin and Stanley, of course, and now you—but I am not sure she could ever put herself in a man's power willingly."

Rose stood before him completely naked, but strangely powerful. As her breasts rose with desire Bennet stared at her, his heart thumping in his chest and his member already throbbing with arousal. What puzzled him was how he had kept himself in check for so long. He began shrugging off his clothes as frantically as possible.

Rose laughed at him, tossing their nightclothes on the floor with the rest of her things, and slid between the sheets naked. Bennet hastened to follow her and explore again her body. He had never touched a woman before who actually had muscles in her legs and slender arms.

This was how a woman was meant to be, he thought, not some lump of flesh, but a live, moving being, with as hot a desire as a man. When he plunged inside her he reveled at the hot strong surges of muscle that wrung his passion from him as urgently as he could mount it. Rose did not wait for him to take her, but met him halfway on the field of love. Her kisses were every bit as demanding and ardent as his, her satisfaction as complete, and he knew that after they had slept the night through, her reawakened appetite would be just as voracious as his. He chuckled deep in his throat as he contemplated their future, their thousands of nights together.

"You are very powerful, Bennet," Rose whispered as he held her in his arms, her flesh hot against his.

"I don't always feel that I am."

"Just think, even as we lie here, your business is going on, moving grain, wool and iron ore to be made into bread, uniforms and guns."

"I had thought you meant myself," he said with a weak laugh.

"But your business is an extension of yourself. How much do you suppose you move in a day?" Rose asked in awe.

"Oh, tons and tons," he replied happily, nibbling on her neck.

"That's what makes you so attractive. You don't flaunt your power, like a scar or a saber. Your power is just there, under the surface. Like a riptide, unfathomable and inescapable."

"You have your own pull. Do not underestimate yourself. I really had vowed never to marry after my last disaster. That is one promise I am glad I broke. Together, Rose, we are unbeatable."

Chapter Thirteen

The next morning Bennet and Stanley consumed a substantial breakfast and then bolted from the house before Rose had got through even one cup of tea. There was no announcement of their nuptials in the *Morning Post* yet. Perhaps tomorrow. But many of the ton would find out tonight. She wondered what the reaction would be to a supposedly staid businessman with some pretensions to society marrying a woman who had been the talk of the town for days. The unkindest would assume she had trapped Bennet somehow. It would take years of sobriety and scandal-free living to make them forget the gossip of the past week.

Edith Varner seemed somewhat resigned to the fact of her son's defection. Since Rose's mother lent a sympathetic ear to a recital of all Edith's troubles over the past twenty years, their old friendship seemed to be on the way to a revival. Edith even spoke of visiting Bristol.

She went with them to call on Alice, but Stanley's wife would not leave her bedroom, even when Rose's mother knocked on her door. Apparently she considered her hair unsalvageable, or else was too mortified by the gossip to show her face. Edith vetoed a visit to the Gravelys' residence to inform Harriet of their changed circumstance. Edith now spoke of her daughter as the troublesome headstrong child rather than Bennet.

They returned home to find the preparations well in train for the evening, Mrs. Marshall having borrowed all the staff she needed from Change House. They had little to do but tweak a flower arrangement here or there and think of their own toilettes.

Harriet stared despondently into her teacup as she read the invitation card Lady Catherine had thrust at her. "I shall not go," Harriet said, pulling Cassie's too large dressing gown closer about her. "I shall never set foot in that house again."

"Never is a very long time, Harriet. What does Bennet mean, a reception? Is there some foreign dignitary to be entertained? Whom are we supposed to be meeting?"

"Unfortunately, I think he must mean this to be for Rose. Bennet has always been much too persuadable. Depend upon it, Rose has tricked him into throwing this reception to recognize her and the Walls. I would not be at all surprised if Bennet and Rose did announce their engagement."

"I won't have it, I tell you. Bennet will marry Cassie or no one."

"What are you going to do?"

"I'm going, of course," Lady Catherine said decisively.

"I do not think that would be wise. You cannot talk him out of something once he has decided on it."

"I won't have to talk him out of it. I've sent for Axel. When he comes send him up to me. After tonight, Bennet will recognize what a misstep he has made. He will offer for Cassie if he does not want his name dragged through the filth with that of Wall." Saying that, Lady Catherine marched upstairs to begin her toilette. Harriet had been shocked at how old her hostess appeared in the morning light and could not see how such a transformation could be achieved at all, let alone in two hours.

Harriet tried to think clearly. One thing was for certain. She could not long take refuge with the Gravelys if they declared war on Bennet, especially if they lost. Gossip and innuendo were all very well to give someone a subtle nudge, but to create a truly remarkable scandal one had to have proof, witnesses. Harriet could bring down Gwen Rose, but she would need Axel's help, and for that she might have to bargain away all she had. It would be worth it.

When Axel strode in the door she waylaid him in the hall and lured him into the breakfast parlor with promises of food.

"I'm starved," he vouchsafed. "I no more get home from the club than I am commanded, commanded, mind you, by that harpy to attend her." Axel filled his plate with eggs and sausages and set to eating with a voracity that fascinated Harriet. If he did everything with so much enthusiasm he was sure to be an accomplished lover. She hastened to serve him extra coffee as she set her plan before him. He listened to her with interest and did not interrupt her but ate thoughtfully as the edge wore off his hunger. "And why should I do this for you? What do I get out of it?"

"I will accept your proposal of marriage."

"Left it a bit late, did you not, Harriet dear?" He finished chewing a mouthful of bread and washed it down with coffee.

"I will...I will also agree to your terms."

"Give me control of your affairs, as it should be?"

"Yes," she whispered passionately.

"Very well, I will write it out."

Harriet hastened to get Axel ink, pen and paper as he finished his coffee. She signed the short document he produced without even reading it. He added his name to the bottom with a flourish. From that moment on she considered herself his wife.

"Now I must hie me to the harpy and see what she wants. Mayhap I will refuse her this time. With this—" he held the document aloft like some battle prize "—I need no longer take orders from Lady Cat."

Harriet stood on tiptoe to kiss him and was pleased when he grabbed her roughly and bruised her lips with a savagely hungry kiss. He was gone then, leaving her swaying on her feet. She knew she would never get used to such a man, and rather liked the idea that he would always take her by storm.

Rose chose to wear the palest of blue silks to show off her ring and the blue diamond necklace Bennet had presented her with. She did not know where he found the time to shop with a war to supply. She feared Bennet and Stanley would both be late, but on this occasion they had managed to tear themselves away from business in good time to change into their evening clothes. Bennet was the handsomest man in the room in his black evening suit and snowy cravat. And he looked happier, Rose thought, than she had ever seen him. If anyone might have come suspecting a forced marriage they would not hold that impression long, for Rose knew she must be smiling foolishly in her joy at being Bennet's wife.

Bennet and Rose stood in the receiving line for an hour only at the top of the grand stairs. Anyone making a fashionably late appearance would have to seek them out to be made welcome. Rose was enjoying mingling with her guests in the gold salon. These were mostly friends of Bennet, and assured her they were delighted to see him so comfortably settled at last. And they meant it. Those who were of the ton were rather subdued. There was no buzz of gossip behind her back, no turned-up noses or sidelong glances. The gossipers would be outnumbered.

"Enjoying yourself?" Leighton asked her as she moved skillfully from one cluster of people to another.

"Immensely. Have you seen Dowd, by any chance?"

"He just got here and plunged into the refreshment salon when he discovered he'd fallen into a nest of cits."

"I must speak to him."

"Cutting at him again? May I listen?"

"Just laying a little trap," Rose said mysteriously. She led the way into the red salon where the champagne and wines had been set out. "Ah, Mr. Dowd," she said, emphasizing the "Mr." to get his attention. "I believe you know Leighton and…and…not really anyone else actually."

"You have invited scarcely anyone of consequence. A bunch of bankers and—"

"And men from the Foreign Office," Rose said. "Isn't it exciting? They were all closeted in the library this afternoon for hours. I suppose it has something to do with Napoleon. Oh, excuse me. I must find someone. Leighton, have you met…"

"What the devil was that all about, Rose?" Leighton demanded. "I am from the Foreign Office and I was not in Bennet's library this afternoon."

Bennet came up to them. "Is the bait laid?"

"I thought his eyes would bulge from his head," Rose replied.

"Leighton, can you keep an eye on Dowd without being conspicuous?"

"Of course, but what the devil is going on?"

"Didn't Gaspard get word to you? Rose believes Dowd to be our imperial sympathizer."

"You're joking."

"Just let me know if he goes into the library."

Bennet was just congratulating himself on having deflected Stanley's attention from the army when a scarlet uniform walked through the doorway to join the glittering throng that had gathered at Varner house.

Stanley looked hard at the sun-burned face and fair hair above the scarlet coat and then shrugged and turned his back on Axelrod Barton, Lord Foy. The snub was not lost on Axel, Bennet or the dozen people who saw it. Bennet smiled knowingly.

Rose left the sofa where her mother and Edith Varner chatted to come and take Bennet's arm. "How goes the war?" he asked.

"I think your mother is beginning to warm up to me."

Bennet chuckled. "She knows what side her bread is buttered on."

"Bennet, she is a rather lonely old woman, trapped between the predatory Gravelys and..."

"And my vindictive sister."

"Did you send Harriet word of the reception? It would be best for her to put in an appearance."

"Yes, I sent back a note for her when Lady Catherine's man called for her trunks."

"You did tell her we are married."

"Let me think. Did I mention we are married?"

"Bennet, don't be so provoking. Why didn't you tell her?"

"Don't you see? For the first time in years something has happened in London that she and the Gravelys know nothing of. It was too good a piece of news to simply tell them."

"You want them to make a misstep," Rose accused, "to say something stupid to someone who knows about our marriage. Harriet and the Gravelys will feel like fools then.''

"Well, yes.''

"So the Gravelys do not know either.''

"As a matter of fact I sent an invitation to the Gravelys as well, though I failed to mention what event we are celebrating.''

"Do you think that was wise?''

"I thought it might get Harriet here, but I see I was wrong. Here come Lady Catherine and Cassie without my sister.''

"Perhaps it shows that Harriet has some shred of decency left," Rose said optimistically.

"Or that she is a coward.''

"Kindness costs so little," Rose repeated, smiling artificially at the Gravelys.

"I was simply practicing telling the truth. You do want me to reform, don't you?''

"Yes, my dear, but not tonight," Rose said with a laugh. "Shall we make them welcome? They have to speak to us, since they came.''

"Yes, we've trapped them there." Bennet moved forward and greeted the enemy. Lady Catherine smiled acidly. Cassie could not quite manage to wipe the resentment from her face. Rose nodded to a footman and he brought them champagne. Rose and Bennet moved on then to greet Fortney, the banker, and his wife.

"How dare she?" Cassie asked. "She is acting as if she were the mistress of the house. Mother, we must put a stop to this.''

Lady Catherine's usually smooth face was marked by creases between her eyebrows. "Something is not quite right here and I mean to find out what is going on.''

"Mother, don't leave me.''

"Go and talk to some of your friends.''

"Other than Axel I do not see that many people I know. These are all cits and politicians."

"Oh, I wash my hands of you." Lady Catherine turned on her heel and walked away, trailing her lavender demi-train on the floor.

For the first time in her life Cassie Gravely felt like an outsider. She saw Axel move toward the refreshment salon and went after him. If there was to be dancing she would need a partner, and he at least matched her dress. Her mother had warned her that scarlet was not the sort of color a girl wore but she had insisted and got her way. Now, with so many raised eyebrows, she wondered if she had not pushed fashion a bit too far with this latest creation. Her bosom was much exposed but that was true of many ladies—well perhaps not the dowdy women in attendance tonight, but at a true society function she would be a hit.

"Axel, what are you doing?" Cassie demanded when she saw him down two glasses of champagne in quick succession.

"What does it look like? I'm getting drunk. I shall have to in order to do what has been asked of me tonight."

"I need you sober. I need someone to dance with me."

"I've got no time for you. I'm going to get drunk and then I'm going to get Rose back."

Axel stalked to the sideboard and discovered a brandy decanter. He sloshed this into his wineglass and emptied it down his throat as well.

"You cannot just walk in here and claim her. Not when she is hanging on Bennet's arm."

"I have a plan," Axel said proudly. "Not your mother's plan, exactly, and not Harriet's, but my own plan. Rose will come to me. She will have no choice."

"But what about Harriet's idea of abducting her?" Cassie asked, coming to take his arm. "I thought you were to take her to your house at Epsom and hold her there."

"I want Rose to come to me because she has nowhere else to turn." He poured another draft of courage from the brandy bottle and drank it down. "Now get out of my way."

Axel did not push her, but by snatching his arm of support away so vigorously he caused Cassie to stagger into someone who stared at her and murmured an insincere apology. She found herself left in a room full of men, who were, except for an occasional raised eyebrow, ignoring her completely. It was maddening.

She went in search of her mama, who had finally worked her way around to Edith Varner, who was sitting on a sofa shooting desperate looks from side to side, in the obvious hope of a rescue. Suddenly Cassie's mother dropped her champagne glass and it shattered on the floor. She sat down limply on the sofa. What drew Cassie to her side was not so much concern as curiosity.

"Saturday morning," Edith confirmed. "It was the greatest shock to me, as you may imagine."

Cassie noticed that her mother's face was even paler than usual and her hand was thrown up to her throat as though she had drunk a glass of poison. "What is it, Mother?"

"They are married."

"Who?"

"Don't be so dense, child. Bennet and Miss Wall. They were married Saturday morning. That's why Harriet found her here. When I think of the people I told. My God, they will think me deranged."

"You gossiped about Bennet?" Edith asked.

"Married?" Cassie said in a small voice as the blood drained from her face. There was a roaring in her ears and she sat down on the sofa, nearly sitting on the lap of

Edith, who just managed to wriggle out of the way in time.

"Yes, they say it was a lovely ceremony at St. Giles's. Of course I was not well enough to go," Edith replied smugly, as though anyone cared about that.

Cassie was vaguely aware of the voices petering out, and when she opened her eyes she found Mrs. Varner peering into her face. "Are you quite well, my dear?"

Cassie saw the footman sweeping up the glass shards at her feet and thought that her life was now shattered, too. As long as her marriage to Bennet was something to look forward to in the future, life was bearable. But who would marry her now? "I am feeling a trifle light-headed."

"Here, try my vinaigrette."

Cassie sneezed and heard her mother's vicious undertone reminding her not to embarrass them by fainting. As though it were something one could control.

The couples were all waltzing now, all the brilliant silks whirling past her, interspersed with the dark evening garb of the men. There were uniforms too, splashes of scarlet, white and gold, even blue and dark green, many uniforms spinning past, but not one of them for her. As soon as the dance was over she would try to make it upstairs, failing that the front door, anywhere but here. The music stopped along with the spinning, Cassie opened her eyes but did not trust herself to stand.

The voices went on and on as though she did not exist.

"How can you bear to receive such a woman?" her mama demanded.

"I must receive her," Edith said. "She is married to my son."

"How could you let that happen after the promises you made?"

"In case you have not noticed Bennet is a grown man.

He makes his own decisions and will not take any advice from me.''

Cassie sobbed. "You promised he would offer for me."

"There was a time he almost did," Edith recalled.

"When?" Lady Catherine demanded.

"When he was recovering from his wound."

"What stopped him?" Cassie asked tearfully.

"He overheard you shredding someone's character. I do not recall whose. But he came away with a sudden disgust with you that the years and your subsequent actions have only enhanced. You lost Bennet, the pair of you, and I can only say that I am glad." With that Edith rose and left them.

Axel plunged through the doorway near the sofa with a garment draped over the end of his saber. "Miss Glen Rose Wall," he mouthed loudly. "May I have this next dance?"

Rose crossed the room to try and quiet him. "I am promised to my brother, Axel. Besides I fear you have had too much punch and would not be able to dance without treading on me."

"I wanted to return this to you," he mumbled, letting the scarlet robe slither off his saber at her feet.

"What is it? A flag?"

"You left it at my apartments."

There was a shocked gasp from the cluster of people near the door as Rose stared at the crumpled scarlet nightdress. But she did not blush. She simply smiled and said, "Don't be absurd, Axel. Scarlet? I would never wear such a color. You must have me confused with someone else."

Axel hesitated, then laughed wickedly and hoisted the gown with the tip of his saber again. "My mistake. Yours, I believe, Miss Gravely."

The sheer fabric slithered off into Cassie's lap and she screamed and pushed it to the floor as though it were a hideous animal. Axel fell flat on his face but no one paid much attention to him, for Cassie had gone into strong hysterics.

"Stanley, we need water," Rose said as she attempted to quiet the girl yet stay out of range of the kicking feet and flailing arms.

"Look out, Rose," Stanley said as he tossed a bunch of flowers out of a vase and emptied the contents over Cassie. This put a stop to the noise, for Cassie gulped like a fish for several minutes before she could be led away, weeping, by Rose's mother and Edith Varner. Rose searched about for Lady Catherine but she seemed to have melted into the floor. Rose shrugged and turned her attention to Axel, who was being shouldered out of the room by Bennet and a footman.

"Now for our dance, Stanley." Rose nodded toward the players and they struck up a waltz.

"I must say, Rose, you have not lost that knack of landing on your feet."

"When one has had as many emergencies in life as I have it is second nature. I do wish you could have prevailed upon Alice to come. She might treasure the memory of Cassie in hysterics."

"She says she is going back to Wall to let her hair grow out, and I am inclined to let her go home with Mother. I have work to do here. Besides I can stop in at Wall on my way. I will be using the Bristol house for now. I have even begun to think that it is a mistake for Mother to remove there. Alice will have no idea how to go on at Wall."

"I'm sure that will all work itself out in time. I am so glad you are going to help Bennet. He cannot be everywhere, you know, although he does try to be."

Bennet returned from loading Axel into a hackney to find that the debris had been cleared away and that the party was in full swing. After the dancing a late supper was served in the blue-and-white dining room. By then Cassie had been sent home with a housemaid. Bennet surveyed the long table as though counting his guests.

"What is it, dear?" Rose asked.

"There are two of our party missing."

"Who?"

"Magnus Dowd and Leighton."

Just then Leighton appeared in the doorway, gesticulating wildly and attracting not only Bennet's attention but that of half the guests in the room.

"Come, Stanley," Bennet said, almost leaping out of his chair.

"You're not leaving me out of this," Rose said as she scampered after the two men.

"He may be armed," Bennet warned.

"With what? His mouth?" Rose whispered.

A goodly number of the guests crowded out of the room after them so there were plenty of witnesses when Bennet threw the library door open to discover Mr. Dowd backed up against the mantel with Gaspard's sword at his throat. Three guardsmen were there as well to make the arrest official.

"Check his pocket," Gaspard said in French.

Bennet strode forward and removed the documents. "Our plans, Stanley. For shipping arms to Wellington."

There was a murmur from those guests who had crowded into the room. Dowd was sweating and not entirely from the fire that was singeing his coattails. "I was—I was looking for some paper."

"Well, you found some, didn't you?" Bennet said with a chuckle. "Paper that will land you in prison or perhaps on the gallows, depending on how far your involvement has gone."

"No! No, I had nothing to do with Napoleon's escape."

"But you did. You shipped him great trunks of books with the false bottoms full of English guineas. I wonder what you were promised. A title, perhaps?"

"No, you cannot send me to prison. I would never survive. Please!" Dowd pleaded.

"Take him away. Good work, Gaspard."

As Dowd was hauled away by the soldiers the word *traitor* spread through the crowd who began to find their way back to the dining room to report the news to the others.

"Sorry for spoiling the party, Rose," Bennet said, "But this was a matter of national security."

"After watching Axel's drunken fiasco and Cassie's tantrum, they will think nothing of seeing one of their number arrested for spying."

Leighton came up to them. "You certainly know how to entertain, Bennet. Your parties are never dull."

"But Magnus Dowd is only one man," Rose said. "If there are, as you say, other such cowards undermining the war effort, the struggle has only begun."

"But we will win in the end," Stanley vowed. "It almost makes me want to buy a pair of colors."

Rose caught her lip between her teeth in apprehension.

"I mean," Stanley explained, "if I had not more important work to do here in England."

"It does not seem quite fair," Leighton offered, "having to fight Boney twice."

"No," Bennet said. "The most Napoleon can accomplish is to weaken France's position at the peace talks, especially because he has found so much support."

"You all seem so sure we will be victorious," Rose said worriedly.

Bennet smiled at her. "No matter what anyone says, wars are not won or lost by courage or cowardice, but by economics."

Stanley stared at Bennet as he continued.

"In spite of our war debts we are in much better frame than France, whose trade has been destroyed, and most of her men, both young and middle-aged, have been used up by the army. Whereas we have resources and allies."

Leighton nodded. "This last feint of Napoleon's is only dangerous because of its boldness and quickness. If we can be ready for him…"

"That's the trick," Bennet agreed, "getting enough arms and supplies to the right place at the right time. A big undertaking, but we can do it." Bennet looked meaningfully at Stanley.

Rose noticed that the blazing anger had died out of Stanley's eyes, to be replaced by a set look of determination. "Yes, I would be better employed helping you than joining a regiment."

"Much better employed. We must be at the docks at first light."

"Then I'm for bed," Stanley said, draining his glass and coming to peck his sister on the cheek. "See you in the morning, Rosie."

"What a night," Bennet said as he lay naked between the sheets and watched Rose undress. He thought she was taking a long time over it and was inclined to get up and help her but he was tired.

"Yes, you caught a spy ring."

"Modesty prevents me from calling it a ring. There are more than a few pernicious aristocrats such as the Hollands with a fondness for Napoleon."

"And you put both Axel and the Gravelys to rout. Of course we have not got Harriet back, but Mother has finally convinced Edith to call and see if they cannot persuade her to turn her coat."

"I would as soon she never returned."

"You have not the same fondness for her as I have for Stanley."

"No, Rose, I have not. It was killed a good while ago."

"Kindness costs so little." She cast the last of her garments aside to walk boldly to the bed and lay her hot flesh beside him, stroking his manhood teasingly.

Bennet was amused at how quickly Rose had lost her shyness around him. He grasped her buttocks and slid her up on top of him. "If Harriet comes home she may stay for all I care, but I will make no overtures. She has caused too much harm for me to pretend nothing happened. Let us speak no more of her for now," he pleaded, cupping Rose's breasts in his hands.

Rose kissed him as he guided her onto his enlarged manhood. For a horsewoman she seemed very unsure of her seat and clung to his arms for support, laughing as he bounced her on top of him. She could not know that every move she made was exquisite torture for him, that those muscles trained from years of riding were exciting him beyond his wildest imaginings. He rolled Rose over and captured her whole attention with his mouth on her lips, her breasts, her whole aching body.

She had thought she was tired. No sleep last night, an entire reception got through, and it looked like no sleep again tonight. But Bennet brought her vividly, hotly awake to his need and her desires. He fit inside her now as naturally as they argued or sparred with words. He knew, as always, what she wanted, and it was the same goal as his, to be entwined together for as long as possible before they reached the heights, and then to sleep in each other's arms. Would she sleep, or lie awake watching him sleep? She was in love with every breath he took and studied him the night through. There would be time enough to sleep in the morning when Bennet was at the office. When he would sleep she did not bother to wonder. He would manage somehow as he managed everything else.

Chapter Fourteen

Rose did not see how Bennet could have awoken and dressed without rousing her but he was gone in the morning and she felt restless. She put on her green riding habit and sent Cynthie to tell Martin they would take the horses out this morning. It was earlier than their usual hour to ride but she must do something. Bennet and Stanley would simply have to let her help with the preparations. She could not be frivolously playing while others worked at such a desperate project. But for this one morning she was inclined to wallow in her success. The day was crisp and clear. The sun lay as bright on the cobblestones as her future lay before her. Three days ago she would not have thought it could all turn out so well.

Rose and Martin had cantered nearly through Hyde park and had seen no other riders. The horses were frisky with the cold and ready for a real gallop. The sound of hoofbeats behind them surprised Rose. She did not think Bennet would have found time today. Rose glanced around and the smile froze on her lips, for it was Axel and another soldier on very fresh horses.

"Martin! It's Axel! Split up and ride to Varner House as fast as you can. Get help." It was the presence of the other soldier, more than Axel's grim face, that frightened Rose. She might have dealt with Axel alone, but since he had brought reinforcements he meant mischief.

When it became clear they could not outrun the men Martin halted Bright Valor and drew his pistol instead. Axel fired and the boy tumbled off the horse, which pulled away, but stood there uncertainly, not knowing what to make of this new development.

Rose threw herself from Gallant's back and bent over Martin, locating the wound high on his shoulder by the growing bloodstain on his black coat. His eyes fluttered open. "Listen Martin. The only way you can save me is by pretending to be unconscious." She had her handkerchief bound round the wound by the time Axel dismounted and grabbed her, forcing her to her feet. "Wait, I will go with you if you let Martin be."

"You are in no place to make conditions," he said as he snatched up Martin's pistol and pointed it at the boy's head.

"Then I will scream and you will have to kill me. Or I will walk away with you if you leave Martin here to be found."

"I don't want him anyway. Walk toward that carriage in the trees, and not one squeak from you."

"What about these horses?" the other soldier asked, sidling his mount up to reach for Gallant's reins.

"Leave them," Rose said. "They will go home."

"That one is your favorite, isn't it?" Axel pointed the pistol at Gallant's noble head.

Rose lunged in Axel's grasp, throwing his aim off. This second pistol report sent Gallant bucking and careening toward Varner House, so Bright Valor followed him at a trot, holding his head up to keep from stepping on the dragging reins.

Rose said nothing, for Axel might still murder Martin

if she detained him. She picked up the tail of her riding habit and walked resolutely toward the carriage, noting the lone driver. Unless the place they were taking her had more servants, there were only three of them. Only three! What was she thinking? She might overpower one man, but never three. What did one do when outnumbered? she wondered. One waited for reinforcements. One bluffed and delayed and used her wits. Above all, one did not panic. She opened the door to the coach and climbed in without assistance.

Axel got in beside her and the soldier rode alongside the window, leading Axel's horse. "My servant will shield any early-morning risers from your screams."

"Come now, Axel. Have you ever known me to scream?"

"Once I did, when Bennet Varner was hanging by one hand off the edge of my roof. That made you scream. And I think there was one other time. Do you remember it?"

She looked at him, a man who would do murder, rape or shoot a beautiful horse just because she liked it, and she knew she had to be very careful how she answered him. "Yes, I remember it well. I screamed when you and father were fighting over my maid as though she were some spoil of war."

"You did not just scream. You tried to murder me."

"You do not even remember what happened. You were knocked senseless for days by the stallion."

"That was no horse that hit me over the head. It was you."

He took her face in one hand and she wasn't sure how best to make him disgusted with her, but she had to try something. "Yes, I did scream 'Axel, no!' just before I tried to kill you with that shovel. My luck I did not grab an ax instead."

"You always were the bloodthirsty one," he said with a wicked chuckle. "If I mistake not, you did in your own father."

"My father was trampled to death by Redditch," she said, looking away from him at the curtained window.

"He was not trampled by any horse, not a horse over which you had complete control. You killed him and put the blame on the animal."

Rose thought that if she insisted it was an accident she might lead Axel to suspect Martin of dispatching her father, and that was not a direction in which she wanted his thoughts to go. "Very well, he was a brute and I killed him. Now Mother doesn't have to be afraid anymore."

He reached down and pulled her skirt up to the top of her boot. Her breath hissed at the coldness of his touch, but other than that she did not respond. "Where is it?" he demanded.

"What?"

"That knife you carry in your stocking."

"Suddenly so cautious?" she asked callously. "You were rather careless last night. Do you remember what you did?" Rose bent down and slowly withdrew the boot dirk from its scabbard and handed it to him, hilt first.

"Not perfectly."

"You as good as called Cassie Gravely your mistress."

"What of that? She is."

Rose turned her head to stare at him, her lips parted in surprise.

"Finally after all these years I have shocked you," Axel said with satisfaction.

"But Cassie and her mother. They are pillars of society."

"Pillar is a good word to describe Lady Cat. She does not lose that stonelike aspect even in bed."

"You are joking."

"Why would I lie about them?"

"But you were going to marry Harriet, and they are her intimates."

"Yes, that was the plan, after I completely disgraced you. But the more I thought of it, the less I liked it. I wasn't sure I wanted my wife forever conspiring with those two."

"Harriet knows what you are doing?"

"Lord, Rosie, it was Harriet's idea. What's the matter? Don't you believe me?"

"Unfortunately, I do."

"Then I got to thinking, what do I need with such a cold fish as Harriet, if I can have you?"

Rose bit her lip and stared at the leather curtains again. She thought for a long time about whether to tell him she was already married or not. She finally decided against it. The news would not save her and would only mean Axel would go after Bennet later. Bennet. Would he know where to look for her? They were heading south, perhaps toward Axel's place near Epsom. Axel might have a long lead, but Bennet had better horses. If only Martin had survived it would be worth anything that happened to her to have carried Axel away.

"Is it true?" Axel asked suddenly, breaking in on her reverie.

"Is what true?"

"Have you really married Bennet Varner as Harriet says?"

Rose glanced at him, schooling her expression to show no fear. "Yes, what choice had I? My reputation was ruined. Being a gentleman, Bennet convinced me marriage to him was my only alternative."

"And you listened to him," Axel said gruffly, some meanness glinting deep in his brown eyes.

Rose sighed artificially and said, "After that hideous

letter the girls sent to my mother I felt I had to do something. And as neither Bennet nor I particularly cares about anyone else I saw no impediment—"

"What letter?"

"Ah, they do not tell you everything, do they? They sent a fictitious catalog of my transgressions to Wall. The wedding was the only thing that could stop Mother from worrying herself sick."

He snorted a derisive laugh. "That has the feel of Lady Cat about it, though Harriet is such an apt pupil...."

"You do not mean to marry Harriet, then?"

"I am here with you now, am I not?" He ran his hand along the wool cloth covering her thigh and she schooled herself not to cringe.

"I am glad you had nothing to do with that letter. I always knew you for a passionate fool. I would not like to think you an absolute villain."

"Not this time, at any rate. There's a deal of irony at play here. Lord, it would make a drama if anyone cared to write it."

"Yes. Cassie thought to drive me from town so she could have Bennet. She should have guessed he would do the honorable thing. Isn't it ironic that the same sort of gossip you used five years ago to revenge yourself on me has now put me beyond your reach?"

"If I cared anything about vows. You are not beyond my reach by any means. You are right here."

So saying he took her in his arms, and sought her mouth. Her gasp of disgust he must have interpreted as surprise, for he made no comment after the kiss, but continued to hold her, staring at her in a puzzled way.

"What are you thinking?" he asked. "I never know."

"We seem to be destined to be together," Rose replied, "the two outcasts."

"You should have accepted my offer of marriage. Now I won't be so gentle."

"You were never gentle, Axel. I don't expect it of you."

He grabbed her shoulders and forced his mouth over hers in another disgusting travesty of a kiss, then had the nerve to look at her to assess its effect.

Rose gasped for air. "Where did you get brandy so early in the morning?"

"Sweet Harriet gave it to me."

"Don't be absurd. The Gravelys would never receive you after what you did last night."

"Harriet came to me at my lodgings this morning to make sure I was awake enough to meet you. Lady Cat told her about your marriage. I did warn you that these morning rides are dangerous."

"I don't believe you. Harriet could never be so…so lost to all sense of propriety."

"Propriety? It's a bit late for any of you to worry about propriety. I've decided I like my plan better than any of theirs. Lady Cat's idea was to kill you and throw you in the Thames."

Axel released her finally and she staightened her habit. "Not very original of her."

"You are a cold-blooded little wretch. This is your life we are speaking of."

"If you really intended to kill me you would have done so when I broke our engagement. You might shoot my horse, but you won't kill me because then you lose control of me…and my money. Did you know it all goes to Stanley if anything happens to me? There is no husband mentioned in my will."

"Well, we shall have to take care of that, at our leisure, of course."

"My money is mine to do with as I will. You cannot get it unless I give it to you."

"Is that why you think I took you?"

Axel's eyes burned with avarice, but the way his gaze raked Rose's body she believed him when he said it was not for money. "You did it to please Harriet, who, in her misguided way, thinks this will matter to me."

"I took you for myself and for revenge. I have never lost a woman to Bennet Varner yet. You may be his wife, but before the night is out you will be my mistress, willingly or not."

Rose reached up to push the blind aside, feeling Axel's hot gaze observing her closely. They had left town and were driving now past snow-sprinkled fields and walls, and coppiced hedgerows, grotesque under caps of white. She had been wrong about spring coming. She let the curtain fall shut again, knowing there was no help to be had from anyone unless Martin could get back to Varner House. She tried to remember how bad his wound was. If Martin died she would most definitely feel no compunction about putting a period to Axel's existence. Firing at an armed man was the reaction of a soldier, but doing so in Hyde Park was the instinct of an animal, a very dangerous animal.

"Where do you stand with your regiment now that Napoleon needs trouncing again?" she asked suddenly. "Will you be recalled?"

"I have been already. I leave from Portsmouth within the week."

"I shall go with you. I have been promised Europe and I mean to see it."

"Even if there is a war on?" He looked at her almost with admiration.

"Better yet. No stupid conventions to worry about flouting."

"I rather hate to take a beauty of your caliber with an army train. Anything might happen to you."

"Anything won't. If I have kept you at arm's length this long I do not imagine the rest of the army will be much of a bother."

Axel laughed harshly. "I wish I believed you cared for me."

Rose looked surprised. "But I don't, not any more than you care for me. That's what makes our relationship so perfect."

"So perfectly hellish. You ruined me."

"You ruined me. Now we're even."

"You are the most exasperating woman. I have the feeling that I would never win an argument with you even if I held a pistol to your head."

"Yes, Axel," Rose chanted tiredly. "Now hand me that rug. If I am going to be worth anything at all when we reach our destination I must have some sleep."

Axel grabbed the traveling rug and threw it over her impatiently. He even let her curl up in the corner of the coach. Just for safety's sake, though, he retreated to the opposite corner.

Damn, Rose thought. No chance to steal the pistol or the knife back if he should fall asleep as well. Rose tried to gauge the amount of time they had been on the road. She pretended to sleep but always when she lifted her eyelids, Axel sat in the corner gazing at her and smiling like a cat toying with a mouse. After at least another hour of this the carriage lurched so violently Rose was almost thrown to the floor. Axel caught her in his arms.

"Where the devil did you find that driver?" she complained.

"He's an army muleteer," Axel said, righting her on the seat. "You will encounter roads much worse than this in France or Belgium."

"Yes, but I will be on horseback then, and better able to see the ruts. I have been thinking I should send for some better horses than the ones you have. Can we afford to wait for them?"

He stared at her, thought about it, then shook his head no. "We will need money, though."

"That is no problem. Stanley and I had already made arrangements for transfers of funds to Europe. So long as the banking houses are still operating at Paris, Venice or Brussels…"

He nodded his head in the affirmative.

"Then we shall have all we need. Are we on our way to Portsmouth?"

"No, Epsom. We are nearly there."

The coach skidded to a halt, which threw Rose onto his lap again. "Axel, I can drive better than that maniac."

Axel laughed, set her to rights again, then jumped out of the coach to help her down. A wan sky showed her what decades of neglect can do to a small country house. He took her arm and led her inside.

"Your banister is dustier than your yard," Rose said, running her fingers along it as she tramped up the wooden stairs. She shook the dust from her hand. "Don't you have a housekeeper?"

"There's an old crone who cooks, but she's deaf, which suits my purposes."

He followed after Rose and pushed open a door at the head of the landing.

"I suppose there's no point in cleaning now if we are going to be leaving," Rose decided, looking at the dust-webbed ceiling of the hall. "But I will need some traveling clothes."

He pushed her into the bedroom suite and wrenched open a wardrobe. "Everything you require should be in there."

Rose went to the cabinet and pulled out one scarlet-colored dressing gown. "Just on a hunch I would say they are Cassie's."

"They are worn by whomever I bring here."

"I see, well, that will have to stop. And I need some hot water and—"

"Will you listen to yourself?" he demanded. "You are in my power, my prisoner. I am the one who is giving the orders."

"Then order me some hot water. You have servants. They should do some work." Rose busied herself searching through the gowns for one a bit less shocking.

"Ahhhrg," Axel growled, clutching his hair. He went out the door grumbling and locked it from the outside.

"And bring some wine or brandy, whatever you can find," she shouted through the panel. As soon as she heard him thump down the stairs, mumbling, she pushed a chair back under the door latch, then made a thorough search of the room. It yielded little: a pair of hair scissors, which she secreted in her boot scabbard, two rusty sabers, which she removed from their plaque over the mantel and an old horse pistol, empty. Frantically she searched for powder and shot. They finally turned up in the very last drawer she flung open. She knelt on the carpet, desperately loading the weapon, yet trying to be careful to do it right. The pistol also was rusty with disuse but the flint was good. It might just fire.

Three of them, plus the deaf cook and only one uncertain shot. Perhaps if she could wound Axel, she might be able to bully the other men into letting her go. She had noticed the other soldier had a bandaged head. Probably he was the batman Bennet knocked out at Axel's lodgings when he rescued Gaspard. The driver looked stupid. Yes, Axel was the one to fire at. Leaderless, the others might be capable of being bribed.

She heard the door being unlocked and suddenly knew she would not be able to shoot even Axel. She ran to the window and flung it open. The driver was posted in the yard and jumped to attention at the unexpected noise. But she saw a heavy traveling carriage on the main road. She grabbed the scarlet coverlet off the bed and shook it vigorously outside the window as any good housewife would, then she closed it with the blanket hanging in the sash like a pennant.

"Rose, damn you. What have you got against this door?" Axel demanded.

"I wouldn't want to make things too easy for you," she said. "If this is an abduction, you should have to work for your reward."

"I'll wring your pretty neck if you do not let me in now."

One in the yard, Axel on the stairs. Where was the other man?

She was answered when the burly soldier heaved the door open and let Axel in. Axel snatched the bottle off the tray as he let the can of water crash to the floor. "You really should not have done that," he said as he removed the cork. He took a long drink from the bottle and wiped his hand across the back of his mouth. Apparently confronting a woman with a pistol in one hand and two sabers in the other was no deterrent. He began to advance on her just as there was an exchange of shots in the yard. Running steps on the stairs heralded the arrival of the driver.

"How many?" Axel demanded.

"Two and a groom."

Rose and her small arsenal were all but forgotten in the efforts of the three men to barricade the door again and reload all their weapons. More footsteps, then both Bennet and Stanley shouted to her as they heaved against the solid oak of the door.

"I'm all right!" she shouted back from the other side of the bed. Rose aimed her pistol at Axel.

"I've got a gun to her head," Axel lied.

"No, I have a gun to his," Rose replied, causing a dead silence from the other side of the door. Finally the heaving renewed.

"On my signal, let them in," Axel commanded the soldier and the muleteer.

"It's a trap," Rose shouted as Bennet and Stanley plunged through the door. Five weapons were set off in short order with amazingly no one taking a hit that Rose could see, but there was so much powder smoke she could scarcely tell one man from another as they wrestled in hand-to-hand combat. Stanley was playing at fisticuffs with the soldier while the driver held Bennet down and Axel beat him with his fists. Rose brought the pistol to the soldier's head and he ceased struggling. She tossed the sabers to Stanley, who waded into the fray and managed to arm Bennet and get him to his feet. The muleteer grabbed his empty rifle to hold off Stanley with the bayonet and Axel drew his own military saber to have at Bennet. Under such an onslaught the blade of the older weapon was soon broken and Bennet had to resort to pushing the chair around in front of him to keep Axel at bay.

The soldier glared at Rose. "What is to keep me from taking that pistol away from ye?"

"A bullet through your brain. What sort of allegiance do you owe Axel anyway?"

The man bit his lip. "Let me go and I'll not help him."

"I prefer to make sure the odds stay even."

"When Axel kills him—"

"I shoot Axel," she replied. "If Axel loses, I'll let you go. Either way you live so long as you hold still."

The logic was overwhelmingly simple and the man froze again.

The chair was quickly disemboweled and its frame carved to flinders with the bed Bennet leaped on soon to follow.

"Rose, shoot Axel," Bennet yelled, his saber by now a worthless hilt.

"Where?" Rose yelled.

"Anywhere."

"Face the wall," she demanded, and got compliance from the soldier. "There will be a knife in your spine if you so much as move." Rose pressed the scissors into his back.

Bennet was backed against the headboard with feathers everywhere and not so much as a pillow sham to defend himself with. Rose swung the pistol toward Axel's rump, but he laughed at her triumphantly. "That pistol hasn't fired in years." He raised his saber for the death stroke as she pulled the trigger. The hammer snapped down and she froze when nothing happened. Axel was still laughing when Bennet kicked his feet from under him. The powder hissed in the pan and the gun finally went off. Axel fell on top of Bennet.

"You can run now," Rose said to the soldier, who leaped for the window and was through it, disregarding the one-story drop.

"What shall I do with this one?" Stanley asked of the muleteer he had pinned to the floor.

"Let him go and help me," Bennet demanded in a muffled voice.

The muleteer ran from the room as Rose and Stanley rescued Bennet from Axel's limp weight.

"Is he dead?" Rose asked apprehensively. She grabbed the scarlet dressing gown and began shredding it for bandages.

"No, just surprised," Bennet said. "Or he will be when he wakes up. You caught him a grazing shot to the head. There's a lot of blood, but he should be fine."

"Bennet, you're hurt." Rose's hands frantically searched his body for the wound.

"No, I think this is all Axel's blood. Let's bandage him up. Is there anyone else about the place?"

"Just his deaf cook. Are you sure you are not hurt?"

"Not a scratch," Bennet said. "Stanley, what about you?"

"A gash on the arm where the bayonet caught me."

"Oh, Stanley." Rose bandaged and crooned over her brother's wound while Bennet tied a serviceable strip of cloth around Axel's head. Footsteps trudged up the stairs and they all leaped behind the door until they discovered it was only the cook. She shook her head, tsking over the mess, and when she saw the disheveled trio said, "I suppose you'll be wanting dinner now."

"We would not think of troubling you," Bennet mouthed. He plunked some gold coins into the grimy hands and shouted, "Get him a doctor," as they gathered up their pistols and pelted down the stairs.

"It took you long enough," Stilton said as they piled into the open carriage. "You cannot run this team like that and then leave them standing. I have been walking them, of course, but that is not a proper cooling down."

"Stilton," Rose said. "How is Martin?"

"He'll be fine. Lost a lot of claret, but young lads have such hot blood anyway."

"Well, Stilton," Bennet said. "If they're too tired for the return trip, we'll have to stable them and hire some job horses."

"I never said they were tired." Stilton grumbled as he turned the carriage, and Stanley crawled up on the seat beside the groom to give the lovers some privacy.

"I am a lucky man to have married such a good shot," Bennet said, "moreover, a woman who can keep her head."

"Axel was right about that pistol. It had not been used in years."

"Fortunate that you knew to wait."

"Fortunate that it went off at all. You're not going to have him arrested this time either, are you?"

"Rose! How could I? Think of the scandal."

Rose opened her mouth to rant at him, but found herself laughing instead. Even this was soon stopped with a long, lingering kiss that warmed her as nothing else could. She had waited for Bennet and he had come through in the end. Even better, her brother had shown himself a valiant man, as much a hero as Bennet. And with that arm wound there was absolutely no chance Stanley could be seduced into the army. Rose halted her kisses long enough to inspect Bennet's split lip and swelling eye.

Bennet stilled her hand with his. "If you say one word about leeches I will make love to you right here in the carriage. I earned these wounds valiantly and I would like to get credit for them."

"No more leeches," Rose said. "Of any kind."

Harriet was unused to traveling without a maid. The girl who had been waiting on her at the Gravelys' house refused to come when Harriet ordered a trunk be packed for a fast trip into the country. No matter. The fewer people who knew she had anything to do with the Wall woman's abduction the better. By now, Rose was tied up at Axel's house in Epsom, awaiting her fate. Just what that was to be, Harriet had not quite decided. Perhaps they would hold her until Bennet realized Rose had absconded with Axel. But Harriet had to see her to make victory complete. She wanted to witness Rose helpless and friendless, begging for mercy.

The house was quiet with only a few windows lit when the hired carriage stopped in the weedy drive. One of the postboys flung down her trunk, and since Axel did not come out to meet her, she paid them off herself.

There was another reason she had come. Harriet was afraid Axel, left to his own devices, might enjoy himself with Rose, and that was a pleasure she wished to keep for herself. She had promised to marry Axel if he would perform this errand for her. Now she would give herself to him. Her body throbbed with the thought of how he would take her. With Rose crying in the basement they would make wild, passionate love, and Axel would be hers. Leaving the trunk on the drive she knocked on the door, then tried the latch and entered. A single candle stood on the hall table and she took it up. There was no one crying or begging for mercy. Heavens, had he had her already? She hastened up the stairs and went into the open door.

She gasped when she saw Axel sitting on the mangled bed, a bloody bandage wound round his head. "I knew you would come," he said, rising slowly and walking around her to kick the door shut. "I knew you would not be able to stay away."

"Where is she?" Harriet demanded.

"We can talk about that later. For now, I want my reward."

"I am yours," Harriet said, throwing off her cloak.

"Bennet, you are hurt," Rose said as she pulled off his torn shirt in the privacy of their bedchamber. "Look at all these cuts and bruises."

"For once I feel I deserve you, having actually rescued you instead of the other way around. What do you think of your unemployed Galahad now?'' He sat tiredly on the edge of the bed.

"As always, I am lost in admiration." She wet a cloth in the basin and began to wash his chest. "But what will you tell people about your face?"

"That you got a bit rowdy in bed."

Rose smiled and took his head to her breast to hold him. "I'm so glad you came in time."

"Me, too. Finding Axel's corpse, drawn and quartered, would have been hard to explain to the authorities."

Rose laughed again. "You trusted me to handle him. But I confess I have always been afraid of Axel."

"But you are smart enough not to show it."

"I only knew Martin and Stanley as boys. I actually used to think all grown men were beasts, until I met you." She took a towel and carefully dried him so as not to hurt him.

Bennet looked up at her. "Rose, you have been unfortunate enough to have known the worst of men just as I have known the worst of women. I venture to think we have finally changed each other's expectations about the opposite sex."

"You have changed my expectations about everything."

"What about you?" Bennet asked as she stepped out of her bloodied and mutilated riding habit. "Axel did not hurt you?"

"He worried me."

"I'm sorry for that."

"Not about myself. He said that you could never have a woman he could not take away from you."

Bennet was silent as he watched Rose disrobe. "That is why I vowed never to marry. After Trudy and April, then Robin, I was afraid to put another woman at peril."

"You never knew he followed us on our rides?" Her boots thudded to the floor.

"Not until you told me. What an obsessed fellow. But it's over now. He will marry Harriet if he knows what's good for him. Besides, his regiment has been called up."

"I cannot understand why Harriet would want him. I did warn her what Axel is like."

Rose walked naked to the bed. Bennet put his arms around her and held her to him. "You must understand not all women are like you. They cannot enjoy kissing a man. They must be kissed. They cannot make love. They must be made love to."

"You mean they want to be victims?" Rose asked, running her hands through Bennet's hair. "Axel said some such thing to me once, but I could not credit it."

"For Harriet or Cassie, being a victim is easier than being courageous. They can always blame someone else, their lover or husband. Nothing is their fault."

"But it is their fault," Rose insisted.

"Even if they do not realize it?" he asked as he slid into bed and made room for Rose.

"They lie to themselves."

"Rather skillfully, I might add." Bennet began kissing her in that intoxicating way that made her whole body throb with desire.

"So there is no way to save Harriet from Axel," she mused.

"No more than Harriet can save Axel from himself. We must each find our own salvation."

"Or at least live with the consequences of our choices."

"I imagine Harriet and Axel will be too occupied with each other to be much of a problem for us in future."

"But not happy," Rose concluded.

"In their own way, they will be happy. There are people who enjoy discord, fighting, torturing each other. At least once they are married, Axel will let us alone.''

''You are an optimist, Bennet. It is very nearly your only flaw.''

Rose kissed him again, then lay still and held him, not at all surprised when he fell asleep. She watched over him, savoring this privacy as a secondary joy to their love-making and waiting for the morning when Bennet would be rested.

Epilogue

They were having afternoon tea, just the two of them, in the gold salon. A plate of scones made their joy complete. Stanley had been dispatched to Bristol on the mail coach. Alice, Maryanne and Edith were making the trip to Wall in Bennet's plush traveling carriage.

"I am surprised your mother wished to visit Wall at the height of the season," Rose said, wandering to the window to watch the afternoon sun warm the bricks of the houses across South Audley Street.

Bennet looked up from his perusal of the *Times*. "Just lying low for a bit. Did I tell you Gaspard managed to convince Dowd to confess?"

"Really? How?"

"By recounting his experiences in the Bastille. Some of them sounded a great deal worse in French than English."

"Did Dowd implicate anyone else?"

"Only one person. Dowd had been engaging in a secret correspondence with Bonaparte via this intermediary."

Rose stared at him. "Who?"

"Someone totally above suspicion because of her social position and her lack of interest in matters military."

"Lady Catherine," Rose said, clapping her teacup into her saucer with finality.

Bennet cast a pleased smile upon her. "Correct, my dear."

"So that was the connection, what she had on Dowd. But will she be arrested?"

"If they could find her." Bennet cast the paper aside and crossed his booted legs. "Cassie is staying with some distant cousin in Highmarket, but she has no idea where her mama has got to."

Rose glanced out the window to see Harriet marching up the steps to Varner House with her reticule clutched tightly between her hands. "Bennet, Harriet is coming."

"Oh bother."

As they waited Rose reflected on how strangely Harriet's position and hers had been reversed.

"Lady Foy to see you, Mr. and Mrs. Varner," Hardy said, a smile tickling the corners of his normally impassive mouth.

"Show her in." Rose got up and went to take Harriet by the hand. "So, you have married Axel. We got your letter this morning."

"Yes, I accepted his offer. We were married yesterday. His regiment leaves for Belgium by midweek."

"Is he...well enough?" Rose asked as she led Harriet to a chair.

Harriet stared at Rose belligerently as the new mistress of Varner House handed her a cup of tea. "No thanks to you."

"Axel is a big boy," Bennet said, "He should know better than to go about abducting other men's wives."

"Will you have him arrested?" Harriet asked.

"It's a tempting thought," Bennet said, helping himself to another scone, "but compared to unleashing him on Napoleon..."

"You must know that if you bring charges against Axel, Rose's character may be compromised."

"Only if Axel lies through his teeth," Bennet said with a grin that made his injured lip ache.

"Abducting Rose was my idea," Harriet said, then clamped her mouth shut.

Bennet glanced at Rose, who did not even blink. So she had known all along, he thought.

"I have stopped asking myself why you hate me," Rose said.

Harriet gave her a cold look and turned her gaze to Bennet. "If you want to see your own sister in prison..."

"That, too, is a tempting thought," Bennet said, rubbing his sore eye.

"You wouldn't dare," Harriet chided.

"But compared to unleashing you both on Napoleon..." Bennet got up and wandered toward the fireplace where they had not even bothered to start a fire. The spring breeze was licking warm and fresh through the window.

"What are you talking about?" Harriet demanded. "Of course, I am not going to Belgium."

"What are you going to do?" Bennet asked, folding his arms and leaning on the mantel.

"I thought I might as well stay here until the war is over."

"Here?" Bennet demanded. "And I thought Axel had cheek. You very nearly get four people killed, five if you count Axel as a person, and we're supposed to welcome you back with loving arms? No, Harriet. We will meet you politely on social occasions, you may come to tea, but that is the extent of it."

"I must live somewhere. That disgusting house at Epsom is uninhabitable."

"What about Axel's estate in Yorkshire?" Rose asked.

"We will have to go there when the war is over, but I require a house in London."

"Well, I suppose it would be just as convenient for Stanley to stay here and let you have Change House," Bennet remarked.

"That—very well. I'll have my things moved from the hotel."

"But you haven't even inquired about the rent yet?" Bennet taunted.

"Rent? You would charge your own sister rent?"

"Sister, I have come to the conclusion that you are the one who was adopted from a foundling hospital. You are no longer my sister as far as I am concerned."

"Very well, then. Fifty pounds a month," Harriet said with decision and stood. "It's not worth a penny more. Good day to you."

When Harriet had left, Rose came to embrace Bennet. "You were very...firm."

"No more lectures on kindness costing so little?"

"I know you have said she has chosen her own fate, but I still feel uneasy about her marrying Axel."

"Face it, Rose. They deserve each other. Now, back to work. You and I have armies to feed and clothe, ships to lease, grain to buy."

"Yes, we will be very busy for the next month or so, perhaps even the next year or so," Rose said as she stood watching Harriet walk down the street. In point of fact she did not understand women, most of them, nearly so well as she understood men. Even Axel, if he could be considered a man, was no real puzzle to her, and Stanley was now an open book. Bennet was like the other half of herself, that missing piece of her life she had been seeking. But Harriet and women like her, Rose would never understand. Harriet Varner had thrown away everything. She would live on the fringes of society now rather than at its center, and would for a good part of the year be exiled to the ruined house in Yorkshire, where the weather was so unkind to one's hair and complexion.

Bennet thought they were safe now, but Rose knew Axel well enough to know that was not so. They were safe only so long as Axel was out of the country, but if he survived the army again, Rose would always keep a pistol or knife handy just in case. Not a dull marriage by any means. Why did the prospect of a lifelong danger not daunt her more? When she thought about her adventures with Bennet, the rescue at Axel's lodgings and the desperate fight at Epsom, she knew she and Bennet were equal to anything so long as they remained together. Danger was what she was used to, and Axel would add that element of spice to an otherwise idyllic existence.

"Happy, Rose?" Bennet asked, turning her face up to look at him.

"Happier than any woman on earth so long as I have you."

He kissed her, and she knew they would always be together, keeping each other safe through the long sunny days and velvety dark nights.

*   *   *   *   *

Don't miss these Harlequin favorites by some of our bestselling authors!

HT#25721	THE ONLY MAN IN WYOMING	$3.50 U.S. ☐
	by Kristine Rolofson	$3.99 CAN. ☐
HP#11869	WICKED CAPRICE	$3.50 U.S. ☐
	by Anne Mather	$3.99 CAN. ☐
HR#03438	ACCIDENTAL WIFE	$3.25 U.S. ☐
	by Day Leclaire	$3.75 CAN. ☐
HS#70737	STRANGERS WHEN WE MEET	$3.99 U.S. ☐
	by Rebecca Winters	$4.50 CAN. ☐
HI#22405	HERO FOR HIRE	$3.75 U.S. ☐
	by Laura Kenner	$4.25 CAN. ☐
HAR#16673	ONE HOT COWBOY	$3.75 U.S. ☐
	by Cathy Gillen Thacker	$4.25 CAN. ☐
HH#28952	JADE	$4.99 U.S. ☐
	by Ruth Langan	$5.50 CAN. ☐
LL#44005	STUCK WITH YOU	$3.50 U.S. ☐
	by Vicki Lewis Thompson	$3.99 CAN. ☐

(limited quantities available on certain titles)

AMOUNT	$ _____
POSTAGE & HANDLING	$ _____
($1.00 for one book, 50¢ for each additional)	
APPLICABLE TAXES*	$ _____
TOTAL PAYABLE	$ _____
(check or money order—please do not send cash)	

To order, complete this form and send it, along with a check or money order for the total above, payable to Harlequin Books, to: **In the U.S.:** 3010 Walden Avenue, P.O. Box 9047, Buffalo, NY 14269-9047; **In Canada:** P.O. Box 613, Fort Erie, Ontario, L2A 5X3.

Name: _____

Address: _____ City: _____

State/Prov.: _____ Zip/Postal Code: _____

Account Number (if applicable): _____

*New York residents remit applicable sales taxes.
Canadian residents remit applicable GST and provincial taxes.

Look us up on-line at: http://www.romance.net

HBLAJ98

HARLEQUIN ULTIMATE GUIDES™

A series of how-to books for today's woman.

Act now to order some of these extremely
helpful guides just for you!

*Whatever the situation, Harlequin Ultimate Guides™
has all the answers!*

#80507	HOW TO TALK TO A	$4.99 U.S. ☐
	NAKED MAN	$5.50 CAN. ☐
#80508	I CAN FIX THAT	$5.99 U.S. ☐
		$6.99 CAN. ☐
#80510	WHAT YOUR TRAVEL AGENT	$5.99 U.S. ☐
	KNOWS THAT YOU DON'T	$6.99 CAN. ☐
#80511	RISING TO THE OCCASION	
	More Than Manners: Real Life	$5.99 U.S. ☐
	Etiquette for Today's Woman	$6.99 CAN. ☐
#80513	WHAT GREAT CHEFS	$5.99 U.S. ☐
	KNOW THAT YOU DON'T	$6.99 CAN. ☐
#80514	WHAT SAVVY INVESTORS	$5.99 U.S. ☐
	KNOW THAT YOU DON'T	$6.99 CAN. ☐
#80509	GET WHAT YOU WANT OUT OF	$5.99 U.S. ☐
	LIFE—AND KEEP IT!	$6.99 CAN. ☐

(quantities may be limited on some titles)

TOTAL AMOUNT	$
POSTAGE & HANDLING	$
($1.00 for one book, 50¢ for each additional)	
APPLICABLE TAXES*	$ _____
TOTAL PAYABLE	$ _____
(check or money order—please do not send cash)	

To order, complete this form and send it, along with a check or money
order for the total above, payable to Harlequin Ultimate Guides, to:
In the U.S.: 3010 Walden Avenue, P.O. Box 9047, Buffalo, NY
14269-9047; **In Canada:** P.O. Box 613, Fort Erie, Ontario, L2A 5X3.

Name: _____

Address: _____ City: _____

State/Prov.: _____ Zip/Postal Code: _____

*New York residents remit applicable sales taxes.
Canadian residents remit applicable GST and provincial taxes.

◆ HARLEQUIN®

Look us up on-line at: http://www.romance.net

HNFBL4

MEN at WORK

All work and no play? Not these men!

April 1998

KNIGHT SPARKS by Mary Lynn Baxter

Sexy lawman Rance Knight made a career of arresting the bad guys. Somehow, though, he thought policewoman Carly Mitchum was framed. Once they'd uncovered the truth, could Rance let Carly go...or would he make a citizen's arrest?

MEN
IN
UNIFORM

May 1998

HOODWINKED by Diana Palmer

CEO Jake Edwards donned coveralls and went undercover as a mechanic to find the saboteur in his company. Nothing— or no one—would distract him, not even beautiful secretary Maureen Harris. Jake had to catch the thief—*and* the woman who'd stolen his heart!

MEN of STEEL

June 1998

DEFYING GRAVITY by Rachel Lee

Tim O'Shaughnessy and his business partner, Liz Pennington, had always been close—but never *this* close. As the danger of their assignment escalated, so did their passion. When the job was over, could they ever go back to business as usual?

TALL, DARK AND SMART
E=MC

MEN AT WORK™

Available at your favorite retail outlet!

 HARLEQUIN®   Silhouette®

Look us up on-line at: http://www.romance.net   PMAW1

From the high seas to the
Scottish Highlands,
when a man of action
meets a woman of spirit
a battle of wills—
and love—ensues!

Ransomed Brides

This June, bestselling authors Patricia Potter and
Ruth Langan will captivate your imagination with this
swashbuckling collection. Find out how two men of action
are ultimately tamed by two feisty women who prove
to be *more* than their match in love and war!

SAMARA by Patricia Potter

HIGHLAND BARBARIAN
by Ruth Langan

Available wherever Harlequin and Silhouette
books are sold.

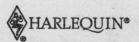

HARLEQUIN®   Silhouette®

Look us up on-line at: http://www.romance.net   HREQ698

Looking For More Romance?

Visit Romance.net

Look us up on-line at: http://www.romance.net

Check in daily for these and other exciting features:

Hot off the press — View all current titles, and purchase them on-line.

What do the stars have in store for you?

Horoscope

Hot deals — Exclusive offers available only at Romance.net

Plus, don't miss our interactive quizzes, contests and bonus gifts.

PWEB

COMING NEXT MONTH FROM

HARLEQUIN HISTORICALS

- **MIDSUMMER'S KNIGHT**
  by **Tori Phillips,** author of SILENT KNIGHT
  Betrothed against their will, a confirmed bachelor and a free-spirited widow try to hide from one another, only to discover that they are soul mates.
  HH #415 ISBN# 29015-2 $4.99 U.S./$5.99 CAN.

- **RUNAWAY**
  by **Carolyn Davidson,** author of THE FOREVER MAN
  The bearer of a dark secret, a beautiful fugitive finds love in the arms of an honest cowboy. But will their love survive the terrible truth?
  HH #416 ISBN# 29016-0 $4.99 U.S./$5.99 CAN.

- **WIDOW WOMAN**
  by **Patricia McLinn**
  Feisty rancher Rachel Terhune must win back the heart of Nick Dusaq, the man she once refused to marry, and the unknowing father of her child.
  HH #417 ISBN# 29017-9 $4.99 U.S./$5.99 CAN.

- **INFAMOUS**
  by **Laurel Ames,** author of NANCY WHISKEY
  Dashing nobleman and spy Bennett Varner finally meets his match in the Lady Gwen Rose Wall, a woman determined to flee both his passion and her past.
  HH #418 ISBN# 29018-7 $4.99 U.S./$5.99 CAN.

DON'T MISS THESE FOUR GREAT TITLES AVAILABLE NOW!

#411 LION'S LADY
Suzanne Barclay

#412 JEB HUNTER'S BRIDE
Ana Seymour

#413 THE WILDER WEDDING
Lyn Stone

#414 TWICE A BRIDE
Rae Muir